WANDERLOST

ALSO BY JEN MALONE
Map to the Stars

Wanderlost

JEN MALONE

HARPER TEEN

An Imprint of HarperCollinsPublishers

HarperTeen is an imprint of HarperCollins Publishers.

Wanderlost
Copyright © 2016 by Jen Malone
All rights reserved. Printed in the United States of America. No part of
this book may be used or reproduced in any manner whatsoever without
written permission except in the case of brief quotations embodied in
critical articles and reviews. For information address HarperCollins
Children's Books, a division of HarperCollins Publishers,
195 Broadway, New York, NY 10007.
www.epicreads.com

ISBN 978-0-06-238015-9

Typography by Kate J. Engbring
18 19 20 PC/LSCC 10 9 8 7 6 5 4
❖

First Edition

To Emma and Mary, the grandest of grands

ONE

I'm wedged into the pantry, between forty-seven rolls of toilet paper and an industrial-sized box of Raisin Bran. Oh, and a chunk of my hair is hopelessly snagged in the joints of a metal shelving unit.

Seriously?

All I wanted was to grab a roll of paper towels for the inevitable moment beer pong went bad.

What I got was an epic fail.

Rule #1 of horror movies or Those of Us with Lives That Sometimes Resemble a Horror Movie: Always, always turn on the light. Never assume that just because you've been inside your own pantry eleventy billion times in the last seventeen years, you will therefore be able to navigate safely around your mom's latest Costco finds.

Now I have a bump on my head that's gonna look super-fantastic in all my graduation photos and there's the chance this may not end well for my hair, which, my mother would say, serves me right for having it long enough to reach my elbows. Except she isn't the one who had to endure seventh grade, when Brady Masterson said my bob reminded him of Edna in *The Incredibles* and got the entire class on board with the nickname. It took five years of growing my hair out to put that in my past, and I'm sure if I studied this year's yearbook messages carefully I'd still find a mention or two.

Rule #2 of horror movies or Those of Us with Lives That Sometimes Resemble a Horror Movie: Don't ever say, "I'll be right back." Those guys NEVER make it to the credits in one piece. And it's exactly what I said to Madison before I made my paper towel run.

I stretch my arm toward the doorknob, but each time I pull away from the shelves, my scalp yelps. This is so not good. If I could reach the light, I could maybe see enough to untangle the stupid hair myself, but no such luck on that one either. At this point, it's snarled in so many places, I'm worried all my efforts in the dark are making things ten times worse.

Yelling is an option, but my secret (from Mom and Dad at least; definitely not from anyone in the senior class) pre-graduation party—which was supposed to be six of my friends getting together for a night of tiki torches and margaritas by the pool and somehow turned into a raging kegger with half my grade in my living room—is in full swing. I already have sort of a reputation among my classmates for being . . . not always "pulled together." No need to let the whole senior class in on yet another lovely episode worthy of rehashing at our ten-year reunion.

At some point someone has to come looking for me, right? I strain my ears and pick out voices coming closer. Oh thank God!

"Did you see the smoke show in the feminazi T-shirt?" Damn. It's the class creeper, Matt Grafty-Hamm. I'd rather wither away to nothing in here than be rescued by Matt "Grabby Hands." I smother my cry for help.

"'Feminism is the radical notion that women are people,'" a mocking voice quotes. "Yeah, but did you see her rack in that shirt? Dude, she's so hot." Sounds like Brad Worthy, who, unlike Matt, in no way, shape, or form lives up to his last name. It's really no wonder I'm single.

"Hells yeah she is. I think she's Aubree Sadler's sister." I instantly snap to attention. My sister's home? She isn't supposed to get back from college for another four days.

Matt gets zero-point-zero points for class when he follows up with, "Total piece of ass if you can pry the stick out of it. That chick's name was on every sample paper my English teacher handed out last year and she graduated forever ago."

"Dude, but she's hot *and* a college girl. Think I could hit that?"

Oh, ick! I throw up a little in my mouth as their voices fade away. That said, why am I not surprised to hear Elizabeth's papers are still circulating as shining examples of perfection. "Shiny perfection" pretty much fits my sister to a T. We're talking about a girl who made my entire extended family fill out evaluations of her third grade piano recital performance so she could "better identify her weak spots."

Okay, this situation is now officially borderline pitiful. I'm gearing up to shout for help (even if it means suffering through Grabby's attempts to cop a feel) when a bright light assaults my eyeballs.

"Aubree? Bree, are you in here?"

My sister.

"Hey." I blink about a hundred times as my eyes adjust to the bulb. "What are you doing home?"

Elizabeth shuts the door behind her, closing us both into the tiny space.

"My last exam got canceled. I'm officially a college grad. I just bumped into Madison—she's been searching all over for you and she's freaking out. Which you should be too, incidentally. Mom and Dad are going to flip when they find out about this."

I know my friends have probably helped themselves to a few beverages by this point, but really, how hard would it have been to think of opening a few doors and peeking inside? Elizabeth found me, no problem. Then again, she *is* Elizabeth. And Mom and Dad cannot know about this party. Ever. Period.

"Are you hiding from the guy in the 'I'd Wrap That in Bacon' hat? Because if so, permission to carry on," she stage-whispers, reaching around my side for a twenty-pack of Purell. She unwraps a bottle and squirts a blob into her hand before offering it to me.

"Yeah, not hiding. I'm kinda, um, stuck." I gesture to my hair and Elizabeth does a comical double take, then gasps. To her credit, she does not laugh, though I can see the effort that's taking her.

"Go ahead," I groan. Blessing given, she collapses in giggles. I manage one last woe-is-me sigh and then I crumble too. Even *I* can admit when I'm too lame for words.

And I also have to say, it's kind of nice to laugh with Elizabeth. The four-year age difference was only kind of a thing when we were younger and lumped together in the backseat of the car and at the kiddie table at Thanksgiving dinners, but it became pretty pronounced when she left for college. She was barely around during breaks and always took summer internships near her campus outside Chicago. Once she got an apartment there, she basically never came home for more than twenty-four hours. There's only so far that bonding over the turkey wishbone as six- and ten-year-olds can carry a relationship.

It's not that we don't like each other. More that we don't *know* each other. Not to mention the fact that her shining beacon of perfection casts a loooooong shadow behind her that's pretty hard to step out of.

Laughter is good. It's a start.

When we get our composure back, Elizabeth slips out to find Madison and a pair of tweezers. She returns with both and I endure their wisecracks as Elizabeth carefully unwinds my hair. Freeing me, she then produces a brush from her purse because, being Elizabeth, she has one on hand at any time to maintain all that gloriousness.

Then she puts both hands on my shoulders. "All fixed," she says.

"My hero!" I clutch at my heart and pretend to swoon at her feet. Madison snorts.

"And don't you forget it!" Elizabeth says. "Okay, how about we clear this crowd outta here? I had big plans for a quiet night on the patio. I'm in the middle of the *best* biography of Eleanor Roosevelt. Seriously, you should read it. Wanna help me ditch Bacon Dude?"

I do. I really do. Bacon Dude and the rest of them crashed my own plans for the night, but at the same time I'm kind of pissed that Elizabeth thought she could show up out of the blue and just reclaim the house. What if I'd wanted this party? What if I'd planned and plotted for it and was psyched to bid high school good-bye with a bang? She's not the boss of me.

"Nah. I'm good with them here. I'm gonna go grab a beer." I wait to see if Elizabeth's eyes widen. They do. Well, maybe there's a lot about me she doesn't know. I'm grown-up Aubree now and she's gonna have to accept it (even if I don't exactly embrace it myself).

Besides, I may as well soak up every chance I get to hang with my friends before they head off to college and leave me behind to commute the twenty minutes to classes at Kent State. Though, truth be told, as much as I'll miss them, I'm perfectly fine being the one holding down the fort here. There's a reason they call it home *sweet* home. I love it here.

"Mmm-hmm," Elizabeth says, and her disapproval is written all over her face. She probably waited until her twenty-first birthday to sip from a glass of classy white wine and the odds of her having a house party when she was in high school were negative one billion to one. I try not to remind myself that my own track record was not so different before tonight's accidental rager.

Elizabeth frowns. "Well, on your way to the keg, I suggest you stop by the living room. Someone threw up in Mom's ficus. I'll be upstairs. Try to keep the noise under control, okay?" Elizabeth slips from the closet and I slump against the wall, making sure I'm nowhere near the shelves this time around.

"Do you think she'll rat you out to Nancy?" Madison asks, joining me on the wall.

Oh God. It's a major miracle my parents went away for the weekend in the first place, given my mother's addiction to *Dateline* and her related belief that strangers dangling candy from their van windows at her youngest daughter lurk around every corner. She was halfway to DEFCON 5 the one time I was three minutes late for curfew. The second any of us coughs, she's on WebMD.

Hands-off, Mom is not.

And yet she made a big deal about going away with Dad for their anniversary, given the fact that I was almost a college student and, even though I'd be living at home for school next fall, had earned myself the right to some independence. Wait. Was that just for show? Did she turn right around and summon Elizabeth home? Because I don't need her to babysit me. Um, with the small exception of me being held captive by a set of shelving units.

"Why couldn't *you* have found me," I whine, bumping my shoulder into Madison's, but we both freeze at the quick whir of a siren.

It sounds close. As in driveway close. We swing open the door and are nearly mowed down by a crowd of people scurrying for the back door as if Godzilla's appeared in the living room.

"Cops!" Madison says. "Oh God, oh God, oh God. I'm so dead. I can't lose my scholarship!" She puts her hands over her eyes and leans against the kitchen doorframe.

"Don't answer the door!" I order anyone in earshot as a pounding sounds from the front hallway. "They can't enter without permission, can they?" I whisper to Madison. I sneak a glance around the now-empty kitchen at the abandoned keg and an assortment of beer cans that form a fairly impressive pyramid. Hudson High should be proud; at least one of my classmates mastered engineering.

"What do I do? Okay, get back in the pantry!" Madison tugs me inside again and we tumble against a stack of cleaning supplies and a hand vacuum.

The house is eerily quiet. And then the pounding starts again. "Police! Open up!"

Inside the pantry, all is still. The last bottle of Clorox stops wobbling on the floor and stands at attention, much like Madison and me. The knocking ceases once more, and then I hear something that turns my blood to ice. My sister's voice.

"Good evening, officer. How can I help you?"

What is she DOING? Madison grabs my arm and she mouths the words, "Is that Elizabeth?"

I nod, confusion wrinkling my forehead. I miss the policeman's next words, but Elizabeth responds, "Yes, sir. Everything is fine here. I'm so sorry the neighbors felt we were being too loud. I'll be sure to monitor the noise level more carefully."

I can picture the cheeseball smile she's giving him. It's the same one she used to use to con me into sharing the last of the mint chocolate cookie swirl ice cream with her. Worked on me every time, so I'm not surprised when I don't hear the cop's voice anymore. But then suddenly he speaks and it sounds like he's right outside the pantry door.

Oh man, I think he *is* right outside the pantry door.

"Looks like quite a party," he's saying. I'm guessing the beer pyramid does not impress him.

"Hey, don't I know you? Did we go to high school together, Officer Dixon?" Elizabeth asks.

It's quiet for a second, and then the deep voice answers, "You don't even remember my first name? That figures. Too busy being valedictorian to notice us little guys, huh?"

On the other side of the door, he snorts, and I gaze wide-eyed at Madison, who returns my expression. Should we go out there? If Elizabeth knows this cop, chances are he isn't going to bust us. Then again, it doesn't sound like they were cozy lab partners or anything. If I needed proof he didn't know her well, it would be right there in the way he described her. My sister is super-accomplished and confident and everything, but she's not stuck up. She's pretty friendly to any and all normal people. Emphasis on *normal*, which this guy doesn't seem to be.

"I'm sorry. Can you remind me?" my sister says.

"Whatever," Officer Scorned replies. "Looks like there's quite a lot of alcohol here."

"Oh, well, not really. The cans are left over from an, uh, experiment we were conducting. We didn't drink all those or anything. Really, this is just an intimate gathering."

The cop isn't buying it. "So intimate your friends felt the need to run for the hills when my cruiser pulled into the driveway?"

"What? No, of course not. They were on their way out anyway." Elizabeth coughs delicately.

"You find this funny?"

His voice has an edge to it that makes Madison clutch my arm again.

"Of course not. Not at all. I had something in my throat."

All is quiet for a second and I exhale carefully. Maybe he'll be leaving now. Obviously there's no more noise violation, so the complaint is handled.

"You have any ID on you?" he asks.

"We just established we were in the same class. You know exactly who I am."

"ID, please."

I say a silent thank-you to the birthday gods that Elizabeth turned twenty-one last spring. Of everyone here, she's the only one actually old enough to drink. Still, why the *hell* did she open the door?!

"This a fake ID?" the voice booms, even closer now.

There's true indignation in Elizabeth's voice when she answers. "Are you kidding? Of course not!"

Officer Douchecanoe has a definite edge to his voice when he says, "You're gonna want to be careful of the tone you take with me, miss."

"Excuse me, *sir*," Elizabeth says, and her "sir" drips with contempt. "I'm a private citizen, of legal drinking age, on private property, and I'd like you to leave now."

"Like I said, Miss Sadler, you don't want to cross me. You may be twenty-one, but if anyone drinking here tonight was underage, you could be held liable for supplying minors."

"That's ridiculous. Besides, do you see anyone else here?" Whoa. It isn't like Elizabeth to get worked up like this. She held top honors in her university's debate club and I'm guessing she didn't earn them by losing her cool. "Listen," she says. "You no longer have my permission to be in my home. If you don't leave right now I'm going to have to file a report against you."

"Guess what, prom princess? You got a problem. I have the

power now. So you're just gonna have to deal with it." Whoa again. This guy is not fooling around.

"Please just leave. I'm asking politely."

Footsteps move away from the pantry and I crack the door a centimeter so I can peek out. The officer is now standing in the doorway that opens off the kitchen, peering into the back-yard for any hovering partygoers. He turns to Elizabeth again and my sister puts a hand on his arm to guide him toward the front hall.

Before I can process what's happening, there's a sharp clanging of metal, and then a set of handcuffs are out and around my sister's wrists.

"What the hell!" My sister screeches and I cover my mouth. Madison tugs me out of the way so she can spy for herself. She steps back and mouths, "OMG!"

Is my sister getting arrested? For *what*?

That's obviously what she'd like to know as well. "Why are you handcuffing me?"

"You put your hands on me and I felt threatened. You can't threaten an officer, Miss Sadler."

"Are you insane? I put one hand on your arm to show you out. It's not remotely possible that you felt threatened."

What do I do? Do I go out there and defend my sister? I had two margaritas a few hours ago, so I should be good, but I don't know what Madison's intake has been, and if I expose our hiding place, she could be the proof he's looking for to arrest Elizabeth on real charges, ones that could stick. Charges of supplying minors with alcohol. Which she also didn't do, obviously. This guy must be totally nutso or carrying the monster of all grudges over an unrequited high school crush or something. I move back to the door to peer out, but beyond that I'm paralyzed in place.

"You're welcome to plead your case in front of a judge if you have a different opinion of how things went down tonight. For now, you're coming with me for processing."

Elizabeth struggles against him and it's nearly enough to make me burst through the door. Nearly. Madison and I have a whole conversation with just our eyes as we weigh what to do, but in the end it doesn't matter. In the span of thirty seconds, the front door closes, two car doors slam, and an engine starts up in the driveway.

And my sister heads off to jail.

TWO

Elizabeth has a folded washcloth across her forehead and her eyes closed when I wander into her bedroom the next day. I hesitate near the doorway.

"Close the door behind you, please," she says, without lifting the cloth.

I drop a pile of graduation cards addressed to her on her desk and, because she looks so miserable, take a second to straighten them into an orderly pile to match their surroundings.

"You need anything?" I ask.

"Have you *met* our mother?" She waves at her nightstand, where a glass of ginger ale with a straw in it sits next to a plate of dry toast and the TV remote. As if my sister's fighting off a cold and not a criminal record.

I'm impressed my mother has this level of care in her, despite being awoken at a B and B two hours away to post bail for Elizabeth, not to mention the subsequent hours she spent yelling at me.

"Um, so I just wanted to say again how sorry I am about what happened last night," I offer my sister. "If it makes you feel better, I'm grounded forever."

Elizabeth slides the washcloth off her face and uses her elbows to push up to a sitting position. She leans back against the headboard of her canopy princess bed and lets her head tap against the wood.

Then she bursts into tears.

Whoa.

"Hey. Hey, it's gonna be okay."

She wipes her nose with her sleeve, which honestly freaks me out more than her tears. I can't remember ever seeing her the least bit out of control, and the Elizabeth I know would *never* walk around with snot stains on her shirt.

Then again, it's not like I really do know her that well. Everything about her is a mystery I've tried to crack from the time I was a toddler. How did she ride that two-wheeler so perfectly when my tricycle barely kept me upright? How did her cherry lemonade lip gloss stay on when mine tasted so good I licked it off in ten seconds? How did she get the cute lifeguard to watch her with interest every time she climbed the ladder to the diving board? How did she get the grades she got and still have time to be the president of every other club on campus when I could barely get myself to school before the late bell? Seriously, do we even share the same genes?

But for now, the only mystery I want to solve is why she opened the door last night and why on earth she'd mouthed off even a tiny bit to an obviously power-tripping cop.

"So, *what* happened? I mean, I know what happened. But *how* did this happen?"

She smears mascara across her cheek when she swipes at her eyes. Her breath hitches over a deep inhale and then she exhales slowly and says, "I screwed up."

In spite of the situation, I almost laugh. I would be willing to bet the entire contents of my room that she's never uttered those words before.

"You didn't screw up. That guy was Crazytown."

"Obviously. But I should have recognized that and not antagonized him. Anyway, how would you know? You ran for the hills." Oh. Somehow it hasn't quite come out that I witnessed the whole thing from the pantry.

"Well, it's not like I knew you'd open the door."

"I was trying to cover your ass. I answered the door because I thought I could just smile and assure the officer we'd keep the noise down and your little shindig wouldn't get busted. You said you wanted the party, so I was looking out for *you!*"

And now there's a knife of guilt lodged in my chest. I'm a little surprised too. Usually Elizabeth is wrapped up in her own things and doesn't pay me much attention.

"Thanks," I mumble, then I add, "Seriously, though, once you tell the judge your side of the story, he or she will have to see what a mistake was made."

"Maybe. The lawyer Dad hired definitely thinks so. He said it's laughable how weak the case is. But it doesn't matter, because either way the damage is done. I just can't believe that in the span of, like, ten seconds, all my dreams for my career are dead."

"What are you talking about? You just said the lawyer will get you off. There's no way you'll end up with any permanent record or anything! You'll be *fine* to start work on the campaign this fall."

Elizabeth has a grunt job helping a congressman with his reelection campaign, but we all know that's just the start of things for her. Pretty soon she'll be the one running for office and no one who knows her has the least little doubt about that.

She sighs. "Chances are really good I can get the arrest expunged. But as for the job: nope. It all hinged on this tour guide gig this summer. When the congressman's biggest donor asks him for his help finding a last-minute replacement guide and he chooses you, you don't earn a whole lot of brownie points by skipping out on it at the last minute. The conditions of my bail mean I can't even leave the state, much less head off to Europe. I don't see how they could possibly find anyone else to replace me on such short notice. And if I leave his donor in the lurch, there's no way Congressman Willard's going to think I'm responsible enough to work for him. Honestly, if he even gets word of the arrest, that's probably it for me. He needs the soccer mom vote to win and he's not gonna want some girl who hosts keg parties for high school kids helping with his campaign."

"But you didn't!"

"I know. And maybe I could convince him of that. But

the hint of a scandal coupled with a pissed-off donor? Forget it. It's over."

This time she sinks low in the bed before losing it with a fresh batch of tears. I stare slack-jawed for a second at my typically stoic big sister, then scoot across the quilt to wrap my arms around her. The pillow she's been hugging squeezes between us.

Obviously, it's not like I haven't hugged my sister before, but I don't think I've ever consoled her, and the role reversal feels awkward. This is usually her job. She's the one who offered me half her Halloween candy the time I was on crutches and Mom thought it would be too dangerous to go trick-or-treating. She's the one who made the attendant at the top of the log flume at Cedar Point let us out so we could walk down the attached steps since I was freaking out so bad I couldn't breathe. Our roles are clear.

She's the big sister.

I'm the baby.

I pretend to mind, but secretly I love having my mom put away my laundry and set out vitamins next to my juice glass every morning. I still sleep with a stuffed animal and have the same friends I did in nursery school, and I'm okay with those things. More than okay. They're comforting. Safe. Home.

Elizabeth sniffles a few more times and her sobs subside.

I ease out of the hug and say, "It can't be as bad as you're making it sound. You'll figure something out."

She clears her throat and straightens. "The thing is, I

actually do have one idea that would solve everything."

I grin. "See? I knew you would. You wouldn't be Elizabeth if you didn't."

Thank God. She'll be fine and I can let go of the crushing weight of guilt on my chest. Already I can feel it getting lighter, floating away.

Elizabeth glances at me from under her lashes. "It's simple, really."

She pauses and collects a breath before blurting, "You just need to go to Europe as me."

THREE

My jaw drops to the floor along with the tissues I was getting ready to offer Elizabeth.

"You can't be serious!"

My sister's eyes flash. "I wouldn't be in this position if it wasn't for *your* party. You have no idea how big the stakes are for me right now. What if this scandal follows me around and I can't land a job on *any* campaign? Do you have any idea how screwed I'd be? If I cancel this Europe tour, the congressman is going to need to know why. But if I go—or everyone *thinks* I go, at least—he won't have a reason to suspect anything is wrong."

"Yeah, but—"

"Bree, please. Just take a little bit of time and think about it. It's only for a month. What were your plans for this summer? Lounging by the pool with your friends?"

"*Noooo.*" I pause. "Well, okay, yes, but I was also going to work on some new jewelry techniques and finally launch my

Etsy shop. Everyone says my designs are good enough to sell."

Elizabeth's voice is sticky sweet when she says, "I'm sure they are. But as far as jobs go, you *could* put that one on hold without letting anyone else down. Or better yet, you could bring your beads and your supplies with you and do them on the bus." Her tears have dried completely and she seems pleased as punch with her quick solution. She continues, "Most girls, most *people*, would be over the moon about a chance to go to Europe."

"Would they?" I ask, having a hard time controlling the sarcasm. "Would they also be over the moon about the chance to lead A BUS TOUR OF SENIOR CITIZENS through Europe? I don't even think I *like* old people."

"How can you say that? You don't know any old people. All our grandparents died before you were born."

"I've seen at least ten reruns of *The Golden Girls*! That has to count for something." My mind is whirring. How could she possibly think I would go for this? Doesn't she know me at all? If she *did*, she'd know I barely cross county lines.

"Oh, and Aunt Mira," I offer. "I know Aunt Mira. She's a few pixels short of a picture."

"Aunt Mira has dementia. These people are in complete control of their faculties. It's totally different and you know it. At least let me tell you more about the job before you say no."

I don't reply, which she takes as permission. "Okay, so you'd be leading a twenty-two-day tour of Europe for six senior citizens. They keep the tours super-small so you have more mobility. Plus it's really expensive and exclusive, so deluxe accommodations all the way. You'll fly to Amsterdam to meet up with them and then you'll do all of your travel by bus. Netherlands, Germany, Austria, Czech Republic, Italy, Monaco, Spain, Portugal, more France, Belgium, and then back to Amsterdam for the flight home. The schedules are very low-key for the seniors. It sounds like a lot, but there's actually tons of downtime."

It sounds like a lot? It sounds like A LOT? Is she serious right now? I throw my hands up and drop my voice to a growling whisper. "I've never been *anywhere*."

She leans back and looks me straight in the eyes. "That's not an argument, Bree. That's a reason right there. I've been considering this plan since last night and I think maybe this could be really good for you too. A sort of win-win, if you will."

I won't. I let loose with a big sigh. She so doesn't get it. "What I'm saying is, I wouldn't have the first clue how to get around. Or how to talk to anyone. I wouldn't even know how to get francs or lira or whatever."

"Euros." Elizabeth is fighting to keep the amusement out of her voice, but I can hear it.

"Huh?" I ask.

"Most of Europe uses euros. It's not that hard, really. You just use an ATM, same as here."

I wind my hair around my wrist. Does this mean she really thinks I can do this? Like, seriously believes I can handle something like this? That's actually flattering. "Okay, fine, euros. But . . . everything else. The tour guide stuff. I'm not a leader. And I don't know the first thing about Europe except that they make really good chocolate there and they call soccer *football.*"

"I'd help you. I promise! We have two weeks before you'd need to be in Amsterdam. I can quiz you and I'll make you one of my signature study guides. Everything you need to know."

I groan. Those things are legendary. At one point in high school she started a side business selling her study guides and the entire class GPA rose by 0.5 points in one semester.

I don't admit this to myself a lot, but the fact of the matter is that I miss my sister. We used to hang out when we were little and do sister stuff, like push each other on the swings and fight over who got to climb the stepladder to put the star on the Christmas tree or whose ice cream cone had more sprinkles. As much as I wouldn't want what would be waiting at the end of it, two weeks' worth of my sister's undivided attention would be . . . amazing.

Elizabeth isn't done with her hard sell yet. "Even though almost everyone speaks English and I doubt you'll need them, I'll put language translation apps on your phone. Currency ones too. And you'd have the tour company. They're totally there for you whenever you need them. You just place a call and they'll handle things from here in the States. Easy peasy."

I am *not* considering this. "There's no way this could work."

"It could! I've been thinking about all the angles, trust me. The company's based in Dayton, but I've never been there in person. I interviewed over the phone. They had the referral from the congressman's office, and my transcript, and, well, I think they were pretty desperate, so that was enough for them. Believe me, they won't be asking many questions. Anyway, point is, they've never seen me. All they have is a copy of my passport, and that photo was taken back in high school, the time I went to Canada for the debate team competition. It looks just like you, honestly. They'll have no reason to suspect you aren't Elizabeth reporting for duty."

Except that I'm seventeen and she's twenty-one. And she's Miss Perfectly Put Together and I'm . . . me. For example, it's one p.m. and I'm still in pajama pants.

"What about Mom and Dad? I'm grounded, remember. And even if I weren't, there's zip-zero chance Mom is letting me jet off to Europe."

"I have a plan for that too. You just let me handle them." She tugs a hand through her hair and continues, "It boils down to this. All I need is that letter of recommendation at the end of the trip. If the owner gets good evaluations from the tour participants, she's happy, which means the congressman is happy. I'll have my job and I'm golden. I won't have to lose everything I've worked my whole entire life for. Bree, you know how badly I need this job. It means *everything* to me."

This must be why she did so well on the debate team. I half expect to hear a tiny violin playing in the background.

Apparently she sees my resolve crumbling because she goes for the kill.

"I wouldn't even be in this position if it wasn't for you."

Ouch. Low blow, even though she's right.

The thing is, I don't know what it's like to want something the way Elizabeth wants a career in politics. When other kids were playing Four Square, she was turning cardboard boxes into voting booths and making me and preschool friends cast ballots for her. I don't have a clue what I want to do when I "grow up," but Elizabeth has always known. Always. Now she's watching her best shot at that dream slip from her grasp and I have the power to help her.

There are thirty-seven-hundred reasons why this would be a monumentally T-E-R-R-I-B-L-E idea. I'm the least qualified person on the planet to put in charge of anyone. Elizabeth wins Most Likely to Succeed awards while I count myself lucky I haven't won a Darwin Award yet.

"Please, Bree?" Elizabeth's eyes are like saucers now, as wide as an anime character's. It's a total put-on, but for just a second I see the utter desperation behind it and it throws me.

She needs me. *She* needs *me*.

My sister has never (not once, not ever) needed me.

I'm going to regret this with every single fiber of my being. I already am.

But that still doesn't stop me from whispering, "Okay."

FOUR

The day of reckoning is here.

After all the plotting and planning, I'm finally at the airport check-in area, trying to soothe my tear-stricken mother. It should be noted that aliens would need to inhabit the body of Nancy Sadler before anything resembling permission for me to fly off solo to a foreign land would escape her lips, so Mom is blissfully (read: nervously) under the impression that I will be accompanying Madison to the summer camp she's attended and then worked at since forever. I will be in charge of handling boat rentals for a slew of tween girls. I'm a little surprised Mom bought that this would be something I would want to do, but Elizabeth can be very persuasive (as I know all too well). She's even convinced Mom a summer in the backwoods of Maine will get me far away from the "negative influences" that led to my "poor decision making with regard to that party incident."

Oh, she's good.

Somehow Mom has managed to hyperventilate only once this morning. I, however, can't say the same.

"Mom, *yes*. I have my photo ID."

"Okay, well, make sure you keep it out because you'll need it when you go through security."

"Mom, I know. We've been over this."

"And what about your phone? And the snacks I packed you for the flight? You know what a picky eater you are and you'll be lucky if they serve so much as peanuts on the plane. I should have packed you a whole lunch. I can't believe I let you and your sister talk me into this."

Madison makes her way over, hunched to one side by the weight of her shoulder duffel. She waves a few sheets of paper at us. "I've got both our boarding passes."

It's exceedingly helpful to have a best friend who majors in devious. She was all over perpetuating my little charade for Mom's benefit.

"I don't know, sweetie. I'm just wondering if I should walk to the gate with you," Mom says. "I'll bet if I talked to someone with the airline, I could get one of those passes to accompany a minor through security."

"Mom! Those are for five-year-olds! I'm not exactly what they mean by a minor!"

"And she's got me, Mrs. Sadler. I do this every summer, remember?" Madison practices her most innocent expression on my mother. Mom's shoulders relax.

"Okay, okay. I'm sorry. I thought I'd be at the airport today waving Elizabeth off on her European adventure, not sending my baby to Maine. It's just, it feels like yesterday Aubree was clinging to my leg at nursery school drop-off and now my little girl is going halfway across the country from me."

Or halfway around the world. But who's getting technical? At least she's not suspicious about the way my departure date aligned with Elizabeth's. Having Madison willing to leave a few days early helped big-time.

"Mom, I'm good. I promise. Besides, Dad's probably circled the airport twice by now waiting for you."

Mom wipes her eyes with the sleeve of her shirt. "I know, you're right. Madison, you have to excuse this. She's just never been away from home before. You can't blame a mom for worrying."

When Mom looks away, I roll my eyes at Madison, who stifles a laugh. Although, as much as I'm following proper teen protocol on the outside, inside I'm a mess just like my mother.

Mom sniffles one last time, then straightens. "Okay, okay. Give me a giant hug. And promise to text me when you get on the plane."

I wrap my arms around her. Madison used to have a bumper sticker on her binder that said, "A hug is just a strangle you haven't finished yet," and I sort of get it at the moment. It's probably a good thing Mom's acting a tiny bit annoying, because otherwise I might be falling apart too, in a way totally inappropriate for someone my age who's only headed to a summer camp in Maine.

Who am I kidding? I am absolutely *thisclose* to falling apart. There's a lump in my throat that refuses to be swallowed away and tears prickling my eyelids. I've never been away from home for more than the occasional sleepover and suddenly I'm feeling overly sentimental about good old Hudson, Ohio.

I backtrack with Mom to the sliding glass doors, allegedly to claim one last hug, but also so I can make sure she gets into the car and pulls away. I can't risk her seeing me switch terminals to get to where my actual flight departs.

Dad pulls up to the curb and gives a light tap on the horn. We said our good-byes at home, so he leans over the passenger seat and blows kisses.

Then they drive off. And I'm alone.

Well, not really. As soon as they're out of sight, Madison races over from where she's been hovering a few feet away. "Are you okay?"

I swipe my hand across my cheek before she catches the tear and grin at her. I can tell she's not fooled. She steals a look at the clock in the center of the terminal and says, "Crap. I wish I had time to hang until you're feeling like yourself again, but the line for security is huge and if I don't get in it soon, neither one of us will be in Maine to send home those postcards you wrote. I hate leaving you like this. Are you gonna be okay? Your sister's waiting outside?"

I nod, forcing a smile.

But instead of hoisting her duffel farther up her shoulder, Madison lets it drop to the ground and grins back at me. "Wow. I still can't believe you're actually going to see the Eiffel Tower. And the *Mona Lisa*. And the Alps. I'm insanely jealous, you know that, right? I expect email updates by the hour—they'll be waiting on my phone when I make trips to civilization. And I know I've said this a zillion times, but seriously don't worry about your mom. The camp director was my counselor way back when I was still a camper there. She's beyond awesome *and* she owes me big-time for sticking me in charge of a cabin last year that was one case of head lice after another. I've already emailed her all the deets. She'll totally cover for you if your mom or dad calls."

As she talks, she helps me tug a lightweight hooded rain jacket over my head.

"If you meet hot European boys, I expect pictures. Or videos. That way I can hear their scrumptious accents. Ooh la la."

I snort. "You do know I'm going to be spending all my time with octogenarians, right? I can send you videos of old-guy ear hair, if you insist."

Madison makes a face as I twist my hair into a low ponytail and tuck it under my jacket before yanking on a baseball cap. Disguise complete. Not that I'm expecting my parents to circle back around, but you know, I wouldn't put it past my mom to come wailing through the terminal, looking for "one last good-bye" as if I'm headed off to war.

Nodding at my transformation, my best friend grabs me into a hug. "You're super-brave. I'm in total awe. I cannot *believe* you agreed to this, but I'm so, so excited for you. You're gonna be amazing. I just know it."

I didn't realize how much I needed someone to say exactly that to me right at this very second. Elizabeth has been saying things like this these last two weeks and I still don't believe the words, but I believe that she, and now Madison, does, and that counts for something. I nod hard and we squeeze it out before I help her settle her giant duffel back on her shoulder.

"Go take on the world!" Madison calls, working her way toward security.

I give a final wave as Madison takes her place at the back of the security line; then I quickly slip through the glass doors, back onto the sidewalk. Ten cars up the row, I find my sister slumped low behind the steering wheel of her friend's borrowed Toyota. I giggle at the lengths we've gone to in order to pull the wool over my parents' eyes. It's been like planning a spy mission.

In fact, the best thing about all of this is that the last two weeks with Elizabeth have been everything I hoped for when I said yes to this crazy scheme. She's been really patient with me—even when I've had periodic quasi panic attacks whenever reality hit that this trip was an actual thing that was happening—and we've spent nearly every day together running errands, reviewing her binder of information, and snorting with laughter at the testimonials in the tour brochure (where one women exclaimed, "I couldn't believe the copious amounts of time I was given to get my teeth back in before departure every morning!"). It's the most time we've spent together in the four years since she left for college and I think she's finally, finally seeing me as something other than that middle school kid who borrowed her clothes without asking, and maybe even acknowledging that, with me starting college, the age difference between us doesn't have to mean so much. I think maybe she finally sees me as an equal. Or at least, as someone she could be friends with.

Elizabeth doesn't notice me approach from behind, and through the rolled-down window I can hear her on the phone.

"I mean, I'm taking a pretty big gamble here. What if she can't do it?" she's saying.

I pause and step back, just out of her view.

"I know," she continues. "But you've never met my sister. She's just not . . . not . . . I don't even know what the right word is. Assertive, maybe? Resourceful? She's basically completely codependent on my mom, who does ev-er-y-thing for her."

I'm stunned. This entire time Elizabeth has had cheerleader-level enthusiasm for her plan. *Her* plan. It certainly wasn't *my* idea to go traipsing around Europe with a bunch of grannies. And whenever I expressed the slightest doubt, she talked right over it, telling me how easy it will be, how great I'll be. And the whole time she was hiding these feelings?

Elizabeth continues chattering into the phone. ". . . I know . . . I know. Right. She hasn't ever been out in the world. I don't even think she drives into Cleveland ever. She's never had a real job before . . . yeah. Yeah, I guess. Okay, but let me rest my case with this: she had my mother pack her snacks for the plane ride. . . . No, I'm not kidding!" Elizabeth giggles into the phone.

I go from stunned to furious in two seconds flat. She's laughing at me? After everything I'm about to do to save her ass? I'm furious. I tap twice on the back window and then fiddle with the handle, before yanking it open and dumping my suitcase and backpack inside.

"Gotta go," my sister hisses into the phone. I exhale a sharp breath and slide into the passenger seat. My sister plasters on a big smile as we move out into traffic, headed for the terminal that houses the airline the tour company uses.

"How'd it go with Mom and Dad?" she asks brightly.

I'm in no mood for her fake friendship. All the confidence Madison's words gave me—and then some—was just wiped away in one overheard phone call. Elizabeth has been insisting I was overreacting every time I got nervous about something or other to do with the trip. All along she kept telling me to trust her, trust the binder full of information she compiled for me, trust that the tour company could have my back. Trust myself. How many times had she said that to me over the last two weeks?

Was it all a big show on her part?

It's one thing for me not to have faith in myself, but finding out my sister doesn't have faith in me either feels like a punch to the gut. And I can't hide it. I'm quiet for a long moment as she circles to the farthest terminal. Finally she repeats her question.

"I heard your phone call," I snap.

"My—? What?" She acts all innocent but I see her hands clench the steering wheel so tight her knuckles turn white.

I roll my eyes, even though she's now busy looking for a spot to pull up along the curb at the terminal, and can't see me. "You know. Where you told your friend that I'm probably about to ruin your life because I won't be able to keep it together."

Elizabeth puts the car in park and reaches across the console to place a hand on my knee. It feels condescending, like I'm a small child she's trying to reason out of a temper tantrum. "You didn't hear that, because I didn't say that."

"No, not exactly. You just said I'm a baby who needs my mommy." I sit spine stiff in my seat, ignoring her hand and staring out the window at the terminal entrance, where a couple is kissing like their very lives depend on it.

"I didn't mean it like *that*," Elizabeth says in a soft voice, and I snort.

It feels like every good minute of the last two weeks has just been erased. I can't have this conversation right now. I lurch out of my seat and slam my door behind me. Elizabeth yells "Bree!" in a shocked voice but I ignore her and grab my bags from the backseat. She reaches for her own door handle and hops out of the car, but I move faster, striding toward the terminal. I know she can't leave the car on the curb in a no-parking zone and I quicken my pace. When the glass doors of the terminal swish closed behind me, I steal a tiny backward glance at my sister. She looks completely perplexed and a little lost, her head tilted and her shoulders raised. I swallow another lump in my throat.

That was not at all the send-off I'd envisioned. Not one tiny bit.

This trip isn't even two minutes old and already it's a disaster.

FIVE

Mom's always telling me I can't say I don't like something until I've tried it. She's usually talking about bologna. Or Zumba classes.

Well, you know what, Mom? I've tried flying now.

And flying and I will *not* be achieving bestie status.

I'm somewhere over the Atlantic in a tin box of death and the curved walls are closing in on me. Every time I pick my head up to look around, my eyes can't help but land on the TV screen at the front of the cabin. The one that shows a tiny animated version of our plane arcing in marching red dots across the ocean—the giant, sprawling, endless sea represented on the screen by a crap-ton of blue. Seriously, it's like watching a slasher film. I know I should look away. I *want* to look away.

I can't look away.

"Nervous flyer, huh?" The businessman next to me touches my arm lightly.

"Sorry?" I tug my headphones out of my ears.

"I was saying, you seem on edge." He passes me a fresh napkin.

I look down at the one already in my hands and realize I've shredded it into pieces so itty-bitty, it's like my seat-back tray has dandruff. Awesome.

"Thanks," I say.

So. Embarrassing.

As is the fact that I'm clutching Mr. Pricklepants, my obviously well-loved stuffed hedgehog. I may be a bona fide high school graduate of all of six days, but there are times a girl needs her snuggly.

"Hey, don't worry about it. I used to be a wreck on planes too," he says.

"How did you stop?" I shift to face him, eager for tips.

He laughs. "Six months of hypnotherapy."

"Oh. I was hoping you'd say something more immediate, like, 'You just have to do a headstand and count to twenty.'"

He laughs again. At least someone is enjoying himself on this flight.

"In the here and now, the best thing I've found is to go to sleep and let time take care of the rest. Can't be panicked if you're fast asleep."

"Can't be fast asleep if you're afraid you're going to snore through the oxygen masks dropping from the ceiling," I counter.

This time his smile is rueful. So's mine. In fact, I'd say

rueful pretty much describes my mood in general, ever since the Great Sister Switch idea was hatched by perfect (HA!) Elizabeth. I'm trying not to think about how, even *if* I survive this flight, that is so only the beginning of things.

I tuck Mr. Pricklepants against the egg-shaped window and snuggle into him. My seatmate has turned his attention back to his laptop, so I close my eyes and try to figure out how *this* became my life. The plane gives the tiniest of lurches and I grab for the armrest. Instead I'm horrified to find myself clutching the businessman's arm.

"Um, sorry," I say, but my eyes are glued to the ceiling, waiting for the oxygen mask.

He gently uncurls my fingers from his forearm and pats my hand.

"Words of wisdom didn't help, huh?"

Yeah, no.

He sighs and says, "Look, I probably shouldn't offer this to a total stranger, but I would feel bad if I had a way to help you and didn't suggest it. I have trouble adjusting to the time difference, so I always travel with sleeping pills. Would you like one? It'll knock you out for the flight."

Okay, so of course Mom's *Dateline* obsession means I know never to take any drugs not prescribed to me, much less from a stranger, but it's not like he's targeted me for this or anything. There *is* a legitimate reason behind his offer. Plus, the guy has a copy of *The Tale of Peter Rabbit* in his carry-on case and he read it over the phone to his kids while we were still parked at the gate, before blowing them good-night kisses. He really blew them too, even though his kids couldn't see if he was or wasn't. Surely *this guy* doesn't have plans to put me under and auction me off to some underground sex trade.

"That would be amazing, if you have one to spare," I say.

He reaches into the carry-on and withdraws a small toiletries kit. "I can't promise you'll have your wits about you when we land. You're only supposed to take this if you have eight hours to devote to sleep and we land in"—he glances up at the evil screen of death—"four hours and eighteen minutes."

I accept the pill he offers as he continues, "So maybe you'll just want to take—"

I pop the pill in my mouth and swallow.

"—half."

My eyes grow big as I process his words.

"Ah, okay," he says. "I'm sure it will be fine."

"Right. Well, thank you so much." I give him a grateful smile and adjust my pillow, aka Mr. Pricklepants.

"My pleasure. Sweet dreams."

I coil the cord of my headphones around my cell and tuck it into the seat pocket alongside Elizabeth's "Everything Bus-Tour Related" binder before snuggling under the paper-thin blanket the airline provided.

Finally, I can turn off the noise in my brain. This sustained level of adrenaline can't be good. The flight attendants are reassuring with their constant bustling and offers of drinks up and down the aisles as I close my eyes and burrow in.

"Miss? Miss! You have to wake up now, miss."

I squint my eyes open. Where am I? Mmm . . . so sleepy. I flutter them closed again, until a hand shakes my shoulder. Pesky, pesky person, leave me alone.

"Miss, I let you sleep as long as I could, but the flight's empty now and we've got a quick turnaround before we're wheels up."

I jerk upright and wipe a trail of drool from my cheek, hoping the flight attendant hovering over me doesn't notice it. Oh wow, I really crashed out. The plane is parked at the gate and there are only a few people still shuffling off. The seats all around are perfectly empty. Even my friendly pill-dispensing businessman has deserted me.

"I'm so sorry. I'll . . . I'm going now."

I move Mr. Pricklepants to the seat beside me, unclip my seat belt, and pop up, only to bump my head on the overhead compartment. Ouch!

"Can I give you a hand? Is this your bag up here?" The flight attendant gestures to the open overhead compartment.

"I can get it," I say.

Sliding out of my row, I reach above her for my backpack. It's the only thing left in there, but it doesn't budge when I pull on it. I give a hard yank and something tugs free, sending the bag flying out and me tumbling into the row of seats behind me.

"Oh!" exclaims the flight attendant. She offers me a hand and helps me to my feet.

"Oh dear," she says, this time examining the contents of my backpack, which are now scattered across the aisle and multiple rows.

I snatch my bag from the floor and begin cramming items into it, with no particular rhyme or reason. The flight attendant retreats a few rows and returns to delicately hand me the spare underwear I included in my carry-on in case my checked luggage got lost.

Dear God, shoot me now.

"I think this is the last of it," she says discreetly.

"Thank you so much."

"Don't mention it. Enjoy your trip." Gee, what gave away the fact that I'm a visitor and not some suave European returning home? I try in vain to zip my backpack closed, but the zipper head refuses to line up in the track.

Instead, I force the bag onto my front, tugging it over my shoulders and hugging it to my chest to keep it closed. Mr. Pricklepants peeks over the top. The bag is wider than I am, so I bump seat edges the whole way off the plane. When I reach the exit, the pilot does a double take.

So much for leaving the drama at home.

I could really go for some coffee. And a shower. Anything that will clear the cobwebs out of my brain. I guess there's a reason people coined the term "medicine head" because I'm feeling fuzzier than a pair of slippers right about now. I trail the few lingering passengers up the Jetway and into the terminal.

It doesn't look so very different from the airports in

Cleveland or Philly, where I made my connection. I'm not sure what I expected, but this is Europe. Shouldn't it feel totally foreign? Like maybe the air should be different somehow? Even the signs are in English and there's a banner advertising a McDonald's in Terminal One.

Somehow this is both a huge relief and oddly disappointing.

I follow the crowds to the passport control line and fumble for my passport inside my shirt. Elizabeth made me get a ridiculous-looking money belt, which is like a flat fanny pack I'm supposed to wear buckled around my waist on the inside of my clothes. She says it will keep my money and documents safely on me at all times, yet protected from pickpockets. Apparently there's this rumor online about thieves on trains who wrap bundles up to look like babies and then throw them at tourists. Because who wouldn't reach up to try to catch a tiny infant sailing through the air? Which is exactly when they rob you blind. These are the stories I wish she'd kept to herself. Nonetheless, I'm sort of grateful to her at the moment because at least I don't have to worry about my passport lying abandoned underneath an airplane seat.

I reach the front of the line and slide my only identification under the glass divide to the security guard. Even though I have Elizabeth's to show at hotel check-ins with the tour, I draw the line at committing international fraud. I hand him Aubree Sadler's brand-spanking-new-and-extremely-expensive-to-procure-last-minute passport, with every page boringly blank. Kinda like my brain right now. Ugh.

So. Groggy.

The man looks at it for two-point-five seconds, riffles all the empty pages, and settles on a random one to press his stamp onto.

"Next!" he calls as he slides it back to me.

And just like that I'm in Europe, officially. I thought the occasion would be more noteworthy somehow. I shuffle away, hugging my backpack—er, *front*pack—as I navigate to baggage claim and watch, dazed, while the luggage comes bubbling up from a conveyor belt below to thump onto a circling carousel.

I grab my suitcase, then head back upstairs to grab something to eat. Step by step, that's how I'm going to take this whole experience, because if I think ahead past the next step, the panic attacks threaten. Elizabeth and I reviewed my arrival in painstaking detail and I know from her online research there's a food court in Lounge One upstairs with real American fast food chains. I'm not ready to take my chances with Dutch food just yet. My sister even included a map of the airport facilities in the Amsterdam section of my binder.

I stop sharp in the middle of the walkway. A small child pushing a doll in a stroller and chattering away in a foreign language nearly crashes into me.

"Sorry," I say. But inside I am screaming.

My binder!

My binder *and* my phone are tucked inside the seat-back pocket.

On the airplane.

Oh my God, oh my God! If I hadn't been so out of it and in such a rush to get off the plane, this never would have happened. I can't believe I did something so totally stupid. That binder has everything, EVERYTHING, I need for this trip. And my phone! My phone is my only method of communication.

What am I supposed to do now?

SIX

I race back toward the gate, but as soon as I reach the security line, I hit a roadblock. I've already exited the secured part of the airport and there's no way they'll let me pass through without a boarding pass for an outgoing flight.

This is a nightmare.

I veer to the side of the line and flag down one of the officials. He doesn't look all that friendly, but maybe it's because he has passengers asking him stupid questions all day. I explain my situation and his eyes soften.

"I'd like to help you," he tells me in perfect English with only the faintest of accents. "But I'm not permitted to leave this area. Perhaps you'll have more luck talking to an AirEuro representative at the check-in desks."

He points me in the right direction and I take off at a run. I'm fairly sure I look like a certifiable crazy person as I attempt to race through the terminal, dragging my suitcase behind me and keeping one hand wrapped around my could-spill-forth-at-any-moment frontpack.

I'm huffing by the time I reach the airline attendant.

"Um, hi, do you speak English?" I ask.

She smiles easily. "Of course," she says in flawless, accentless English. Okay, why does everyone here sound more American than I do?

"I left my whole life on the plane," I tell her. Total understatement too.

"Well, I'm here to help. We can file a report for your missing item and when we locate it, we'll alert you."

I stare at her for a beat or two before saying, "No, please, you don't understand. I can't file a report and wait to hear from you. I'm supposed to lead a bus tour of senior citizens through nine countries over twenty-two days starting *tomorrow morning* and all of the information I need to do it is in a binder I left in the seat-back pocket along with my cell phone. So, see, you wouldn't even be able to contact me to let me know you found it because I don't have a phone. And I'd say you could call me at my hotel, but I don't have a hotel. Well, that's not true. I *do* have a hotel, because the tour company booked one for me, except I don't remember the name of it, because I didn't think I'd have to memorize it, since every single detail I need is in a binder my sister made me. And she's home waiting for her court date because she was arrested and she sent me here instead, which is insane because I've never even been farther away from Ohio than Evanston, Illinois, where my sister went to college, and . . ."

I run out of breath. The desk clerk has every right to call security and have me tossed into the Netherlands version of an insane asylum, but she doesn't. Instead she picks up the phone and rattles off something incredibly fast in a language that sounds like most of the letters are formed in the grunting part of the throat. She pauses and places her hand over one of mine.

"What flight were you on, love?"

I give her the details and she's off and running again. Finally she replaces the receiver.

"I sent someone to the gate to see if we can flag down the plane before it takes off, though it's very possible the cabin doors are already closed. But don't worry. We'll also check with the lost and found to see if the cleaning crew has turned anything in. And there may be some of the attendants from your flight still lingering in the airport, and if so, we'll do our best to locate them."

My knees go weak at her kindness. Someone to take care of me. This is all I want right now. I'm groggy from the sleeping pill and sticky from the running and panicked from, well, the panic, and this woman's eyes are puppy-dog friendly. Maybe she can take me home with her.

"This will all take some time," she says. "Perhaps there is something you need to take care of while you wait? Exchanging money or having a meal?"

"Yes, please. The food court?" I use my shirt's sleeve to wipe a bead of sweat from my forehead. A cup of coffee would be heavenly.

"Of course. Let me tell you where you can find it."

She whips out an airport map identical to the one in my binder and circles Lounge One.

"Now, my name's Marieke, so if someone else is here when you get back, you just have them ask for me, okay? M-A-R-I-E-K-E. Like Mary Kay, the makeup company, yes?"

I want to throw myself into her arms. "Okay," I manage over the lump in my throat.

I cling to the airport map. Marieke is back on the phone before I'm even out of sight.

This is in fate's hands now.

The caffeine from the steaming cup of coffee adds to the jitters I already have from worrying about the binder and my phone. But I try to block it all out and just focus on the aroma and the American-ness of my accompanying bagel.

I am calm, I am zen. I am calm, I am zen. I figure if I can repeat this enough, maybe I can trick my brain into believing it. It sort of works.

When I feel human again, I head back into the terminal. All around me people are moving efficiently. Zooming by with luggage carts, walking with authority to their terminal, pausing to buy cheese at the cheese store.

Holy crap, there's a cheese store. An entire store selling only . . . cheese. In the airport. Somehow this strikes me as ridiculously exotic. These Europeans. They like their cheese enough to have a whole cheese shop in the airport. If the airport has cheese shops, what amazingness could possibly be waiting for me outside here?

For one of the first times since Elizabeth hatched her crazy plan, I allow a twinge of excitement to float above the fear of the unknown. I have no binder, no phone, and no clue where I'm going, so how is it remotely possible that I'm a little bit giddy? Over a cheese shop.

Is this hysteria? Am I about to lose my marbles in the middle of Schiphol Airport in front of people from nearly every nation in the world? I don't know, and at the moment, I don't even care. I just know I have to keep moving before the enormousness of everything hits me.

On my way back to the AirEuro counter, I stop in a gift shop and buy six travel sewing kits, each containing one safety pin. There. My backpack now looks like Dr. Frankenstein stitched it up, but at least I can wear it properly again.

Is it time to go home yet?

"I'm sorry that took so long," I tell Marieke.

"That is no problem. But I'm so sorry, too. I do not have your belongings."

Well, so much for my mini bubble of zen. It pops.

I slump against the counter as Marieke tries to comfort me.

"We are doing everything we can to locate them. We've left word for the plane, so when they land again in Philadelphia, we'll have them do a thorough search for your items and they'll be sent directly back here. We'll take care of messengering them to your hotel. How long are you in Amsterdam?"

"Only for two days. But I don't know the hotel. Oh God. I'm supposed to meet my passengers tomorrow morning in the lobby restaurant and now I'll never find them. How many hotels does Amsterdam have?"

"More than a thousand." Marieke looks worried I'll pass out.

Instead, I thump my head onto the counter separating us. She places a hand on top of mine and pats it gently. "I'm so sorry. Do you remember anything at all about it?"

If I could have any superpower in the world, right now I'd pick photographic memory. I strain to remember the printouts I studied on the plane. Honestly, I didn't read too far ahead because every time I tried to, I got overwhelmed. My brilliant plan was to just peek at the next day. And now I can't even remember that much.

"I think it was something Polish. I remember in the photo there was a tall statue in front of it." I blush. I don't want to tell this perfectly lovely woman that the reason I remember that is because I giggled at how much the statue in front looked a whole lot like a giant, er, part of the male anatomy. "Um, and I'm pretty sure it said something about a royal palace nearby."

Marieke's face lights up. "Does the statue look a bit, hmm . . . how do I say this in English? Ah. Phallic?"

I nod hard.

"By any chance, could it be the Grand Hotel Krasnapolsky?"

Polsky, Polish . . . "Yes! I think that's it!"

"Let's be sure." She picks up her phone and places a call. I hear a whole lot of a mumble jumble with my name in the middle. Dutch is a very strange-sounding language. As she talks, Marieke catches my eye and smiles, nodding.

She hangs up. "They have your reservation and your room is being prepared for you as we speak. It will be ready upon your arrival." Her eyes sparkle. "You're leading quite the fancy tour. That's one of the nicest hotels in the city and it's centrally located in Dam Square. It's very easy to board a train here and take it to Centraal Station. From there, it's less than a kilometer walk straight up Warmoesstraat. I can write that down for you."

I try to remember if a kilometer is longer or shorter than a mile. Shorter, I think. Marieke is looking as proud as if she just solved the *New York Times* Sunday crossword puzzle.

"You see? It's not so bad after all. Besides, you must be very capable if you are entrusted with leading a tour group. That is quite a lot of responsibility."

"Trust me, they didn't pick me for my troubleshooting skills. They didn't even pick me at all."

I'm tempted to smack my head back onto the counter. Marieke steps around the counter to stand beside me and places one hand on my arm.

"Well, *I* see a very resourceful young woman in front of me. You are dealing with a difficult situation, but you have not let it get the best of you. You remembered enough about your hotel to help us locate it. I see you have even problem-solved your broken backpack. I think you are not giving yourself enough credit."

I have to fight to contain my sniffles. Does she not grasp that I am two seconds away from throwing up all over her pristine Dutch counter? Instead I manage a weak smile.

"Good girl," she says. "Now, I know where to find you if—no, *when*—we find your things. Leave word at the hotel with your next destination when you check out. We'll make sure you get them, one way or another. Okay, so now for the train into town. I can point you in the direction of the platform."

"Um, is, uh . . . is there any chance you could take me there?" So pitiful, I know, but right about now I just want to be led around by the hand somewhere, anywhere.

Marieke looks confused. "It's quite easy, but if you'd like, I have a break in ten minutes. You can wait here and I will walk you over to where the trains depart and help you buy the right ticket."

"Yes, please," I say.

She gives me a friendly smile and says, "Traveling can take the wind out of one's sails. I see it every day. But don't worry, you'll be back to yourself in no time."

And where exactly would that get me?

SEVEN

Marieke kindly walks me through the steps for buying my ticket from a kiosk and for getting euros from an ATM, and guides me onto a ramp right in the middle of the airport to the waiting tracks below. Twenty minutes later I'm stepping off into the chaos of Centraal Station. Centraal—it's practically English except for the extra *a*. They seem to like their extra letters here, judging by the street names on the map Marieke drew me. Prins Hendrikkade, Sint Olofspoort, Warmoesstraat.

I wonder how many tiles the Dutch version of Scrabble has.

I let the people stream past me for a few seconds, trying to take it all in, processing everything into two categories: "mostly familiar" and "WTF."

Mostly familiar: the station itself looks like your standard-variety train station, the signs are also in English, and the people look pretty normal except that they're freakishly tall and wear waaaay cooler shoes.

WTF: the voice on the announcement over the loud-speaker and the general chatter around me sound like someone has taken a regular soundtrack and amped it up to Alvin and the Chipmunks speed. The suitcases everyone rolls beside them are mostly hard plastic in bright colors, totally different from what people at home use. Oh, and the snack bar where I stop to grab a water has something like forty thousand varieties of black licorice, including salted. Blech.

I've been dropped in a land of awesome-shoed, licorice-chomping, giant people.

I clutch Marieke's map in my fist and pull my non-primary-colored suitcase behind me as I step into the hazy sunshine of Amsterdam. I'm greeted with the sight of super-old-looking buildings splaying out on roads leaving the station like bicycle spokes. And speaking of bicycles . . . Holy bicycles, Batman.

They are everywhere. Like, seriously thousands of them. I stop in my tracks, earning two angry dings from a handlebar bell on one of them.

But whatever, because *oh my God*, I'm in EUROPE. It looks so . . . European!

I spin in place, trying to implant every detail into my brain. I may be in completely over my head, but I'd be an idiot not to notice how the buildings are so beautiful with all their scrolls and fancy windowsills and their turrets. And the church spires! I feel like I'm in Peter Pan's London. Look at the canal I'm about to cross over! There are funny long boats

floating on it. I stand in place in front of the station for probably five full minutes, just drinking it in, while people stream
past me.

Eventually I register that my backpack is getting heavy
and when I shift, I feel a prickle where my brand-new "perfect
for walking all over Europe" sandals are starting to rub a tiny
blister on my heel. Plus, a bead of sweat down my back tells
me I could really, really use a shower. Adrenaline gives way to
a deep-boned fatigue.

I let the promise of a drawn-curtained hotel room, a room
service lunch, and a nap pull me down Warmoesstraat, a wide
boulevard with a streetcar chugging through it. According to
Marieke, this street will drop me in the center of Dam Square,
tourist mecca of the city. The road is nonstop souvenir shops,
each one displaying orange soccer jerseys, tulip bulbs in pretty
packages, entire walls of felt slippers shaped like wooden clogs,
and windmill *everything*. Basically, all the things you'd think
of when you think of Holland. You couldn't buy a single one
of these things in Ohio. Not one.

I see the seedier stuff too: youth hostels that have signs
decorated with cartoon drawings of pot leaves, a sex museum,
ads for tours of the Red Light District, where prostitution is
legal—your basic "Vegas, the European edition" stuff—and it
just adds to the we're-not-in-Kansas-anymore feeling. It's all so
exotic and I can't even process whether that's a good thing or
a bad thing right now.

It's only about a fifteen-minute walk, but I'm on full

sensory overload by the time I roll my suitcase past the penis statue and spy the blue awning of the Hotel Krasnapolsky.

I knew the bus tour would be first class all the way, but wow. The lobby looks like something out of a movie. I pass Elizabeth's passport over to the desk clerk, snatch the key she hands me, and stumble to my room. It's only eleven in the morning, but I feel like I've just spent a day chopping firewood (not that I've ever actually done this. But it looks tiring).

After five failed attempts to get the door unlocked, the little light finally clicks to green and I push it open, drop my bags on the floor, and flop face-first onto the bed.

And this is only the first *morning.*

I wake up several hours later, totally disoriented.

After a room service meal (a burger! Fries! Just like at home, despite the fact that they serve mayonnaise with the fries, instead of ketchup) and a soak in the ridiculously long bathtub (custom-fitted for the ridiculously giant Dutch people), I'm feeling . . . I don't actually know what I'm feeling. My internal body clock is so screwed up it seems like midnight even though it's four p.m., and somehow being on the other side of the world is almost this physical sensation where I can just *sense* every bit of the distance in my bones. Plus, I can't even wrap my head around the suckitude of not having my binder and phone. There may be canals and cobblestones and museums and streetcars out my window, but at the moment I just want my mom.

Or Elizabeth. Well, it's not so much that I want her, because I'm still incredibly pissed at her, but I do have to face facts and admit that I need her. I'm counting on her having backups of her backups of all the material in my missing binder and overnighting them to me STAT.

I grab the card that has directions for placing international calls off the top of the phone and when I uncover the keypad beneath I see the message light blinking. No one else knows I'm here, so it could only be Elizabeth, calling to tell me how sorry she is and how badly she underestimated me. I pick up the receiver and push the button. Immediately, Elizabeth's voice is in my ear.

"Hey, Bree! If you're listening to this, you must be in your hotel. I hope the flight went well. Listen, I'm not a fan of the way things went down at the airport, but I understand that you were really nervous about the flight and the trip, so let's not worry about it, okay? I just wanted to say congratulations on getting there and I hope you're having an amazing time so far. Don't stress out—this trip is going to be so good for you and will totally expand your horizons and all that. You'll see! If you need anything, I'll be standing by my cell phone, ready to help. I'll even sleep with it, so call day or night. Talk to you soon! Bye!"

Um . . .

I play the message again. I guess someone could listen to it and think, Oh, she's being nice and supportive, but that's not what I hear. "Congratulations on getting there" sounds a little like "Wow, I did not think you would get there in one piece and that deserves major kudos" and "I'll even sleep with it" kind of sounds like "Odds are one million percent that you're going to have an emergency, so I'll just be here ready and waiting to bail your ass out."

And what the actual hell with the whole "you were nervous, so let's not worry about it"? Is she trying to say I didn't have the right to be angry with her or to storm off? What if I don't *want* to forget about it?

It's one thing for *me* to have doubts about all of this, and especially about my own abilities, but for her to have them too makes me feel like shit. She's supposed to be my cheerleader.

Plus that whole "expand your horizons" comment. Fine, so I've never left home before . . . or really wanted to. It's not like I'm missing the sense-of-adventure gene, it's just that, well, I might be missing the sense-of-adventure gene. I like things predictable and familiar and safe and easy. So what? That's practical, is what that is. I don't happen to see that as the character flaw my sister so very obviously does.

I don't know why I ever had any thoughts that doing this tour for my sister would bring us closer. All it's doing is showing me how totally different we are. And how very little she knows me . . . or wants to. It seems like she just wants to fix me, or turn me into some mini version of her.

Well, you know what? Not. Gonna. Happen.

Although this means I can't ask her for help. I *really* can't call her in tears and tell how I've monumentally messed things up right from the start. She'll fix it. Of course she will. But she'll never, ever forget it. I don't even know if I care about having her respect, but . . . yes I do. I totally do. She's my big sister, whom everyone has always compared me to my whole life, and I've always fallen short in those comparisons. If I call her now, it's just one more example of Elizabeth being perfect and Aubree being the screwup.

I drop the phone in the cradle.

I pick it back up. I do have to call her, because otherwise she'll freak out. But I don't have to mention the binder. I'll call her and tell her everything is perfect. Maybe rub it in a teeny-tiny bit how ah-mazing Europe is and drop an oh-so-innocent question about her court case. It's totally passive-aggressive and borderline babyish, but, after all, aren't I the baby in the Sadler family? I'd hate to disappoint.

This is probably going to cost a small fortune, but I don't care even a little bit. I listen to the strange double ring and try to imagine Elizabeth lounging in her bed, reading some boring Russian classic novel even though she'll never have assigned summer reading ever again. Picturing her room gives me a sudden lump in my throat as I calculate just how many thousands of miles away I am.

My mother answers. Why is my mother answering Elizabeth's cell?

"Um, hi, Mom. Where's Elizabeth?"

"Bree? Are you at the camp? Why didn't you call me the minute your plane landed? You sound funny. Are you okay? Do you need me to come get you? Where are you calling from, anyway? The number that popped up is all weird."

Yes, please, Mom. Could you catch the next transatlantic flight, pretty please? I take a deep breath and start spinning a doozy of a lie.

"I'm totally great! I'm here at the camp and everything's great. The kids are really great and Madison's already introduced me around to everyone, which is great. It's just . . . great!"

I wonder if she'll pick up on the fact that I said *great* about eight times in the span of four seconds. But she just laughs and says, "Oh, honey, that sounds fun."

"You know it! The best!" I invent some quick details about the cabins and the drive to the camp and hope my mother buys it all. She seems to. Finally I ask, "Um, Mom, could I talk to Elizabeth now?"

"Oh, sweetheart, she's in the shower. I just love that you girls have gotten so close these last few weeks. I know she'll be thrilled that you asked for her. Do you want me to have her call you back?"

No. No, this is perfect. Mom can tell her I arrived safely "at camp" and I won't need to be fake and pretend our fight at the airport didn't mean anything to me when she's so obviously over it already.

"That's okay. Actually, I had to borrow the camp director's satellite phone because my cell doesn't get any reception out here in the woods, and I should get it back to her. I'm guessing this is costing a fortune so I'll probably just stick to letters from here on out, okay?" There. Hopefully that explains away the international phone number on the caller ID and my lack of further communication. I don't know what numbers satellite phones use, but I'm betting Mom doesn't either. Plus, Madison has enough letters and postcards already written and signed by yours truly to get through the whole trip.

"How am I going to survive without hearing my girl's voice every day?" I try not to groan as Mom adds, "But as your dad keeps reminding me, my baby is all grown up now and I'm just going to have to deal with my empty-nest syndrome. At least I'll have Elizabeth here until it's time for you to come back. I'm glad you're having fun. Oh, and Aubree?"

I pause.

"Don't forget to use bug spray, sweets. If you start to run low, just send a postcard and I'll ship you more."

I mumble something in agreement; then Mom signs off with her typical "Love you!" to which I reply with my equally typical "Loveyoubye," so ingrained by now it comes out as all one word, and place the receiver back in the cradle.

I fall back on the bed. I dodged a bullet not having to talk to Elizabeth, but it does still leave me with the problem of: no binder = no tour information.

I squeeze my eyes shut and force a few deep breaths. It doesn't help in the least. I'm just working up the energy to stand and do something, anything, to try to figure out where to go from here when the phone rings. Dammit, I told Mom not to have Elizabeth call me back. Then again, clearly

Elizabeth wouldn't trust that I actually made it in one piece. Of course she'd need to hear it with her own ears. I snatch the phone off the receiver and huff, "I *told* Mom you didn't need to call me back!"

A deep, warm voice with a whole lot of amusement in it barely misses a beat before responding, "Oh, but you know Mom these days. She's always so distracted. Between her quest for that Mrs. America crown and the beekeeping operation she started in the attic, who can blame her for forgetting to pass along a message here and there."

Wait. What? The voice is American and most definitely male. He sounds young. Well, not little-kid young but more my-age young. Which makes . . . no sense.

"I . . . I'm sorry," I stammer. "I think maybe you have the wrong room."

"Oh, no, that was just me trying to be funny and clearly failing miserably. Let's start over like boring people this time. Hello, is this Elizabeth?"

"No, it's Au—" Oh crap! It *is* Elizabeth. Or at least, it is Elizabeth according to anyone who would possibly have this number. "I mean, yes. Yes, this is Elizabeth Sadler. Sorry. Um, jet lag."

I try to laugh it off, and thankfully there's no hesitation on the other end when the boy responds with an easy laugh and, "Yeah, jet lag is the worst. Hey, so this is Sam. Of At Your Age Adventures Tours?"

I swallow and manage, "Hi. Hey. I mean, hello. At Your Age Adventures. Right. Hi. So, yeah. Everything here is really perfect. Just perfect. More than perfect, actually. Top-notch."

Shut UP, Aubree!

Another chuckle from the boy at the other end of the phone. "Okay, then. Glad to hear all is 'top-notch.'" His voice is definitely teasing, but not in a mean way. At least, I don't think so. I exhale and try to force myself to calm down as Sam continues. "It's just that you missed your check-in call and Bento is waiting for you downstairs now, so we wanted to make sure you'd arrived in one piece and didn't, I don't know, maybe get distracted in one of those Amsterdam coffeeshops."

Check-in call? Bento? I don't know anything about any of this. Maybe I *should* suck it up and call Elizabeth for the backup binder information after all. Maybe winging it is a monumentally stupid Plan B. Besides, having Elizabeth lose respect for me would be way better than having Elizabeth hate me because I mess things up so badly that the whole debacle blows up in both our faces and she loses her job with the congressman.

"Oh, no. Nope," I tell Sam. "I had my coffee at the airport." I need to get him off the phone so I can call Elizabeth pronto, but he probably already thinks I'm a total spaz from this conversation. Might as well make an attempt to sound normal first, so I don't leave him with a bad impression.

Sam's chuckle is a full-blown laugh this time. "Um, Elizabeth?"

"Yeah?" It's so, so weird to answer to that. I wonder if I'll be used to it by the end of the trip.

"You are aware that 'coffeeshop' is a euphemism for a place

you can legally smoke marijuana in Amsterdam, right?"

Oh. Ooooh. "I . . . of course. Yes, sure. I totally knew that."

Sam's voice is warm as he answers, "Sorry. I didn't mean to suggest otherwise. After all, you *are* the tour guide."

"Right," I answer, trying to sound confident. "That I am."

"Well, Tour Guide Elizabeth. I should probably let you go meet your bus driver in the lobby. I'll text him and let him know you're headed down now. Sound good?"

Bento is the *bus driver*! Okay, this feels like progress. And actually, I don't know why I didn't think of this before, but the bus driver, Bento, will definitely have all the information I need to start the tour. Granted, it might not be as detailed as Elizabeth's binder (I don't think the entirety of Wikipedia is as detailed as Elizabeth's binder) but he'll obviously know where we're headed and when. I'm pretty positive I can get it out of him without letting him catch on that I don't have a freaking clue about either.

I suddenly realize Sam is still on the phone, waiting for me to respond.

"Sure, sounds good."

The hint of laughter is still in his voice as he says, "Nice 'meeting' you, Elizabeth. We'll talk soon."

"Sure, okay. You too. Okay, then, loveyoubye." I put the phone back in the cradle and then I pause as my words replay in my head.

Oh God.

I did not just tell a total stranger—my employer, no

less—that I *loved him*. Did not. I roll over and scream into the sheets of my bed.

Maybe he didn't hear me. He probably didn't. I was halfway to hanging up as I said it so the phone was already moving away from my mouth. And even if he did, I bet he thinks he just misunderstood me. After all, I'm guessing he's seen Elizabeth's file and he'd never believe someone as pulled together as her transcript indicates could ever be such a mess.

And she's not.

Aubree, on the other hand? Oh yeah. Aubree is *exactly* that much of a mess.

EIGHT

I don't see anyone looking like a bus driver (not that bus drivers have a particular look, just that no one seems to be glancing around as if they're supposed to be meeting someone) when I get to the lobby five minutes later, so I flip through the postcards outside the gift shop while I wait. I find one showing the penis statue outside the lobby doors, which will not only make Madison laugh but also represents basically the only tourist site I've seen.

I buy it and scribble *Wish you were here (instead of me)* on the back and walk it over to the front desk. The clerk assures me he will attach the proper stamps, post it, and charge it to my room. The service here is even better than Mom's, and that's saying a lot.

I plop into a chair and try not to stare down every male who enters the lobby. A moment later, a man comes through the doors, blowing across the lid of a steaming cup of coffee (which he got where? The pot shop?), and crosses the lobby straight toward me. "Elizabetta?"

He's a stocky Hispanic man who's about in his forties. He has puffy black hair and a healthy-sized mustache. When he smiles, which he does now, he looks like one of the Super Mario brothers.

"Elizabetta?" he repeats.

I stand and stick out my hand. "Hi, I'm Elizabeth. It's so nice to meet you."

"Encantado."

"Oh, sorry, I don't speak . . . um, Italian?"

He stares at me blankly. I stare at him blankly.

"Español?" he asks.

Oh. Spanish. Nope, don't speak that either.

I hold my palms up and grin. "Señorita? Margarita? Gracias? *Uno, dos, tres, cuatro?"*

I've just given him the sum total of my Spanish vocabulary. More blank stares.

Then he begins speaking rapidly. *"No lo entiendo. La empresa de turismo me dijo que sabías español. Yo no sé nada de inglés. Estamos en un lío, Elizabetta."*

I blink slowly, then point to myself. "Um, si, Elizabetta." That was the only word I understood of that stream he just spewed at me. At least I *think* he said Elizabeth.

He shakes his head and begins mumbling. *"Primero me encargan a ese grupo de turistas a última hora. Después me dicen que solo tengo dos días para prepararme y ahora me dan una guía con la que no puedo ni entenderme. Por favor! ¿Cómo se me ha ocurrido aceptar otro viaje después del último desastre?"*

I am beginning to get the distinct impression that this bus driver does not speak any English. I swallow as I remember who minored in Spanish in college: Elizabetta. I mean, Elizabeth. It must have been on her application to the tour company.

I fall back into my chair and blink a few more times. And then . . .

I laugh.

I laugh so hard I almost fall onto the blue-and-gold plush carpet in the lobby of the Hotel Krasnapolsky and I don't even care. Tears stream down my cheeks as I peer up at the bus driver. Now it's his turn to do some blinking. But then he cracks another smile. And then a full grin. Pretty soon he's laughing in a chair alongside me and neither of us acknowledge all the posh people checking in who are shooting us sideways looks.

I stick out my hand again.

"Elizabetta."

He nods and holds my hand in his. Pointing with his other hand, he gestures at himself and says, "Bento."

We might have no other way to communicate beyond charades, but at least I'm no longer alone in the world.

The next morning, my little circle of *compadres* (as it turns out, I'm remembering Spanish words left and right. Thank you, Dora the Explorer) expands even more when, at breakfast, I meet my band of jolly travelers.

Bento and I are the first ones to the hotel restaurant, which is this giant atrium with a ceiling of all glass windows where everything from the chairs to the chandeliers drips in gold. It could be a tourist attraction all on its own.

I prearranged my arrival time with Bento using an elaborate game of Pictionary. I still have no idea what we're supposed to be doing today, but I finally did remember enough to know that the activities are all in Amsterdam because we don't leave the city until tomorrow. There is a stack of brochures from the hotel lobby in the empty seat next to me and I'm planning to do my best at winging it.

After meeting with Bento yesterday and realizing our linguistic dilemma, I gave serious thought to calling Elizabeth. Serious, serious thought. But then I replayed her message a few more times and I just couldn't do it. If I need to I'll call her tonight, but I want to give today a try on my own. Just to see. I'm nervous, but it turns out anger is a pretty good fuel.

I haven't left the hotel since arriving yesterday, which I know is totally lame, but at least at the Kras I know how to obtain food (dinner last night: burger and fries again), make a phone call, and operate the television set. If the *Big Bang Theory* marathon I caught last night is any indication, I think I've solved the mystery of why Dutch people speak English with perfect American accents. If they would let me, I might possibly spend the next twenty-two days leading up to my flight home right here, ordering room service and watching sitcoms.

Sadly, that's not to be. Bento touches my arm and gestures

with his chin at the doors behind me. I spin in my chair.

You know those scenes in movies where the ragtag heroes suddenly band together and they stride in unison down the street in slow motion while the soundtrack blares? Picture that but with six senior citizens. Except in this case, nothing else is moving in slow motion. Just the group.

About twenty minutes later (okay, fine, maybe one minute that just feels like twenty) the ensemble arrives at the table.

"Well, hey there, little lady!" says a bulky gentleman wearing an "Everything's bigger in Texas" T-shirt stretched over his Santa Claus belly. "Are you our fearless leader?"

I smile and take a deep breath. Here goes.

"I am. I'm Elizabeth." Still feels so weird to say. I expand my gaze to cover the group at large. "Welcome to Amsterdam, everyone! Please, have a seat."

Following that simple instruction takes a few minutes of maneuvering as people shuffle around and one of the men holds chairs for the ladies (so cute!). Then all six sets of eyes turn to me. Another deep breath as I stand.

"Well, as I said, welcome. I'm really excited for our trip together. This is Bento, our bus driver."

Bento stands. *"Buenos días. Seguro que ninguno de vosotros sabe español y podría traducir lo que dice mi intrépido guía, pero por si acaso, ¿sabe alguien español?"*

Blank stares greet him. Bento gives a tight smile and mutters something under his breath before sitting again.

"Good golly molly, I thought I was escaping all the

Mexicali when I took off from Texas," says Santa Claus belly.

Seriously? Would you care to file a missing object report for that filter you're lacking, sir? Good thing Bento can't understand a word of it, even if I'm embarrassed on his behalf.

"Well," I say in my most cheerful voice, choosing to ignore Mr. Inappropriate. "Why don't we take a few minutes to do some introductions? I'll begin. My name, as you know, is Elizabeth and I recently graduated, uh, college. I'm a political science major, with a minor in"—whoops, I can't say Spanish, like the real Elizabeth would—"history. And you'll be my first tour group, so I'm really looking forward to having an adventure with you and, uh, please go easy on me!" I finish with a giant smile and my palms up.

Six smiles greet me. So far, so good.

Santa pushes back from the table and stands. If everything is bigger in Texas, that definitely includes his voice. When he speaks, his words boom across the empty restaurant.

"Well, I'm Hank Hermann from Dallas, Texas. This here little woman's my wife, Maisy, and we're here on our fifth honeymoon. We take one for each decade of marriage. Ain't that right, Maze?"

The tiny (maybe she's not from Texas) woman next to him stands, bobs her head, and giggles into the back of her hand. She looks at her husband like he's the quarterback of the football team. Hank pulls her up next to him and slides his arm around her. He is not at all subtle when he grabs her butt. She giggles some more.

I force my face into a neutral expression.

"Welcome, Hank and Maisy."

Everyone else at the table parrots me as Hank sits and pulls a still-giggling Maisy onto his lap.

Next to Hank, a refined-looking man stands. He's African-American, with a full salt-and-pepper beard and a neatly trimmed buzzed haircut. His khakis are pressed with a sharp crease and, even though it's summer, he's wearing a navy blazer over a button-down dress shirt. He clears his throat. "*Goedemorgen*. That was Dutch for 'good morning.' I try to learn the local 'good day's, 'please's, and 'thank you's when I travel." He clears his throat again and continues in his gentle voice. "My name is Mr. Fenton, I'm from Aurora, Colorado, and this is my third organized tour. I'm really looking forward to getting to know everyone."

"How do you say that 'good morning' again?" one of the women asks.

"*Goedemorgen*."

The whole table repeats it.

Mr. Fenton stays standing to pull out the chair for the woman seated next to him. If I were a hundred years older, I'd totally be crushing on him.

The woman he helps up is on the frail side and I finally know what the expression "bird-boned" means. She looks like a flyswatter could topple her over. But her voice is strong and her smile is friendly.

"Hello, everyone. My name is Emma Jordan and I'm from

Connecticut, just outside of Hartford. I'm traveling with my closest friend in the world, Mary O'Brien, and this trip has been a dream of ours since we were little girls listening to the serial *Escape* on my daddy's radio."

"Oh, I loved me that show," Hank booms. A few others nod.

Mary stands too now and holds Emma's hand. She and Emma are like Jack Sprat and his wife, because everywhere that Emma is skin and bones, Mary is soft layers of fat. I'll bet a hug from her would be like being wrapped in towels straight out of the dryer. Her eyes are as warm as melted chocolate and her grin has everyone around the table smiling back at her.

"I'm going to warn you all right now that Emma and I can sometimes bicker, but pay us no mind. We thought it would help us get cast on *The Amazing Race*, but apparently they'd already filled the 'old people team' spot by the time we showed up and we were worried if we waited for next season, one of us might not be around. So here we are."

I stifle a laugh, but it turns out I don't need to because everyone else laughs out loud.

"Anyhoo, if it gets annoying, you just tell me to 'shut up, Mary.' I promise I won't mind. Half the time I walk around saying it to myself anyway."

Emma reaches over and bops Mary on the head, which makes everyone laugh again. With the exception of Texas Hank, I have the sweetest group of grans and grampses possible. Jackpot! Maybe this won't be so bad.

The last woman at the table pushes back and her chair scrapes along the floor. I cringe at the sound. She's got mousy brown hair and a double chin, even though she's pretty thin. Her shoulders hunch in and when she speaks, we all have to lean in a bit to hear her. "Hello, everyone. My name is Dolores Shemkovich. I'm from Dayton, Ohio."

Her voice hits every syllable like she's giving a formal speech to the queen. Wow, though. From Ohio. What are the odds?

"I'm from Ohio too," I tell her. "And our tour company is based in Dayton. What a coincidence."

She looks over at me and gives a tiny shrug. "Oh, no, dear. No coincidence. You see, the company is owned by my daughter."

Her daughter?!

NINE

I'm in a foreign land. With no itinerary of the tour I am supposed to be leading, much less the actual information I am supposed to be imparting to the six individuals entrusted to my care. The driver of my tour bus speaks only Spanish. I do not speak Spanish. I *do* have an English-to-Spanish translation app on my smartphone; however, my smartphone is apparently crisscrossing the Atlantic Ocean considering the hotel still has no messages for me regarding my luggage. The mother of the person who holds my sister's career in her hands is on my tour and about to bear witness to the mega-disaster that awaits me.

I really hope Elizabeth has a fallback career in mind.

Fortunately, about two seconds after Mrs. Shemkovich drops her bombshell, the waitress arrives to take our breakfast orders, so I don't have to wrap my brain around a response.

It turns out pancakes are kind of a "thing" in the Netherlands, at least according to our server. She hands me a menu with topping combinations I guarantee IHOP has never even heard of. Um, shawarma panackes? Pepperoni pancakes? *Rabbit-and-deer*-topped pancakes?! Swear to God. They're on my menu.

"Could I please have butter and maple syrup pancakes?" I ask the waitress. She looks disappointed.

Conversations swirl around for a bit as everyone plays the "Oh, my best friend's cousin's hairdresser lives in Texas, I wonder if you know him" game. It isn't until the waitress is placing pancakes in front of us that attention turns back to me.

"So what's on tap for you today, fearless leader?" Hank says in his freakishly loud voice, which guarantees everyone is now listening.

"Well, funny you should ask," I say. I swallow my panic. "I was thinking we could take a vote to see what everyone would most like to do. I figured it might be a nice way to show right from the start that, as your tour guide, I care deeply about your input into our trip too. What do you think about that?"

"But it says here we're supposed to go on a dinner cruise through the canals at six o'clock tonight," says Mary.

Says here? Where's here? I look down the table at the sheet of paper in her hand. I *must* get hold of that paper. In the meantime, I arrange my face into a carefree expression.

"Oh, *of course* we're doing the canal dinner cruise. I'm sure we've already paid for it and reserved the boat and everything. I mean, we have. I know we have. Now, what does your sheet have us doing this morning? Let's vote on that activity."

"It's a free day until six o'clock," Mary replies, sounding puzzled.

Oh. It's a free day. I busy myself with my pancakes and try not to acknowledge that my grand gesture of democracy just makes me look kind of idiotic. I steal a glance at Dolores to see if she's reaching for a phone to call her daughter yet. Fortunately, she's too busy sawing into plain, dry pancakes. Wow, that's even more boring than mine.

"Elizabeth?"

I rub the butter pat around with the back of my fork to melt it.

"Elizabeth?"

I drizzle maple syrup in a pattern across the top of my stack.

"Elizabeth!"

Hmm? Oh, whoops! Mr. Fenton is talking to *me*.

"Sorry. I was distracted. Actually, I don't usually go by Elizabeth. Um, I prefer Lizzie. If everyone would please call me Lizzie, it would be great."

Okay, where the heck did *that* just come from? Elizabeth would one hundred percent throw herself off a bridge if anyone dared to call her Lizzie. But maybe a little distance from my sister is just what I need in this situation, and my brain somehow knew it.

"Oh, okay, Lizzie," says Mr. Fenton. It's a little weird that he didn't give his first name when everyone else did, but he's definitely the most formal one here so it kind of suits him. "I was just going to say that it is quite nice of you to volunteer your free time to spend with us today. Did you have any suggestions for us to vote on?"

I gave up a free day. Drat.

I hold up a stack of brochures and begin to leaf through them. "There's the Van Gogh Museum, the royal palace, the Anne Frank House . . ."

"I want to see the tulips," Emma chimes in.

"Unfortunately, you've chosen the wrong season for that. The tulip fields close to visitors in May. They won't be blooming now," Mr. Fenton answers.

Emma looks disappointed. "What about windmills?"

"I suspect we'll see plenty of those tomorrow on our drive through the countryside," Mary says.

We're going to the countryside tomorrow? Good to know. I have *got* to get my hands on that printout Mary has.

"This place has a sex museum, ya know. That's my vote." Who else but Hank?

Surprisingly, Emma raises her head and says, "Well, now, that sounds fun."

Wait, what? There is no way in Helsinki I am accompanying six senior citizens to a museum about S-E-X as their *guide*. I would rather drown in one of the canals before having to discuss positions and various aides with Grandma. Well, not my grandma, but I'll bet they're all *someone's* grandma or grandpa.

"Or we could go to the Anne Frank House? Lots of history there." I smile to make my suggestion sound sweeter. I'm trying. Under the table, Bento slips a piece of paper into my hand. I glance at it, but it's just a name and a long string of numbers. I must have a confused expression on my face because he mimes a telephone. Oh. It's a European phone number. Okay, I have no idea who I'm calling, but excusing myself to make a call to a mystery person is way preferable to staying here and getting roped into a sex museum tour.

"I need to run to my room for just a moment. Here, I'll pass around the brochures and we can talk more when I get back."

I race to my room and dial the number.

"Met Corinne."

"Um, hello?"

"Hallo?"

"Uh, hi. This is going to sound weird, but . . . do you know a man named Bento?"

"Bus driver? From Spain?"

The voice on the other end of the line sounds not much older than me and not all that surprised to be answering questions about a random Spaniard.

"Yes! That's him! He gave me your number and suggested I call you but, um, I don't speak Spanish, so I'm not exactly sure why. I know this is strange, but, uh, who are you?"

A sparkly laugh. "My name is Corinne. I've worked with Bento many times. His tour guide companies hire me when they want a local to lead a group around the city for a few hours. You know, get an insider's take on things."

I can do that? I can bring in local experts? This was definitely not in any part of the binder I read. I really should have flipped through more of that thing. I feel a little thrill, like I'm getting away with something; it's like a fire drill sounding two seconds after the teacher announces a pop quiz.

"Yes! Yes! I'd like to do that, please. Would you be available this morning? Oh, please say yes!"

Corinne laughs again. "I'm at my girlfriend's place now. Give me a bit to run home and shower and I can meet you in Dam Square in an hour and a half. Do you know where Dam Square is?"

I stifle a smile. "Pretty sure I can find it."

"Tell me about your group. How many people, what are their interests, any physical considerations I should know about?"

I fill her in on the details and she gives me some suggestions. They all sound perfect.

"Oh, and Corinne? Is there any chance you speak Spanish?" I ask.

"Fluently."

I just might do a happy dance in my hotel room.

Corinne was heaven-sent. She totally and completely saved the day today and I am not ashamed to say I needed major rescuing. Within two seconds she had everyone wrapped around her finger, and I'm fairly sure they would have followed her to the depths of hell (although some might term the Red Light District just that, and we certainly trotted after her there).

Well, everyone except Hank and Maisy, who excused themselves shortly after I announced our pending walking tour.

And I quote: "If we ain't visiting the sex museum, I'm gonna take my little lady there on our own."

I sincerely hope he did not see how seasick green I turned, but I'm pretty sure Mr. Fenton did because he had a sudden coughing fit that sounded suspiciously like laughter.

Too bad for Hank, though, because Corinne started our tour by weaving us behind the hotel and into the Red Light District, where sex was amply on display. Or at least the promise of it. She subtly pointed out the women modeling their wares behind glass windows while I tried to hide the fact that I was blushing.

Then she made a few more twisty turns and we were at the flower market, where shops of every type of bloom made Emma say she wasn't sad about missing the tulip fields anymore. Corinne showed us the buildings that were sloping toward the canals and took us to a secret garden accessed by a totally ordinary door in a wall. It was once a convent, and even though a bunch of other groups had discovered the hidden door too, and clustered inside, no one in there spoke above a whisper.

Our foray through Amsterdam ended with plenty of time for a nap and was so good that when we took the canal dinner tour later that night, a bunch of what we learned was a repeat. Best of all, I am now armed with provisions that are dramatically enhancing my odds of getting through the first week of my tour with all of my limbs and my sanity intact.

The first came thanks to Corinne's superior Spanish skills.

I now know Bento is a total sweetheart who has my back one hundred and ten percent. In return, I have promised him my firstborn. He definitely doesn't know any more than he needs to—such as my real name, for instance—but he *does* know this is my first tour and that I accidentally lost all of the tour information *and* my cell phone (which still hasn't shown up, so fingers crossed extra hard it catches up with me tomorrow in Germany). Luckily, Bento has his own copy of the agenda with all the addresses we need and everything. It's in Spanish, so it doesn't exactly help me much, and Corinne had another tour she had to give, so she couldn't stay and translate the whole thing for me. But at least I know he can get us where we need to be when we need to be there.

The second piece is Mary's scaled-down itinerary, which *is* in English and is currently tucked into my back pocket.

So, yeah, I conned a sweet old lady. I'm not proud of it.

But it was a necessary evil. I convinced her to let me hold her pocketbook (her term, not mine) while she got Emma to take a picture of her in front of the penis statue. I *might* have then asked her for a hard candy, because I've visited Aunt Mira at the nursing home enough times to know that old people always, always have stashes of small candies. Once I had permission to dig through her purse, I pilfered the agenda. I felt *realllllly* bad when she was searching all over for it later, but I figure she'd rather have a tour guide with more than just a vague idea of which country is next up.

Now I'm back in my room after the boat ride and I'm more than halfway in love with Amsterdam. Basically, I've decided it's the most beautiful city on earth. Granted, I have only Cleveland and the suburbs of Chicago to compare it with, but still . . . What could possibly be more beautiful than all those little bridges over the canals with the flower carts on them and the picture-perfect bicycles propped against the railings and the condom shop just as you reach the other side. Okay, well, maybe the condom shop doesn't *quite* fit, but that's just Amsterdam.

I'm even a tiny bit pissed that I wasted my whole arrival day in the hotel room and definitely sorry that we have to leave the city in the morning. With Corinne to lead me around and the Kras providing room service, I'm betting I could even get a little comfortable here.

I'm lying in my bed, feeling more than a little comfortable already, when the phone rings and I jump.

My stomach twists into instant knots. It could be Elizabeth, who has already left me two "Call me right now!" messages today that I am pointedly ignoring because I don't trust myself not to blow up on her yet, or else someone from the tour company—God, please don't be Sam—because I'm supposed to check in with them every day and I forgot to get their phone number from Bento. I also forgot to get Bento's cell number, which is just . . .

I bring the phone slowly to my ear and squeak out a "Hello?"

"This is extremely important, so please take a moment before answering."

Sam. It's Sam. Oh God, please, please, please don't let him

remember my sign-off yesterday. If there is any goodness in the world, he did not hear me tell him that I love him two-point-five seconds after "meeting" him for the first time.

I swallow. "Um, okay."

"Good. Left side or right side? Of the bed."

I sit up. "What?"

"Do you sleep on the left side or the right side of the bed? I know that's pretty forward of me to ask a virtual stranger, but since you went right to the 'I love you's yesterday, I think you, actually, are the one who set a dangerous precedent, and the fact of the matter is, with those words on the table so early, I figure we're gonna be zooming up to marriage and kids before we know it. So I need to know at the outset . . . left or right."

I am torn between sobbing and laughing. He totally heard me. He totally heard me and he's not even going to be polite and pretend like it never happened.

I stifle a moan and answer, "Neither."

"What? How can that be?"

I puff out a breath. One: I haven't had anyone under the age of seventy who speaks my native language to talk with in two days (well, except Corinne, but she was too focused on making sure the seniors were entertained to chat much with me) and Sam is definitely, definitely under the age of eighty, judging by his voice. Two: sure, we share an employer, but would it be worse to shut down the harmless flirting (if that's even what this is) and be all business all the time, or would he respect me more if I played along and befriended him? I'm thinking the latter. Three: he's just a voice on the phone and he's gonna stay that way.

I'm going for it. "I sleep sideways. Oh, and I snore."

"Bold. Very bold," Sam says, with an appreciative whistle. "Just so you know, I can only sleep on the left. Even on my dorm bed, which is the smallest twin mattress known to man. There I am every morning, all rolled up to the edge of the left side."

Hmm . . . dorm mattress. So Sam's a college boy. Or just out of juvie. "That sounds painful," I say with a laugh.

"You have no idea. So, how was your day today? Did you get your 'coffee'?"

I can't help but laugh again. "You know, they also have coffee shops here that serve the real beverage. They even have Starbucks."

"If you say so. Just don't let the barista talk you into any brownies."

"Noted."

Sam clears his throat and asks, "All's going well, then? You met the passengers, obviously. How's the group gelling?"

"Good." I take a moment and give him a short roundup of our day, and even make him snort with my accounting of Hank's introduction.

"Yowza. He sounds like a gem. Every tour seems to have one of those guys who say totally inappropriate things you just have to grin and bear. At least Emma and Mary sound great. How's Dolores? You didn't say much about her."

Oh right, the owner's daughter. Maybe Sam has some recon that could help me make an extra good impression on her so my—Elizabeth's—review could be *extra* glowing. "She's quiet, but good. Hey, have you ever met her? Does she come into the office? Are she and her daughter really close?"

"Um, well, actually—oh, can you hold a sec?" Sam asks.

"Sure." I twirl the phone cord around my finger and try to ignore how my belly goes all squishy when his voice comes back on the line. I'm in Amsterdam, for God's sake. How has a random phone conversation with a boy six thousand miles away somehow become the highlight of my day?

"Listen," he says. "I'm really sorry but something's going on with our internet connection and people here are kind of losing it. I have to hop off now and help." He actually sounds disappointed. "But I'll give your hotel room in Germany a call, same time tomorrow. Does that work? Is this too late for you?"

"Sure, no, it's fine."

"Okay, talk then. Oh, and Elizabeth?"

"Yeah?"

"Likeyoubye."

His laugh is warm in my ear as I hang up the phone.

As pro-tourist as I was a few minutes ago, completely eager to spend tomorrow exploring . . . I kind of can't wait for it to be tomorrow night.

TEN

Cheese and windmills await today.

Hopefully wind*mills* and not just wind. I'm a little reluctant to spend an afternoon on a bus with a bunch of old people who will have just spent the morning hours gorging on cheese. Who knows what bodily functions I'll be privy to on this trip.

After breakfast we meet Bento outside and get our first glimpse at our wheels for the next twenty-one days. The bus is smaller than I had pictured in my head. It looks more like a hotel shuttle than a proper bus, with just five rows of seats, two to a side, except for the last row, where a tiny bathroom is in place of the left row. A pathway runs down the center. The outside is a gray-blue color and there's a smallish luggage compartment door that swings open on the underneath part. But it's plenty big enough for just seven people and a driver, and at least the seats are comfy.

It takes about thirty minutes to load everyone's luggage, sort out who's going to sit where, and make last-minute bathroom stops in the hotel lobby. No one seems eager to christen the one on the bus. We drive thirty minutes outside the city before pulling into a farm with a large barn and a sign promising that inside we'll learn all the finer details of how clogs are made. Oh, and cheese.

"I hope they have jalapeño. That's a Texas favorite," booms Hank as we file off the bus.

"Actually, Hank, Holland is renowned for its Gouda cheese," says Mr. Fenton. "Personally, I'm more excited to see the clogs. Did you know the Dutch have been wearing clogs since the thirteenth century? They're carved from willow or poplar trees and about a million Dutch people wear them as everyday footwear to this day. Mostly farmers."

Wow, someone sure read the brochure.

"Wouldn't catch any ranchers in clogs back home in Texas. Can you imagine, Maisy?" Hank gives his wife's butt another squeeze. Ick.

"Why would you come all the way to Europe to want things just like at home?" asks Emma.

"Everything's better in Texas." Hank has a "duh" look on his face, like the question barely merits an answer.

"I thought it was bigger." Emma snorts.

"Bigger, better, same difference," Hank answers, not bothered in the slightest by her snorting.

"This way, everyone." I'm like a real official tour guide, even though I'm pretty sure my crew can easily figure out that the barn is where all the action will be taking place.

Nonetheless, they fall in line behind me like I'm the mama duck, and we waddle in to see clog- and cheese-making in action.

Two hours later, we file back onto the bus. Emma slip-slides in the clogs she insisted on buying and Mary grabs on to her arm.

"Oh, Em, didn't you hear the woman warn you how dangerous these can be? There's no traction on them at all," she says.

"Pretty risky at our age, if you ask me. No need to go courting a broken hip," says Dolores. It's the first time I've heard her speak today. I noticed she hung back quite a bit during the demonstrations.

Emma grins and clicks her wooden heels together. The tops of her clogs are painted with pink and red tulips. "At my age, how many more chances will I get to throw caution to the wind? Live life to the fullest, that's my motto!"

So far she's my favorite. I love her energy and her giant smiles; she's like a little kid. Sure enough, her eyes widen and dance when she sees Hank hobbling toward the bus under the weight of a ginormous wheel of cheese. It's practically big enough to use as a spare if the bus gets a flat.

"What is *that*?" Mary asks.

"This here is Gouda. Turns out I like it near as much as jalapeño. I plan to introduce it to Texas."

"I'm fairly sure one or two Texas grocery stores offer Gouda cheese, Hank," says Mr. Fenton. He's far too much of a gentleman to do an eye roll, but I can tell he'd like to.

"Well, they haven't had fresh Gouda like this, I reckon."

"Nor will they. Are you forgetting we have weeks left on this tour? Can you imagine what this cheese will smell like by then?" Mr. Fenton sinks into his seat and pulls a handkerchief from his pocket. He places it over his eyes.

"He's got a point, Hank," I say. "You should try to send it home when we get to Braubach or pass it around to everyone here over the next couple of days."

"It would cost a small fortune to send something that heavy internationally." Mr. Fenton sighs. "Looks like we all have some cheese sandwiches in our future."

Hank just shrugs and slides the cheese wheel underneath his seat.

Bento calls, "*¿Estáis todos listos?*" He jangles his keys in a universal can-we-hit-the-road-now? sign.

"Um, sure." I survey my charges. "We good?"

There's a thumbs-up from everyone except Hank and Maisy, who have claimed the last seat on the bus and are making out like teenagers. Although *I'm* a teenager and I've never made out like *that*. I whip my head back around and nod at Bento.

We're off.

We'll be ending the day in Germany, according to my—er, Mary's—itinerary, so I settle in for a long drive. Since I don't have to do anything tour-guide related, for the time being I can relax. I plan to take in every mile of countryside with my newfound appreciation for Europe and its many splendors.

Except after about twenty minutes of this I come to a realization. Holland's countryside can be summed up in one word: flat. Really, really, really flat. Every so often we pass a windmill (which Emma is sure to point out by squealing) but otherwise, it's a lot like being on a highway in a version of Ohio where the street signs have way more letters.

I'm afraid to check, but after a bit it seems as though Hank and Maisy have finally disentangled because the snores coming from the back of the bus echo even louder than Hank's thundering voice. In between exclaiming over windmills, Emma and Mary argue in a totally cute way about whether Emma should try to find lederhosen in Germany to wear with her clogs. Mary dares her fifty bucks to wear the whole ensemble to dinner. She's known Emma for decades and I've only known her for a day and a half, but even I can tell Mary's losing that bet.

Mr. Fenton is reclined in his third row seat with a thick book. The only prop he's missing is a pipe to chew on absentmindedly as he turns pages.

Which leaves Dolores, seated opposite him, calmly staring out the window. She's the x factor on this whole trip so far. Not only is she the VIP guest I need to be extra aware of, but she's also quieter than a whisper, and I'm betting there are turtles who don't spend as much time in their shells. I really need to find a way to cozy up to her.

But for now, I take advantage of the downtime. Once I determine I'm not missing anything life changing out the window, I grab my backpack and pull out a smaller version of my jewelry kit. I won't be able to work with the tiny needle-nose pliers or the even-smaller seed beads because of the bumps we hit periodically, but I figure I can use the time to try out a new technique I'm just learning of making bracelets using embroidery floss that gets woven and knotted around bigger beads in intricate patterns. I make a slipknot on a silver ring and loop the ring over a nail I've hammered into a small wooden board. It keeps the bracelet in place while I practice the knotting pattern.

We cross into Germany, and as exciting as it is to add a whole new country visited to my list of . . . well, two . . . the scenery doesn't change all that drastically. We're on the highway, so there's not much to see, even when we skirt the city of Düsseldorf. After a few hours, we stop for a late lunch in Bonn (hooray for the PowerBars I packed, because I'm not touching bratwurst with a ten-foot pole) and from there Bento steers us onto a two-lane road that hugs the Rhine River.

Now there's scenery. Amazing scenery. The mountains rise on either side, while the river curves in and out beside us, and everyone is glued to the windows. We pass through postcard-perfect villages I swear could have been the setting for "Little Red Riding Hood." The houses have crisscross patterns of wood on the outside and window boxes with flowers cascading over the sides.

"This is unbelievably beautiful," Emma whispers from the seat behind me, and I totally get why she's using her indoor voice. It does feel like you should whisper out of respect, like being in church.

So here's the thing. I've done a lot of worrying, *a lot* of worrying, about this trip and whether or not I could handle it. I'm *still* doing a lot of worrying. But we're on day two and so far the wheels haven't come off this bus, literally *or* figuratively speaking. It's actually, well, going fine.

I never, ever imagined I would be seeing the Rhine River. Or windmills. Or that I'd be taking a riverboat cruise on the canals of Amsterdam. I just didn't.

And now I am.

For seventeen years, I've been perfectly content in my little corner of Ohio and, even when my friends were making plans to go off to faraway colleges, I had no desire to go with them. I felt like I had already found somewhere I truly knew could make me happy forever, so what was the point of leaving? And I still feel that way about my home. I do. But now that I see all this and realize I couldn't even have *dreamed* any of it because it was all so far off my radar, I have this weird uncomfortable twinge in my chest. Because . . . what else haven't I bothered to dream, not thinking things could get any better?

"Lizzie, which castle is that?" Dolores calls from her row, snapping me out of my thoughts. I follow her finger as she points out a turreted fairy-tale building perched high on a mountaintop.

Wow. Just wow.

Except actually not wow, because I have no idea which castle it is and my missing binder, which included interesting tidbits about all the memorable sights along our route, is likely hanging out in the bottom of a drink cart on a 757. Of course the question would have to come from *Dolores*. As in mother-of-the-owner Dolores.

Time for a good ole Aubree-patented truth-stretching. I prop up on my knees, facing backward toward my audience.

"Well, guys, I think you'll love the story of that castle. It was built in the 1800s as a gift from the king to one of his favorite knights. Legend has it that he wanted to ship the knight off far from his own castle, because he suspected the knight was sweet on his princess daughter. Even though the king liked the knight enough to gift him a castle, he didn't like him enough to hand over his daughter in marriage. The story says that the princess was equally smitten with the young knight, so she organized a hunting party one afternoon, from which she never returned. The king sent his troops to that castle there, looking for his precious daughter, but it was so well built the king's men couldn't gain access, and the princess and knight lived there peacefully for many years."

C'mon, we're talking castles and princesses. I needed to give them a happy ending.

"That's just the kind of story a castle that beautiful deserves," says Mary, and Dolores nods as well.

Mr. Fenton clears his throat. "Indeed. Indeed it is."

He looks like he wants to say something else, but thinks better of it. Then he gestures out his own window. "If I may, I would like to point out the castle on the opposite side of the river, Lahneck Castle. In fact, when the Knights Templar were ordered to disband by Pope Clement, all the way back in *1312*"—he pauses and glances at me before continuing—"the last twelve Templars took refuge here, where they perished in a heroic fight to the death."

He looks around to make sure he has everyone's rapt attention (which he definitely does) before continuing. "But the tower is rumored haunted by a far younger ghost. In the 1850s a seventeen-year-old British girl who was visiting the castle with her family wandered off from her group and climbed into the abandoned tower, where the wooden steps collapsed from under her. No one heard her cries for help or could locate her in their searches. It was only years later that her remains were found, along with her diary, which she'd hidden in the walls when she realized she would not be rescued. The last lines say, 'All I know is there is no hope for me. Father in heaven have mercy on my soul.' And below that she drew two little hearts."

Holy moly, Mr. Fenton knows his stuff. I shudder as I think of a girl my age trapped in a tower like a real-life Rapunzel, only without any prince to rescue her. But I shudder even more to realize that Mr. Fenton definitely knew that I needed rescuing myself just then. I try to avoid making eye contact with him.

"Um, so, as you know, tomorrow afternoon we'll be inside

one of the famous Rhine castles. We'll be visiting the"—
I glance down at my itinerary to make sure I get the name
right—"Marksburg Castle. Mr. Fenton, is this another one
you're familiar with?"

To my surprise, Mr. Fenton doesn't look annoyed at having to do my job for me. He looks . . . excited. He pops up
from his seat and asks "May I?" as he gestures to the front of
the bus.

I try to make my shrug nonchalant and smile. Is he serious? Heck yeah, he can!

Mr. Fenton's own smile is wide as he reaches the front,
leans one hip into the empty seat beside me, and addresses his
captive audience, me included.

"Marksburg Castle is unique because it's the only one of
these hill castles that has never been destroyed. It was built
over centuries, beginning with the keep in the twelfth century."

"That's real in'eresting stuff, Fenton," says Hank. Mr.
Fenton grimaces slightly, but thanks him politely.

"It really is. Do you know any other juicy stories about
these castles? Those are the ones I want to hear," says Emma,
her eyes twinkling.

Mr. Fenton laughs. "I do indeed. There are more than
thirty castles just on this stretch of the Rhine. There's one, the
Drachenberg, that was . . ."

For the remainder of the drive to Braubach, Mr. Fenton
entertains us all with funny and interesting stories about the

Rhine castles. I don't know whether to be intimidated, thankful, or scared for my evaluation.

I decide to settle on thankful. I haven't had to make up any more elaborate stories to deceive my sweet and trusting guests, and Dolores looks especially enthralled with everything that comes out of Mr. Fenton's mouth, so I'm fairly sure she's forgotten all about me.

Which is exactly how I want it.

ELEVEN

My sister wasn't kidding when she said there'd be lots of downtime. I get that the tour company doesn't want to run senior citizens ragged with a crazy schedule, but what it means is that, after arriving at our hotel, we're all on our own for the night.

I make sure everyone's luggage gets to his or her room, then excuse myself to head to my own. Even though there's still some time before Sam is supposed to call, I don't want to take the chance of not being there.

I plop on my bed and switch on the TV. The only channels I can find in English are twenty-four-hour news stations that seem to repeat the same five headline stories, so I settle for an episode of *Modern Family* in German, and it's actually kind of fun trying to piece together the sitcom plot based only on visual clues.

When the phone rings I jump and then practically fall off the bed in my eagerness to grab it. I put it to my ear while saying, "My turn to ask the questions. Window seat or aisle?"

"What? Bree, is that you?"

It's not Sam. Not Sam at all.

It's my sister.

As annoyed with her as I've been and as much as I've surprised myself by actually enjoying playing European tourist, I'm completely unprepared for the intense wave of homesickness that hits me when I hear her voice. I don't know where in our house she is, but I picture her sitting out in the backyard, next to the stepping stone path we decorated with our little painted handprints the summer my parents put in the pool. For years after that I used to lie in the grass and fit my palm over the imprint of her hand on the rock, trying to stretch my fingers to cover the purple paint she'd used.

Suddenly I miss those rocks. I miss the pool. I miss my bed. I miss the tomato-soup stain on the countertop by the sink and the way Mom mumbles, "Should have listened to that damn contractor when he warned me about stains and marble countertops" every single, solitary time it catches her attention. I miss the strawberry-lime shampoo in my shower and the tiny gap in the crown molding in my ceiling where the corners meet, which I used to stare at from my bed, waiting for spiders to sneak out. I miss ice in my drinks. Why is it so hard to get ice in drinks in Europe? Is there some kind of shortage?

"Yeah, it's me," I answer over the new lump in my throat. "I, um, I thought you were one of my passengers and I needed to know what side of the bus he wanted to sit on tomorrow."

"Wouldn't he just choose one for himself in the morning? Are there assigned seats with only six passengers? Never mind. Don't need to know. Jesus, Bree, have you been getting my messages? Why haven't you called me? One call to Mom does not cut it! I've been worried sick, thinking all kinds of horrible things, and it really doesn't help that your phone goes straight to voice mail."

I get it. I should have called her and I've been avoiding it. But why couldn't her first assumption have been that I was having too much fun to call home? Why imagine all the things I could be messing up? I sigh. I definitely don't want to tell her I lost my phone because I refuse to give her any further ammunition for Dump on Aubree Day, as it apparently has been declared.

"My cell's turned off because I realized the bill goes to Mom and Dad and I didn't want them to see the international calls."

Actually, I hadn't considered that until right this very second, but wow. Talk about a bullet dodged. Thank *God* I lost my phone.

Elizabeth sounds equally awed. "Damn, for all the planning we did, we never even thought of that. Nice looking out."

Finally, *finally*. A touch of respect in her voice. I savor it and feel my insides unclench. I really hate fighting with her. It's so much worse than the way things have been for the past few years, which was more plain old distant versus ugly emotional. I mean, I haven't really liked the distant thing either, but at least it made sense, since the difference between a fourteen-year-old and an eighteen-year-old (which is how old we both were the last time we spent any significant time together) is pretty pronounced.

"Okay, so tell me everything," Elizabeth orders. "How is it? How are the seniors? Are they nice? Is the tour well organized? Is everything in the binder helping?"

I try not to notice that not one of those questions asks about *me*. How *I'm* doing. I know she's probably just worried about her job with the congressman and whether she'll get to keep it, but c'mon. To be honest, I really do want to tell her all about everything in minute detail. But the weird thing is that, at the same time, I also *don't* want to tell her.

The last couple of days have been an exhausting whirlwind of emotions: I've felt overwhelmed, awed, terrified, amused, frustrated, hungry, tired, amazed. Even though I've been surrounded by people, I've mostly been processing those feelings by myself because I can't exactly confide in anyone here. And that's been . . . okay. Not every minute's been fun, but it's nice to have something that's *mine*, the way this trip has somehow become. As cheesy as this sounds, I'm actually kind of proud of myself for the way I've been problem solving.

If I tell Elizabeth everything in detail, I'm worried she'll get all judgy or tell me how I could have handled a certain instance better, and I might have to scream. Or I might get even more pissed at her, and that's not what I want at all. I wanted this trip to make our relationship better, not worse, but it kind of feels worse right now. I just want her to have faith in my ability to do the damn tour.

So instead of filling her in about the missing binder, or the fact that Bento and I can't get past *hola* and *buenas noches,* or how Mr. Fenton had to bail my ass out on the castle descriptions today, I say, "It's good. Everything is great. I'm just really, really tired. I guess jet lag lasts longer than I thought."

Elizabeth is quiet for a second and then says, "That's it? I've been out of my mind for three days and that's the sum total of it?"

"I mean, the scenery is really pretty." I could give her more. I could tell her about the girl who died alone in the Rapunzel tower waiting to be rescued or how I learned the pointed toes some Dutch clogs have are to help fishermen pull nets from the water, but in reality, I hate how she's gone and made everything all about her again. It's all about how *she's* been worried, how *she's* been feeling. I feel like the scenery in *The Elizabeth Show.*

Across the ocean, she sighs. "It's just weird that you're so quiet and zen now when, before we left, you were so freaked out about going. Could you at least tell me that everything is fine with the people at At Your Age Adventures? Have you talked to the tour operator for check-ins? Do they seem suspicious at all?"

Have I talked to the tour company? Oh hell yeah. I glance at the clock. I should be speaking to Sam again in exactly one hour and I'm slightly giddy about it. I'm sure it's just the fun of flirting with someone my own age, after days among the elderly, that's fueling my mini insta-crush, but whatever. It's harmless. "Yup, I've talked to them every night. As far as they're concerned, everything is one hundred percent perfect." I catch myself before I say "top-notch" and grin a secret smile. Fifty-nine minutes.

Elizabeth says, "Thank God for that. Not that you've asked, but there's nothing to report here. Mom checks the weather in Maine ten times a day and already sent you a care package of homemade chocolate chip cookies. Guess Madison will inherit them. I'm really glad you're holding up over there. Do you think you could *try* calling me from your hotels along the way? I mean, besides Madison, I'm literally the only other person who knows where in the world you are, so it would be kind of nice to actually have confirmation you're in the places you're supposed to be."

She sounds put out or snippy or I don't know what, and I hate that the conversation is going like this. I know I could probably play nice and give her what she wants, which is the sweet, hero-worshiping attitude she knows and loves, but I'm still too hurt by the things she said about me behind my back. I know I need to just get over it, but at the moment it's powering my determination to get one kick-ass evaluation and prove to her how wrong she was, and I need that incentive. I really need that incentive.

So I just reply, "Of course! I'll call you every few days from the hotels. Okay?"

"Yeah, okay." She doesn't sound upset anymore, just quiet. "Hey, I hope you're having fun."

Finally. I smile. "I really am."

She sounds like she's smiling too when she says, "Good. See? I told you you would."

And just like that, I'm annoyed again. God, why is she making it so hard to just be friendly and normal with her?

I puff out a breath and say something I've never said to my sister before. "You know what, Elizabeth? Screw you."

"What?"

"You heard me," I reply.

"What the hell, Bree?"

I grind my teeth. "I just wish you'd save it with the condescending attitude. It's really not helpful."

"Condescending—? Okay, I have no idea what you're talking about. None. No offense, but you're kind of blowing things out of proportion lately. The airport . . . now whatever this is . . . I really don't understand you."

And therein lies the problem. I just snort, to which she responds, "Oh, grow up, Aubree."

"Maybe I already have," I snap, slamming down the phone.

Okay, what just happened? Elizabeth and I never fight over real, actual stuff. Mostly because we're each orbiting our own planets, but still. She pushed a hot button, but immediately I feel bad. Although I have to smirk just a tiny bit. I bet not that many people have hung up on my sister before. She must be pissed beyond belief. It's mean of me to find glee in that, but I kind of do.

However, when she calls back less than a minute later, I'm already cooled off enough to answer with a contrived "I'm sorry."

There's a beat or two of silence at the other end, and then a very male, very *not Elizabeth* voice says, "Love means never having to say you're sorry, Dimples. You're forgiven."

Sam! My mood does the fastest 180 known to man. I stifle a giggle and answer, "Um, did you just call me Dimples?"

"Of course. If we're all in with this, we need terms of endearment. You're Dimples because it's possible I snuck a peek at the copy of your passport we have on file. I'm all for instalove, but I really do need a visual before committing totally. FYI: your dimples are adorable."

Oh good God. Of course he means Elizabeth's dimples are adorable. I have *a* dimple. Singular. Not like it matters because Sam can't see me, but . . .

He's still talking. "What do you want to call me? I came up with a few suggestions for you to choose from. Number one: Your Highness. If that doesn't work, I'm also amenable to: My One True Hero, Captain Amazing, or, while we're on the captain theme, Oh Captain, My Captain. Your pick."

Sam is ridiculous. He's exactly what I need right now. "Give me a second to ponder this," I say, feeling every lingering bad feeling from my call with Elizabeth fly out into the German night air.

Sam whistles the tune from Final Jeopardy! while he waits.

"How about Watson?" I propose.

"Wow. Way to woo a guy. That doesn't sound nearly worshipful enough. Are you referring to the volleyball in *Cast Away*?"

"That was Wilson, you nut."

"Oh, 'you nut' definitely does not work for me either. Let's scratch that. Tell me more about Watson. I'm intrigued."

"You know. From Sherlock Holmes?" I say. "Because he's the supportive sidekick helping out behind the scenes? Like you with this tour."

"Ugh, that's almost as bad as asking me to be Robin to your Batman. How come you get to be Sherlock? Sherlock is way more badass."

"Yeah, well, Jude Law played Watson in the movies. And he was one of *People* magazine's Most Beautiful Men. *Buuuut*, if you don't want me to think of you that way . . ."

Sam laughs. "Now that I can live with, Dimples. Watson it is. So now that we have nicknames established, we're cranking right along. What should we cover next? Where to spend Thanksgiving? My mom cooks a mean turducken. What does yours have to offer?"

I make a face at the idea of turkey and duck in one. "The best mashed potatoes east of the Mississippi. Oh, plus she melts marshmallows *and* brown sugar in the sweet potato casserole. Not even kidding."

Sam's picked a good topic. Nothing cheers me up like my mother's cooking, although picturing the Thanksgiving table reminds me that my diet these last few days has not exactly been well-rounded. Dinner tonight was a Bavarian pretzel.

"Not bad, not bad," Sam says. "Maybe we could time it to hit both. Or do you have to do that holiday runaround already? Are your parents divorced or together?"

"They're together. My dad's in charge of Thanksgiving dessert. Usually that means at least three pies: grasshopper, bourbon pecan, and pumpkin."

"Remind me to invest in some stretch pants sometime between now and then," Sam says.

Is it wrong that I'm kind of loving our fake relationship? I've never even met the guy, but I find myself actually wishing he were coming to my house for Thanksgiving. (I'm also wishing hard that I had a pumpkin pie in front of me right now.)

I lie back on my pillow and let Sam's voice warm my insides. "How about you?" I ask. "Are your parents together?"

Sam is quiet for a second and then says, "Nope. Just me and my mom. As for my dad: never met the guy." I don't know how to answer at first, so I'm relieved when he barely pauses before asking, "Hey, so how 'bout them Yanks?"

I wrinkle my nose. "If you say you're a Yankees fan, I'm going to have to end this call right now."

"Oh, what, because the Indians are such a kick-ass alternative?"

I laugh. Watching baseball with my dad is our thing. We have this ritual before every game where we grill hot dogs (three each), pour big cups of orange Fanta, change into our lucky shirts (which must be switched up after every loss, but can't be washed as long as the Indians are winning), and execute a complicated rally cry while my mother rolls her eyes.

"Maybe," I say. "You have to admit, Santana hitting a home run every year on his birthday is a pretty impressive stat."

Sam whistles. "Too bad his birthday only comes once a year. Still. Girl knows her sports stats. Color me intrigued."

"Yeah, well, I try. At least where the Indians are concerned. It must get pretty lonely being a Yankees fan in Ohio."

"Ah, but I never said I was a Yankees fan, did I? And who's to say I don't like being lonely?"

"Nobody likes being lonely," I answer.

"Yeah, probably true." There's a smile in Sam's voice as he says, "The good news is, you don't have to be lonely when I'm around."

I snort-laugh. Weirdly enough, I actually don't feel lonely at all right now, even though I've never been more on my own in my entire life.

Sam gets quieter when he asks, "You're not, are you? Lonely, I mean. I know there's a big age difference between you and the passengers and it can be kind of a divide after a while, not talking to someone your own age for so long. If you start to go crazy, you know you can always call me."

"Wow, you really *are* a full-service tour company," I tease.

"I would like brownie points for passing on the very obvious dirty joke you just gave me the perfect opening for, and just leave it at 'We aim to please.' But seriously, I want those mad brownie points."

"Noted." I laugh again. I'm doing a lot of that. Sam and I talk about tour stuff for another ten minutes. I fill him in on the clog-and-cheese outing and he tells me he's faxing over a hotel change for Venice, because the one we booked is having trouble with their air conditioning.

"Hey, so, I've gotta sign off and do some more check-ins," he says eventually, and I like that he sounds as though he'd rather keep talking.

"Should I be jealous?" I ask. "Do you flirt like this with all the tour guides?"

"Nah. Raj is up next and he's six foot six and three hundred pounds. Plus he thinks cricket and rugby are better sports than baseball and football. So not my type. Don't worry, I only have eyes—check, make that ears in this case—for the cute ones. You're safe, Dimples. Likeyoubye."

"Likeyoubye."

TWELVE

Braubach has cobblestone streets and houses that look like they were the models for cuckoo clocks and I half expect a tiny bird to come popping out their top windows when it hits the hour. We spend the morning exploring all its nooks and crannies.

Dolores hangs back, as usual, while Mary and Emma buy matching woodsmen's felt hats (complete with red feathers), and she is as quiet as she always is during lunch, but at least she's there with us in body, if not in spirit.

Except after lunch, she decides even that is too much.

We've boarded the bus for a five-minute trip to where we can catch a little train that will take us up to the grounds of Marksburg Castle. Once we park, everyone shuffles out, but when I do a quick head count, I notice her missing. I climb back inside to find her rifling through her bag.

"Dolores? Did you lose something? The train should be here any minute."

"I'm just looking for my yarn bag. I'm not feeling up for a long walk or any stairs this afternoon. I think I'd like to sit out the tour and just enjoy the fresh air and some knitting."

Oh. Okay.

"Um, are you sure? I'm positive the castle guide will allow us to go as slowly as we'd like."

"No, dear. You all go on. I'll be fine. I'd like to find a café and take some time to myself, please."

Got it. I'm not exactly sure how a seasoned tour guide would handle this one. Is it my job to push her into joining us? Or am I supposed to respect her wishes and let her have whatever vacation she chooses? In the interest of preserving my evaluation form, I choose the path of least resistance and go with Option B.

"Okay, well, if you're sure. I know Bento will be hanging here with the bus if you need anything. Should we look for you in the closest café when we finish up?"

"I'll just meet you here at the bus in three hours." She returns to sifting through her giant carry-on bag and I can tell I've been dismissed. With a sigh, I head back outside and follow the rest of the group onto the old-fashioned train. Every time I think I have a handle on things, I realize it's really more like two steps forward, one step back.

At least the castle is interesting, with all its medieval touches. The ladies (me included) love the great banquet hall the best, and Hank seems particularly impressed with the wine cellar. Mr. Fenton keeps the tour guide on his toes with question after question (which makes me ridiculously glad he hasn't drilled me the same way! Does this mean he knows I could never keep up?) and Emma leaves the souvenir shop carrying a knight's metal breastplate decorated with a coat of arms. We're all laughing as our train makes its way back into the Old Town portion of Braubach.

Bento is waiting for us outside the bus, his face ashen.

Right away he starts gushing Spanish and waving his arms around like a crazy person. I know *something* is wrong, but why, oh why, didn't I take Spanish when I had the chance?

"Bento, slow down! Where's Dolores?"

"Dolores. *Sí. Hospital.*"

"I think he's saying she's at the hospital," Hank offers. "Can't help picking up some Mexican when you live in Texas."

Oh good God. This is not the time to inform Hank there is no such language as Mexican or that his comments are unappreciated, not to mention offensive. Besides, obviously he's right about the translation.

My boss's mother is in the hospital!

Bento has us to the hospital in thirty minutes, though it feels longer. As we drive, I formulate the most basic of plans, which consists of "everyone stay right here on the bus until I have more information." Luckily, my crew is on board with this, no pun intended.

The bus screeches to a stop in front of the emergency entrance and I'm already on the bottom step as Bento swings the door open. In seconds I've found the information desk.

"Please, please, do you speak English?"

"Little," the woman at the desk says haltingly, with a very heavy accent.

"I'm a tour guide and one of my guests has been taken here. I don't know what happened. My bus driver only speaks Spanish and I don't, so . . . Oh, never mind, it's not important. I need to find her." I flop against the wooden counter.

"Name, please?"

"My name, or—oh, you mean her name. Dolores Shemkovich. S-H-E-M-K-O-V-I-C-H."

I really hope I'm spelling that right. Why didn't I think to get emergency contact information from everyone the very first minute of the very first day? It's not like I'm dealing with spring chickens here. The best I have is a sheet of paper where I scribbled everyone's names as they introduced themselves so I could keep track of who was who.

But something as responsible as next of kin or lists of medications or allergies? Never even occurred to me. Elizabeth's first move would have been to collect this information. Though of course *she* would never have lost the binder to begin with, so she would already have the forms.

And me? I'm so incompetent people are already landing in the hospital on my watch. Oh God, what if she's dead and it's all my fault?!

The woman at the information desk stops her frantic tapping at her keyboard.

"Yes. She here. Broke this." She bends her arm and pats her elbow. "Room two-three-five. Lift is there."

She points to an elevator behind her and I yell my thanks before running for it.

When I push open the door, Dolores is propped on her bed, staring out the window. She does *not* look like a happy camper. Her arm is in a sling, securing it in position, and she has it resting on top of a pile of pillows so tall the "Princess and the Pea" girl would be jealous.

"Dolores?" I edge into the room and her head turns to examine me.

"I guess I should have gone to the castle after all," she says in a flat voice.

I grimace. "What happened?"

"My ball of yarn dropped and rolled behind me. When I stood up to get it, I didn't realize the string had wound its way around my seat. My chair got stuck and I tripped over it. I tried to put my arm out to break my fall, but I landed on my elbow instead." She winces and I can't tell if it's from discomfort or embarrassment.

"I'm so sorry. Did they give you anything for the pain?"

"They did. It feels alright at the moment. I'm just so darn mad at myself. I never wanted to come on this vacation to begin with. I let my daughter bully me into it and now look what's happened!" She tries to move her hands as she talks, but winces when she lifts her arm from the pillow. She drops it back down with a sigh. "I don't know why she cares so much, but I got a whole guilt trip about how I'm finally old enough to go on one of her senior tours and instead I'm just wasting my days puttering around the house, knitting, and gardening. I *like* to putter. I don't see what's so wrong with that. Who needs to visit all of Europe when I'm perfectly comfortable in my own home?"

When she finishes her speech, her eyebrows crumple and she leans back against the pillow.

"I'm . . . I'm sorry you don't want to be here," I say in a soft voice. If only she knew how much we have in common and how I was guilted into coming too. I guess the big difference is that I'm starting to see the appeal of Europe, and Dolores seems like she'd give anything to be back home.

Her eyes stay closed.

"Um, can I get you anything?" I ask.

"I'm fine. Though someone will need to call my daughter and I don't feel up to it. Would you please do so? I assume you know her?"

"I . . . uh . . . we only had a phone interview. But, um, I can call her. Sure." It probably *does* fall under the realm of tour guide duties, even though I may need to raid the hospital pharmacy first for some antianxiety pills before telling my boss I've broken her mother (or at least let it happen on my watch).

"Maybe I should talk to the doctor first, so I can find out more about what they want to do from here," I say.

Dolores doesn't open her eyes, just nods. I slip out of the

room and head for the nurses' station.

Fortunately, the doctor writes in English as well as he speaks it, so mere minutes later I'm clutching a written description of Dolores's injury and the treatment plan recommended by the hospital. I return to the bus and answer everyone's concerned questions before playing a subtle game of charades with Bento until he finally figures out that I'm looking for the number of the tour operator. He passes over his phone and I return to the quiet waiting room and dial with shaky fingers.

Sam answers. Of *course* he does. "At Your Age Adventures. This is Sam, may I help you?"

"Sam. It's Elizabeth."

"Dimples! My, but you're the impatient one. You know we have a phone date tonight, right? Or was there something I could help you with in the meantime? So far this morning I've located one missing bus in New Zealand, and our tour guide in Koh Phangan had twelve passengers come down with, well, let's just call them intestinal issues, minutes after their bus got hopelessly stuck in the mud. Guess who tracked down a tow truck driver plus a hefty supply of Imodium and toilet paper— which isn't readily available in Thailand, I might add—all from my desk here in Dayton?"

Ew. Even through my panic haze, I make a mental note to stock up on toilet paper at our next stop. But in my pause Sam realizes I'm not laughing along with him.

"What's wrong? Talk to me." His voice is all concern now.

"I think . . . I think I need to talk to the owner." My voice wobbles on the last few words.

"Hey," he says gently. "Hey, it's okay, Dimples. Whatever it is, it's all right. We're really used to tour crises around here. Okay?"

I nod, forgetting he can't see me. Maybe he's right. Maybe this isn't the big deal I think it is. Sure, Dolores is in the hospital, but as injuries go, it's not the *worst* thing ever. I relax a tiny bit and say, "Thanks, Sam. It's, um, it's Dolores. The owner's mother. She had a little accident and, um, she's in the hospital."

"Oh my God!" Sam exclaims and all traces of humor and calm are gone from his voice. In fact, he sounds pretty panicked. "Is she . . . is she okay?"

"She will be. She broke her elbow."

Sam is quiet for a beat. "Can you hold on a second, Elizabeth?"

Elizabeth. Not Dimples.

My heartbeat speeds up. What happened to Reassuring Sam? "Sure," I mumble.

I listen to a few bars of the Beatles singing "When I'm Sixty-Four" and then the line clicks.

"Hello, Elizabeth. This is Teresa Bellamy." Okay, that name I remember from Elizabeth talking about her. She's the owner. Sam dumped me right to the owner without any warning. This must be worse than I thought.

"Um, hel—hi, Mrs. Bellamy. This is Au—er, Elizabeth Sadler. I'm leading the European Indulgences tour. The one your mom is on?"

"Yes, yes, I know. Sam told me she got injured. You should be in Braubach today. Is that where you are? What is the name of the hospital? How hurt is she? Can I speak with her?"

I swallow. This woman has my sister's future in her hands and I have to tell her how her mother injured herself while in my care. Not good.

"Yes, ma'am. We're in Braubach. Or near it, anyway. The hospital is called . . ." I look at the sign in the waiting room. Seriously? ". . . I don't know if I can pronounce it, but I can spell it. It's S-T-I-F-T-U-N-G-S-K-L-I-N-I-K-U-M. Next word: M-I-T-T-E-L-R-H-E-I-N." Wow, German is just as bad as Dutch. I rush on. "Your mom has"—I glance down at my notes from the doctor—"she has an olecranon fracture of her elbow. The doctor said it's really common in elderly people who have a fall. She was using her arm to break the impact, but instead she broke—well, fractured—her elbow."

Teresa Bellamy is quiet. I force myself to breathe.

"I've just come from her room and she's in really great spirits," I add.

Teresa chokes on something. "You're a terrible liar. My mother is most definitely *not* in great spirits. She fought me tooth and nail about going on this trip and I have no doubt she's sitting in that hospital bed feeling sorry for herself right now. That is, when she's not cursing my name."

Hmm. This woman knows her mom. My turn to stay quiet.

"How bad is it?" Teresa asks.

"Well, ma'am—"

"Teresa," she interrupts.

"Teresa, right. Sorry. The doctor says it's a Type I fracture and they don't recommend surgery for this type of injury in the elderly. She'll use a sling to keep her arm straight for a day or so and they'll give her some physical therapy exercises she should do every morning. They want her to get another X-ray in ten days."

Teresa blows into the phone and I can't tell if she's smoking or just really annoyed. When she speaks next, her tone is all business.

"Okay, here's what I want you to do. I'm going to give you a number to fax me the records so I can have someone on this side of the ocean look them over and give a second opinion. It can't hurt to have a doctor here double-check. Damn, but she'll never do any of those PT exercises on her own accord. I need to think about this for a second. Hold on."

The music comes back and this time it's "Still Crazy After All These Years." I wonder if they have a whole playlist of songs about aging to cater to their clientele.

"Elizabeth? You still with me?"

"Yes, ma'am."

"Oh, quit it with the ma'am stuff. Just Teresa, please. I did some Googling and it looks like this is a fairly minor injury, more inconvenient than anything else. She's wanting to come home now, isn't she?"

"I . . . she didn't say."

"Good. Do not let her speak those words out loud. It's *very* important to me that she continues on. She's been holed up in her house since my dad died and, truth be told, a lot longer than that even. This is my chance to show her the world and I'm not going to let a little fracture ruin my plans for her. She needs this; she just doesn't know it yet."

No wonder Teresa gave the real Elizabeth the job so easily. They sound like kindred souls with their I-know-what's-best-for-you attitudes.

Teresa continues, "Now, I know this is your first tour, so I don't expect you to add caring for my mother to your work-load. I feel bad enough that I snuck her on the roster without giving you a heads-up about her connection to me, but I didn't want to give you anything to worry about ahead of time, or any excuse to bag on me. Anyway, I'm going to have a home health aide dispatched immediately and we'll take care of arranging the extra rooms and attraction tickets from our end. You're on to Austria next, aren't you?"

"Salzburg, yes." I say a silent thank-you for Mary's itiner-ary tucked in my back pocket.

"Excellent, excellent. It's beautiful there. I'm going to put an aide on a plane tonight who will meet up with you tomor-row afternoon. Does that sound okay? Can you handle her until then?"

"Oh, um, of course. The hospital says they'll be another hour with the discharge papers, but then she's free to go."

"Good. Perfect. How's the rest of the tour going? Sam says

you're doing a great job, but I'd love to hear things from your perspective. Everything's good?"

Sam said I was doing a great job. Interesting . . .

"Oh, yes, ma'am—I mean, Teresa. It's going really great. Thank you so much for the opportunity."

"Please. You did *me* the favor by sliding into our open spot like that. I'm meeting the congressman for dinner tomorrow night and I'll be sure to thank him again for suggesting you."

"I . . . thank you so much! I'd really appreciate it."

"My pleasure, Elizabeth. Now please, take good care of my mother until I can get an aide there to help."

"Of course."

She reads me the fax number where I can send Dolores's X-rays and then hangs up. I fall back into the chair in the waiting room.

THIRTEEN

The mood is very subdued as we make the drive back to our hotel. Emma and I help get Dolores settled into bed and dosed up on her pain medication before I head back out with dinner orders from everyone. All I want is to climb into my bed, but a tour guide can't rest until everyone else is taken care of. Sigh.

I stumble back into the hotel under a slew of takeout containers and deliver them. I'm tired, I'm hungry, and most of all, I'm completely shaken up by the afternoon's events. Teresa didn't seem to blame me for being neglectful of her mother, but maybe that's coming next, when she's had time to think on things.

I'm hoping against hope that Sam will call, but I'm not surprised when the phone doesn't ring. After all, the tour company is more than up-to-date on the events of our day, so a check-in isn't really necessary. Still, it would have been nice to hear from him that everything is okay on their end and that I haven't just blown my chance at a good evaluation.

I want to sleep for a million years. I tuck Mr. Pricklepants under my arm and curl my legs to my chest.

But just before I drift off, I have an alarming thought.

Tomorrow we head to Austria, and I'm happy for a new country and a fresh start, but it occurs to me that a new location just means a whole new place I know next to nothing about and a group awaiting my brilliant and witty repartee about all the lovely points of interest we'll be rolling past.

I lie in bed for a few more minutes, massaging my temples. Then, swinging my legs over the side of the bed, I groan as I force myself upright and down the carpeted hall. I wonder if Mr. Fenton has ever read *Tom Sawyer*, because I am about to pull the old whitewashing-the-fence trick on him, and here's hoping he doesn't catch on.

I knock on his door. He answers wearing a pajama set under a plaid flannel robe. He even has matching felt slippers. In his hand is a glass of red wine.

"Mr. Fenton, sorry if I'm disturbing you, but I was hoping I could talk to you a sec."

"Of course, Lizzie. Is everything all right with Dolores?"

"Oh yeah, she's fine. Actually, I was wondering if I could speak with you about something else." I take a deep breath and force myself to sound extra sweet. "As you might imagine, one of my jobs as a tour guide is making sure everyone is super happy throughout the trip. So I wanted to check in. Are you happy, Mr. Fenton?"

He tilts his head to the side and looks confused. "Perfectly.

Obviously I'm sorry to see one of our merry crew injured, but it seems as if she'll be able to continue and we won't have any delays. I'm just thrilled to be experiencing Europe again."

"That's good. That's really good, Mr. Fenton. Of course, I'm new to this tour-guide thing and I really would like to go the extra mile to make sure everyone is even more than happy. I'm going for ecstatic, if you know what I mean."

"All *right* . . ." Mr. Fenton now looks wary. Whoops.

I smile my most reassuring smile. "I couldn't help noticing yesterday that you were especially happy—one might even say ecstatic—when you were sharing all of your knowledge about those castles. By the way, you were pretty amazing."

Mr. Fenton looks embarrassed and shrugs. "Well, you pick up a thing or two teaching world history to high school students for forty-five years."

"Ooooh. You're a *teacher*. That explains how natural you were up in front of our group. And the fact that you remember *all* those dates and details. Well . . ."

He shifts his gaze to his slippers and smiles. "Oh, now. You yourself were a history minor. You must have developed some tried and true strategies for memorizing dates, am I right?"

His eyes slide back to my face.

Why on earth would I have *possibly* chosen history from among every single college minor out there? All I had to do was say any one that wasn't Spanish. Applied economics. Astronomy. Underwater basket weaving. But nooooo.

"Right, right," I say. "Of course. But enough about me.

What I was wondering, Mr. Fenton, is if you would like to continue to share your vast wealth of knowledge and years and years of teaching experience with our little group. I could do it, of course, but I *could* also be convinced to step aside. To make you happy."

Mr. Fenton leans against his doorjamb. "You don't say? And to think, you're *only* thinking of my happiness."

"And that of our group, of course." I smile again for good measure, but I have the sneaking suspicion he's very much onto me. "I really think everyone loved hearing you speak so, so much yesterday, and I'm guessing it means that much more to them, learning about these places from a contemporary. The fact of the matter is, Mr. Fenton, you have a true gift for making facts and figures very entertaining. I think we would be depriving everyone if you didn't at least consider it. You really did shine up there."

"Well, thank you, Lizzie. What a nice compliment. And I can't tell you how much I appreciate you making such a huge sacrifice on my behalf. To be perfectly honest, I did get a big kick out of my talk yesterday. It's been years since I've been in a classroom and I miss it every single day. If you're really, truly sure you wouldn't mind *too much*, I think I might like to take you up on your kind offer."

I keep my face straight while my insides bounce around. "It would be my pleasure to step aside."

We stare at each other for a beat or two. I'm getting the distinct impression he might have read *Tom Sawyer* after all, because it sort of seems as if his lips are twitching like they want to laugh.

After a few seconds he says, "Well, if you don't mind, I think I might like to get started on a little lesson plan for our drive to Salzburg tomorrow. The area we'll be passing through is rich with history. But of course, I don't have to tell *you* that, do I?"

"Right. No, of course not. Very rich. Yup. Well, um, fun planning. And I'm really excited for this."

"Me too, Lizzie. Me too. You sleep well."

I spin to face the hallway again and I'm one foot out the door when Mr. Fenton speaks again.

"Oh, Lizzie."

His tone is friendly but it still sends a shiver up my back. I slowly pivot to face him and find his eyes on mine.

"Yes, Mr. Fenton?"

"I was just wondering. That castle you were telling us about, the one with the princess and the knight. Do you happen to remember the name of it? I wanted to research more about that story. It's so sweet."

"Um, the name?"

"Yes, Lizzie, the name." His eyes are friendly as ever, but I don't feel much like smiling. I gulp.

"Um, I can't remember it offhand. I'll have to review my information."

"Uh-huh. I suspected as much. And what about your own name, do you recall that?"

"My own . . . ?"

Mr. Fenton just shifts to his other foot and continues to stare at me with his warm brown eyes. I blink a few times as I weigh my options. Obviously, I am completely busted. The question is, how busted? Will Mr. Fenton keep my secret or will he tell everyone?

"This can be just between us, *Lizzie*." He says my name like it's in air quotes, but he also kind of reads my mind.

When I still hesitate, he says, "Wouldn't it be nice to have someone you could confide the truth in?"

God, yes. But do I dare? Instead I stall for time. "What do you mean? What makes you think I'm not Lizzie?"

"Well, on the first day, you didn't react any time I called it. Then, of course, there's the not-speaking-Spanish thing, and I can't imagine a tour company would have assigned you a Spanish-speaking bus driver without thinking you spoke his language. So they must be under the impression you do."

He spares a look at me to see how I'm reacting, but I'm trying very hard to keep a poker face as I pick at a thread in my T-shirt. I'm not sure how well it's working.

He continues. "And then there was the castle. The one you claimed—with some authority and a great deal of detail, I might add—was built for a knight. In actuality, that *fortress* was rebuilt as a summer residence for the Prussian king Friedrich Wilhelm IV between 1836 and 1842. Now, it's understandable that you might not know the exact date or circumstances of each castle on that route, of course. But I *would* suspect someone with a degree in history to know that knights were a decidedly Middle Ages convention. As the Middle Ages spanned from roughly 400 to 1500 AD, I'd say it is quite unlikely one would still be kicking around in the 1800s, when you claim the castle was built, wouldn't you?"

Um, whoops?

Mr. Fenton leans casually against the wall before saying, "So, what I've been able to piece together is that someone named Elizabeth, who speaks Spanish and studied history, was hired by the tour company to lead this trip." He pauses for effect. "But that someone is not you."

I spare a glance down the deserted hallway, then move another step into his room before saying, in a tiny voice, "My sister."

"Pardon?" Mr. Fenton asks, though I suspect he heard me and just wants me to say it again. I look directly into his eyes, which, thankfully, are still kind. He doesn't look angry, just curious.

"My older sister is Elizabeth. She was the one hired. But she couldn't come—for reasons beyond her control—and she couldn't back out because it would put her real, actual job in jeopardy. She's supposed to start work with a congressman this fall and leading this trip was a favor to a big donor."

"I see," says Mr. Fenton. "And so we get Lizzie."

I drop my hands to my sides and avoid his eyes. And then I crumble.

"I'm so sorry I lied to you. I swear I didn't want to and I

feel horrible about it every day. But please, please, you have to let me make it up to you. If I don't get good recommendations from all the participants, Elizabeth might not get to work for the congressman and . . . she'll hate me forever."

Mr. Fenton reaches out and places a hand on my shoulder. "Lizzie. Or . . . what is your given name?"

"Aubree," I mutter.

"Aubree. That suits you. Aubree, I'm not here to give you a hard time. I hoped to give you a shoulder to lean on. Your secret is safe with me."

I lift my head slightly. "It is?"

He waits until I look him in the eyes. They are forgiving.

"It is. And Aubree?"

Wow, is it weird hearing my name for the first time in days. I raise my eyebrows.

"I'll do anything I can to help you until such a time comes when you're ready to confess to everyone."

As if that will happen. Did he not listen when I told him what was on the line here? But I smile a genuine smile and nod.

"Thanks, Mr. Fenton."

He nods too, then places a hand on the door and swings it gently shut behind me as I ease back out into the hallway feeling about a hundred pounds lighter.

FOURTEEN

We make the six-hour drive to Salzburg in just under eight and a half hours, which is a little miraculous considering how often we need to stop to stretch legs and how long Mary and Emma like to linger in the trinkets sections of every rest stop.

Mr. Fenton is the freaking boss. He seems totally at ease up in front, talking on and on about how the tiny country of Austria used to be a major world power and how the Austrian Empire, under Habsburg rule, dominated Europe, blah, blah, blah.

But he also points out cooler factoids. When we drive through Stuttgart, he drops in that the Porsche logo is modeled after the city's coat of arms, a black horse on a yellow background. And in Munich he tells us all about the Black September assassination of Israeli athletes during the 1972 Olympics held there and, with the way he explains it, it's like he was one of the spectators. Even though everyone else on board besides me was alive and remembers when it happened, they're every bit as caught up in the story as I am.

I work on my bracelets and look out the window at the sights Mr. Fenton points to and feel only a tiny bit guilty that an elderly gentleman is now doing my job for me. At least I can tell he honestly is enjoying himself.

And then, before I know it, we're arriving in Salzburg.

I have to admit, of all the cities on the trip, this is the one I let myself get a teeny tiny bit excited about back home (on any occasion I wasn't fighting off panic attacks, that is). Salzburg is a small city in the Austrian Alps, and even though it was part of such and such empire and this or that revolution, most Americans, including me, know it for one thing only: as the real-life setting of *The Sound of Music*. I have actual fantasies of twirling on a mountaintop, singing "The hills are alive . . ." and skipping around the fountain in the middle of the city to the tune of "Do-Re-Mi" and possibly even climbing trees in clothes made from curtains. I'm not sure where I'll get drapery, much less learn to sew an outfit, but that's beside the point.

As our bus creeps down the city streets, I keep my eyes peeled for any sights that look movie-locale familiar. I'm so busy cataloging the buildings that at first I don't notice the sort-of-skinny guy on the sidewalk beside us as we come to a stoplight, even though he's jumping up and down and waving his arms around like he just stepped on a hornet's nest.

But Dolores notices. "Oh! He's here!"

I squint out the window at the guy, whose limbs now

appear to be flagging down an airplane, then spin in my seat to face Dolores.

"You know that boy, Dolores?"

Her smile, which I realize I haven't truly seen before now, stretches so wide that eight new wrinkles appear.

"Of course I do! That's my grandson!"

I jerk back around and peer out the window. I thought Teresa was sending a home health aide. This guy sure doesn't look like any nurse I've ever seen. I'm guessing he's about my age, and on closer look he's not so much skinny as just not bulky. His dark hair is wavy, with a few curls fighting their way in, and he's dressed in a pair of just-right-fitting jeans, clunky brown shoes, and a short-sleeved white bowling shirt. When he slides his sunglasses off and grins at us, I can't help but notice . . .

He's cute.

Really cute.

In a cool-nerdy, hipster way I don't usually go for, but there you have it. He's also Dolores's grandson. Which makes him Teresa's son.

Which makes me S-C-R-E-W-E-D.

I mean, it was one thing to have Teresa's elderly mom reporting back on me at the end of the tour, but now I'm in serious trouble. Teresa said she was sending someone, but I never expected it to be her *son*. He could blow this all up in my face at any moment.

And the strange thing is, even apart from the whole Elizabeth-would-lose-her-job-and-might-hate-me-forever thing, the idea of having to go home now kind of upsets me.

Cute Boy trails us down the sidewalk until we pull up in front of the hotel a half block away. As soon as the bus is in park, he's knocking on the door, bouncing like Tigger's long-lost relative as he waits. For a guy who must have flown all night to get here, he sure seems full of energy.

Bento slides the doors open and the guy bounds aboard.

"Hi there, party people! Gram!" He rushes down the aisle, maneuvers backward-facing into the empty seat in front of Dolores, then reaches over and pulls his grandmother's head into a ginormous bear hug.

"Tell me if this is hurting the elbow," he says with a laugh, even though he's only cradling her head and her arm is well protected in its sling. Dolores's squeals of excitement are louder than Emma's I-just-spotted-a-windmill noises, which makes our jaws drop. I didn't think Dolores had it in her.

He lets go of his gram and stands, tugging to straighten his shirt. When he catches my wide-eyed stare he gives me a small smile that crinkles the edges of his eyes before turning to face the passengers.

"So, how's it going? I hope everyone is okay with me hitching a ride from here on out. Let me see now. . . ." He points to Mr. Fenton, who has returned to his own seat in the middle of the bus. "You must be our resident ladies' man. Every bus tour has to have one."

Mr. Fenton's answering look is a cross between embarrassed and flattered, and he raises one eyebrow.

Emma and Mary giggle like middle school girls at a boy

band concert as his attention is turned to them. He pretends to lift a hat off his head and mock bows to them. "Ladies." Another gesture to Mr. Fenton. "If this guy isn't pulling his weight, I'm at your service. I have a bit of a thing for older women." They giggle even more when he winks at them.

Oh my God, who *is* this guy? I stifle a giggle of my own, but quick, before he notices me.

Hank and Maisy are cuddling, as usual, in the way back of the bus, and he turns to them next. "And you two must be our honeymooners. Mazel tov!"

Hank guffaws and Maisy hides her smile behind her hand as the guy turns around to face the front of the bus.

"Bento, my man. *¿Qué tal el viaje?*"

"*Ya me conoces, nunca estoy feliz a menos que me queje. Pero me alegro de ponerle una cara a tu nombre.*"

"*Tienes razón, Bento. Eres aún más guapo de lo que me imaginaba.*"

He speaks Spanish. Someone who can translate Spanish. Oh happy day! No, wait, he'll know his mom wouldn't have booked Bento on a tour where the guide doesn't speak Spanish fluently, so he'll be expecting Elizabeth—that is, me—to speak it. Well, crap.

Dolores asks him a question that captures his attention, so I quickly catch Bento's eye and tap tap tap my thumb and fingers together in a universal sign for talking, then move my finger between the two of us and finally to my lips in a shh motion. Hopefully he can piece together this means "please,

please don't tell this guy I can't speak a lick of your language."

He nods, so I think he gets it.

Maybe.

"Elizabeth." The guy is suddenly right over me, then sliding down into the seat next to me with a grin on his face. "I'm Sam. As much as I've enjoyed our phone calls, it's even nicer to meet you in person, Dimples."

Sam?

This is *Sam*?

My Sam?

FIFTEEN

Well, not my Sam, but, you know. *Sam*.

Sam isn't some kid on college break answering phones for *Act Your Age*? Well, he *is*. But he's also the owner's son? He might have thought to mention that! My mouth drops open as I try to process everything. Sam sticks out his hand and I shake it, trying not to notice too much that his grip is sturdy but gentle. He lets go and his expression is suddenly serious as he examines me.

He drops his voice. "Sorry I missed our call last night. It was chaos once we decided I was the one coming. Packing, booking a flight. Plus I wanted to surprise you."

Oh, I'm surprised all right.

Sam doesn't give me a chance to respond, just keeps right on talking. "Listen, I know we had our phone thing going on and it's probably kind of weird that I'm now sitting here, but we don't have to let it be weird, right? And I want you to know that I honestly and truly hope you won't find my being on the tour too intrusive. Especially since, well, the irony."

He waits for me to laugh with him, but I'm not exactly in on the joke. His eyebrows furrow.

"Oh, did you not know? This was supposed to be my tour to begin with. The reason you're here instead of me—or you *were* here instead of me, anyway—is because I landed a spot on the swim team at my college for next year. Coach lined up a bunch of summer training sessions for those of us who could stick around and I figured it was my best chance to get him to notice me."

He shakes his head and makes a little snort/laugh sound. "Enter Chad Harrington and one craaaaazy party. Keg stands on the roof of your teammate's dad's restaurant are never a good idea, for the record. Plus, having most of the swim team busted for underage drinking kind of pisses off a school administration. Enough to suspend all practices for the foreseeable future. My bad luck."

I have to bite my lower lip to keep from smiling.

"Let's just say my summer plans opened up again real fast. And voilà. Here I am. Mom was getting totally annoyed with me moping around the office, so I convinced her to send me instead of a home health aide. But please don't worry. I will totally respect that this is *your* tour."

Um, I didn't really have that concern. To be honest, I've been busy handing off *my* tour to anyone who wants to step up and take the reins: Corinne, Mr. Fenton. But I guess I probably shouldn't mention that to the owner's son or else Elizabeth will be stuck working menial labor and living at home with Mom hovering, and there would go any hope for our sisterly relationship.

But really what's running through my brain on a ticker tape below all these other thoughts is: Sam is here. In person.

"Oh. Um, okay, yeah. Sure. I mean, thanks," I manage. Geez, Aubree, tongue-tied much?

"This is gonna be fun, Elizabeth," Sam says, hopping back up.

"She goes by Lizzie," Mr. Fenton says, and I think he sounds a tiny bit territorial when he does. It's a little funny that he's so insistent on a name he knows isn't even mine. Funny and sweet, that is.

"Got it," says Sam. He leans in close and his breath tickles my cheek as he whispers, "Your preferred name is probably something you should tell a guy *before* you confess your love, Lizzie. Also, your picture doesn't do you justice."

He pulls back slightly and gives me a small wink before standing to face the rest of the passengers. I'm sure my face is the color of a pomegranate.

"So what about the bus?" Sam asks the seniors.

"What *about* the bus?" replies Mary.

"What does the bus go by?"

"Go by?" Emma asks.

"You haven't named this bus yet? What is a proper road trip without a ridiculously named vehicle? Well, we're rectifying that right here and now. I did notice her shade of gray looks a tiny bit purple in the sunlight. Anyone else catch that?"

We all shake our heads. I'm a little dumbfounded, but everyone is wearing a smile. Huh.

"Well, if no one else notices it, that rules that out. Let's see, we could take our location into account. We're about to conquer Austria. We could go with the great Austrian conqueror—"

"Attila the Hun?" pipes up Mr. Fenton.

"Exactly. Attila. I kind of like Attila the Bus."

Mr. Fenton is smiling now. "We're headed to Italy later, though, right? If we're talking conquerors, we can't forget Augustus Caesar, which we could always change to—"

"A-BUS-tus Caesar!" Sam and Mr. Fenton shout together.

I guess this means they're best friends now. So much for loyalty.

"Abustus Caesar it is," booms Hank, and apparently our bus has now been named.

Sam's head bobs in delight. "Okay, everyone, c'mon. I took the liberty of checking us in already, so line up in front of Eliz—I mean, *Lizzie* for key cards."

And just like that, Sam joins our tour.

The rest of the day is another free choice for my passengers, which means I'm officially off duty. After helping everyone get luggage onto elevators and down hallways, I head back to my room with plans for a hot bath to help me process the addition of a new member to our little crew and how exactly

I'm going to handle the fact that he has the potential to blow everything up in my face just when I was getting a teeny tiny bit of a handle on things. I'm running the water when there's a knock on my door.

"Lizzie? You in there?"

Annnnnd speak of the devil.

I throw my shorts back on and yank a T-shirt over my head as I cross the room. Three quick seconds to adjust my hair and then I pull the door open as casually as I can manage. "Oh, hey."

"Hey yourself. Listen, I wanted to see if you might be up for grabbing some dinner later tonight. My gram wants to rest and order room service and I know a good spot not that far from here. I thought, since we're basically the only people under sixty-five on this trip—if you don't count Bento, that is—it might be fun to hang out a little. Thoughts?"

He leans against the frame of the door and smiles right into my eyes as he waggles his eyebrows.

Oh God but he's cute. Danger signs flash in front of my face as I picture the real Elizabeth shaking her finger at me.

Of course I want to say yes, and not only because he looks adorable wearing a grandpa-style fedora hat or because when he grins his eyes light up in this really amazing way. To be honest, I'm intrigued by Sam. The same way he rolled with my loveyoubye thing so easily, he walked onto that bus and had everyone at ease and laughing in mere seconds. And these are people a jillion times older than me, so they know BS when they spot it. He wasn't putting on an act; he was just being himself. I can't even begin to imagine what it would feel like to be *that* in control of a situation. Okay, so maybe I'm intrigued *and* jealous. Plus, it would be kind of nice to hang out with someone my age.

But I can't.

It was one thing to flirt a little bit on the phone with the entire ocean between us, but shit just got real. Sam's the boss's son and his report back to dear old Mom will count more than glowing reviews from all the other guests combined when it comes to Elizabeth's letter of recommendation.

There's a giant list of things Sam's not allowed to know about me:

1. That I have absolutely zero tour information with the exception of a two-page itinerary I pilfered from one of my sweet old-lady guests.

2. That I have no way of communicating with the tour's bus driver short of hand signals and prayers to the gods.

3. That I'm not Elizabeth. Or even Lizzie.

Just for starters.

I might be able to come up with extravagant lies on the spot, but keeping up pretenses for any length of time is not my forte. I would totally dig my own grave.

"Oh, um, thanks, but I was just gonna have a quiet afternoon and some room service for dinner too. I'm beat and, uh, I need to go over the information for tomorrow's sights."

In the name of all things holy, please, please let this hotel have some truly informative brochures in the lobby (or a computer with an internet connection), because I'm not so sure Sam will be down with Mr. Fenton leading the show from here on out. I sense the beginnings of a headache. Much as it kills me to admit, it's entirely possible Elizabeth will be getting that SOS call after all.

Sam's smile falters a little as he takes a step backward. There's a flicker of something in his eyes and I wonder if I hurt his feelings. I don't think hurt feelings are going to make him want to give me a glowing review. Crap. Hanging out with him could get me busted but blowing him off could also be a bad thing. What do I do? I make a game-time decision.

"But, um, I definitely would be up for getting some tour guide advice from a pro, if you're cool with it. Maybe coffee in a bit? I just have to make a phone call," I say.

The smile is back full force. "Sounds good. I want to spend a bit of time with Gram before she crashes anyway. Meet you in the lobby in an hour?"

"Sure."

I close the door behind him and rest my head against the back of it.

SIXTEEN

"Hey, you're here."

"I'm here." I stand awkwardly in front of Sam's chair in the hotel lobby. The only other open seating is a fairly small love seat across the room. Sam glances around and clearly makes the same calculation. I hold my breath, hoping he won't suggest squeezing onto it together.

"Looks like the lobby's a popular spot today. If you're up for it, there's a great coffee shop a few blocks over."

I nod and wait while he slings a messenger bag over his shoulder. He leads us outside, where he turns left and immediately makes the first right without even glancing at the street sign. I hurry across the street with him.

"You know your way around here already?" I ask.

"Hmm? Oh. Yeah. Benefit of a mom who owns a tour company. My mom homeschooled me so we could be on the road a bunch of the time while she got the company going. I'd help her scout out the good tourist sites and hotels or whatever.

We'd basically follow the same itinerary our tours would."

"Wow. That sounds so awesome." I'm surprised to realize I mean it. Definitely not the response I would have had at the start of this trip.

"Yeah, it wasn't the worst way to grow up. Of course, there were a few years when I was pretty pissed I didn't get to join the Little League team because we were taking off ahead of the season ending to go to Lithuania or China or something. I threw a temper tantrum or two over that, before I grew out of my bratty stage."

He laughs and takes me by the elbow to guide me around a street musician playing a cello. Hmm. That's . . . exceedingly nice. I try not to notice how warm his fingers are on my skin.

"And how about now? Do you guys still travel a lot?" I ask.

"Not together as much these days. College keeps me pretty busy, plus summers are her craziest time in the office. Mom's built up a team of tour guides she trusts to keep her up-to-date when hotels slide down in quality or restaurants go out of business. That kind of stuff. So she doesn't need to be out in the field as much."

"Well, anyway, I'll bet it was fun. And you definitely don't need a map to get around Salzburg."

He's kept us walking at a pretty decent clip down a street full of white building after white building, most of which look really old and have elaborate wrought-iron gates or fancy window boxes. It's really a beautiful city. When I look above the rooftops, the enormous mountains are on all sides.

"Yeah, that's the side bonus," Sam says, stopping in front of a nondescript white (of course) building. On closer look, it's a tiny café, and I step through the door he holds open. He places his hand on my back to guide me to a table.

"Bunch of my college buddies are doing the youth hostel thing this summer. You know, Eurail ticket and a backpack, the whole cliché. I was able to put together a pretty sick itinerary for them," he says, talking away as he casually pulls out a chair for me like it's something he does out of habit, without any idea how totally heart-melty the gesture is. He grabs the seat across from me and pulls two menus from between the salt and pepper shakers. Smiling into my eyes, he passes me one.

"So you inherited the tour operator gene," I say.

"Ha! Maybe. Course they'll probably be too busy frequenting the beer gardens to check out most of it," he says, grinning.

I smile too. I've seen tons of backpackers the last few days. They always look a tiny bit disheveled, but also carefree, like they might be going this way, but then again they might decide to go that way. Talk about truly terrifying. At least I have Bento to get me from place to place and an itinerary to tell me what's next. Plus prepaid hotels and set restaurants for at least half of the meals (whether or not I choose to eat the offered food) and . . . Oh. I realize Sam is waiting for me to say something.

"Right. So, um, where do you go to school?" I ask.

"University of Akron. For all my world travels, I wanted

to be somewhat close to home for college. Staying in one place is actually a bigger adventure at this point." He stops when he sees me gaping at him. "You okay?"

"University of Akron? That's right next to Kent State, where I'm going."

"Going? But . . . I thought . . . Didn't you just graduate from Northwestern?" Sam looks totally confused and my breath hitches as I realize what I just did. See, *this right here* is why I should not be hanging out with this boy, even for professional reasons. The past few days, with the seniors, it was enough to just use Elizabeth's name and age. But with Sam I actually have to *be* Elizabeth, the person they hired. The person whose résumé they have in their office. Competent, collected, college-graduate Elizabeth.

Yikes.

I backpedal. "Oh yeah, no, of course I did. What I meant was that I'm thinking about taking some graduate classes there."

Sam relaxes into his seat, but he still sounds a little hesitant when he answers. "Oh. That's pretty cool you'll have time to do that while working on the congressman's campaign. I'm impressed."

Crapola. He's definitely studied Elizabeth's file. What now?

Nothing left to do but dig out. Okay, Aubree. New mantra: WWED. What Would Elizabeth Do? I stare down at my hands and try to channel my big sister. He's expecting someone in control and high achieving and I have to give him that.

"Yes, of course. The position with the campaign *is* exciting. And I'm sure I'll be busy, which is why I'm waiting to sign up for any classes until I figure out how crazy work's going to be. Of course, the University of Akron is a great school too. I grew up in Hudson, which is only a little ways from the campus, so . . ."

Hmm. Somehow, in trying to pull off real Elizabeth's refined pulled-together-ness, I've given her a slightly British accent. I hope Sam doesn't notice.

If so, he doesn't bring it up. "Oh, cool. Well, so far so good. I like it there. I just finished my freshman year and if my swim team can get off suspension in time for winter meets, sophomore year's gonna be a thousand times better." He sighs, then glances at the menu again. "Do you know what you want?"

"Just a coffee. I mean, yes, please, I'd love a coffee, thank you. Lots of cream and four sugars."

Sam lifts his eyebrows. "Four sugars? Does it even count as coffee at that point?"

I shrug. "I inherited my dad's sweet tooth. My sister calls what I drink 'coffee ice cream in liquid form.'"

Okay, that's all me (me, as in Aubree), but no way am I sipping black coffee just to stay in character. Blech! I have to draw the line somewhere.

Sam laughs. "Okay, lemme go grab drinks. When I get back you can tell me more about this sugar-fiend dad and obnoxious sister of yours."

He hops up and moves to the counter. Oh great. Exactly what I want to do: describe my sister while impersonating my sister.

I people-watch until Sam returns a few minutes later with two steaming drinks. The minute he sets mine down, I grab for it and take a long swill to brace myself for his questions.

"Hey! I'm not saying we have to linger all afternoon, but I'd like to think you aren't *that* desperate to get away from me." Sam's eyes are big.

I catch myself and put my mug back on the table. "Sorry. Just eager for a little caffeine, I guess."

His expression grows more sympathetic. "Yeah, you've had a bumpy start to the tour with Gram's injury. Was today rough too?"

Okay, tour questions I can handle. Those aren't too personal, so there's less chance of messing up my identity ruse. Let's keep this going.

"Not too bad. We drove for most of it. It's odd how sitting and doing nothing like that can make you tired, though, isn't it?"

Odd? Isn't it? Ugh. There's no way I can keep up with the affected talk this whole trip. I'm dropping it now and Sam's just gonna have to be satisfied with this version of Elizabeth.

Sam's fingers absently tug on his hair, straightening one curl so that it's long enough to tuck behind his ear. He answers my question without any indication that I'm acting weird, which is a relief given the internal conversations I'm having with myself.

"Well, and having to be 'on' takes its toll, I'm sure," he says. "Talking so much about the sights and all that. I always find that exhausting on my tours after a while."

I jerk my eyes from the curl that's already escaped his ear and snap to attention. Would someone like Elizabeth confess that Mr. Fenton did all the talking, or would she smile demurely and duck her eyes? Then again, if I don't mention it and he finds out from Dolores or someone else . . .

"Oh. Yeah. Well, there's a funny story there. Remember the really buttoned-up guy?"

Sam nods. "Fenton, right?"

He's good. My first day, I had to keep peeking at the cheat sheet I made myself to remember everyone's names while we walked through Amsterdam.

"Yeah. Well, he actually used to be a high school teacher. And when we were driving through the Rhine Valley the other day he suddenly started spouting all these cool factoids about the castles. I mean, obviously I had them in my notes too, but he was getting a total kick out of playing lecturer, so I let him go for it." I peek at him to see if his expression reads anything along the lines of "FIRE THIS GIRL NOW" but he's nodding along. Phew.

I continue, "Anyway, last night he asked me if he could do it again. Since he's missed being in the classroom so much. I can't really say no to that, right?"

Sam nods again. "That's really thoughtful of you. A good tour guide is always looking out for ways to enhance the experience for her guests."

I squirm in my seat, given that my motives weren't exactly selfless. Then again, Mr. Fenton was well aware of what he was getting himself into and who I really am. So I can't feel too guilty.

"I have a question for you," I say, looking for a way to take the attention off me for a minute. I can only handle being in the hot seat for so long, but maybe if I can get him talking about himself, he'll forget about my supposed credentials for a bit. "How do you make it so fun? You were on the bus for five minutes this afternoon and you had everyone smiling, and laughing, and naming buses. I've been with them for five days now and it hasn't exactly been like that."

Is it okay that I'm admitting this? I don't want it to sound like I'm not doing my job well. Then again, as soon as he spends two seconds with us tomorrow, he'll be able to tell that my tour guide style is pretty far from his. I may be getting us from Point A to Point B and fed and checked in to hotel rooms (which is a whole lot, actually), but I can't say I've exactly brought the fiesta. The worst part is that I thought I was doing great. Like, I was actually really proud of myself. My insides twist as I picture the grins everyone wore while brainstorming names for Abustus Caesar. Could I have been making this trip so much more fun for them than I have been?

Sam takes a tiny sip of his own coffee and answers. "Some of it's just a comfort level. I grew up going on these tours with guides who've been doing it for years and years. So I learned from the best." Like he was able to read my mind, he says,

"You can't expect to be great right out of the gate. Obviously, you might be. I haven't seen you in action. But in my experience, it takes a while to get there."

He leans forward and puts an elbow on the table, resting his hand on his chin. "The other part is recognizing that it's human nature to relax around a relaxed person and tense up around a tense person. Goes back to our most primal instincts, right? So I just try to be super chill and laid-back and people usually follow suit."

I nod. Makes sense. Also: I'm pretty sure he's working those Jedi mind tricks on me at the moment, with the way he's all loose and easygoing. Unless he really is just completely relaxed around me, in which case, more power to him. And could he share a little of that?

"The *other* other thing I've learned is your guests don't think of themselves as old," he says. "They just don't. Especially the seniors who take these kinds of trips. I think they mostly want to be seen instead of glossed over, like most people tend to do. So actually, by treating them the same casual way you would treat a friend, you're not disrespecting them. You're acknowledging them."

I glance up only to catch his eye as he grins. "Trust me, I've heard some of the raunchiest jokes you could imagine come out of the mouths of the very sweetest-looking grandmas." I laugh along while silently ordering my blush to leave town.

"Yeah, okay. That all sounds logical," I manage. I don't realize I'm twirling my empty paper sugar packet around and around my finger until Sam reaches over and gently puts his hand over mine to stop me. It lingers there a few beats before he removes it. Damn. Twirling sugar wrappers falls solidly in the Things a Calm, Composed, In-Charge Person Would Never Do category.

He must see something in my expression, because he quickly says, "Sorry, I didn't mean to make you uncomfortable. Can I make a confession?"

As long as he doesn't expect one out of me in return.

Sam's gaze is on the wrapper, and then he brings it to my eyes and smiles, all confident and teasing. "I'm not exactly sure how to act around you right now. I mean, I'm not gonna lie, I was loving the phone thing we had going on, and the fact of the matter is, you *did* tell me you love me. . . ."

I'd just lifted my coffee to my mouth when he says this and I choke a little on the liquid before setting my cup down with slightly shaky hands.

Sam smirks and continues. "I'm just kidding. Look, I know you were probably just playing along to pass the time and make check-ins more fun. I get that things are different in person and I'm sort of your boss, and also you probably think I'm not old enough for you. Though I swear you look even younger than me—I hope that doesn't come across as an insult."

"Oh, um . . . good genes, I guess." I laugh awkwardly. What would someone like Elizabeth say now? *Aubree* would prefer to jump up on the table and shout, "Please, *please* flirt away! I'm only seventeen! *Totally* younger than you!"

But of course I can't, and really, he's just handed me the perfect excuse to keep this crush from going anywhere.

"Um . . . ," I try again. Ergh.

Sam rescues me by saying, "And now I've completely embarrassed you, which was also not what I meant to do. How about we just go right back to talking about tour guide stuff and we can forget that I was ever your Captain Amazing. Or was it Oh Captain, My Captain? I can't remember."

I grin. "Pretty sure we settled on Watson, but nice try."

Sam grins back. "I still maintain Oh Captain, My Captain works way better, but *c'est la vie*." I smile, then drop my eyes, grateful, but also a little disappointed about no more flirting. Even if it *is* a bad idea.

He clears his throat. "Okay, as I was saying. What was I saying? Oh yeah, right. Bringing the fun. Okay, so there's one last thing that's probably the most important."

I'm still afraid to talk because anything I say right this second is going to come out all squeaky. Instead I just nod and raise my eyebrows, urging him to continue.

"Most important of all, *you* have to have fun."

"Me?" Yup. Voice is squeaky. I swallow the frog in my throat. "But it's not my tour. Okay, yes, it's my tour, but it's not *for* me."

"Yeah, but if you're having fun, it's contagious. Everyone will be right there with you and it won't even matter if you're just stopping to fill up the bus with gas."

Ha! He said he's been on a bunch of these tours, so he should know the guests do a fine job filling up the bus with gas all by themselves. Especially Hank.

"You're saying I need to have fun to be fun?" I ask.

Granted, I've been equally excited to see things as some of my guests, and I know I've squealed over the same sights they have, but I'm pretty sure the rest of the time I've been completely focused on getting through each moment and trying to figure out how to stay one step ahead at all times. And whenever we've been on long driving stretches, I've mostly kept to myself, working on my beading or staring out the window. Wow, it's entirely possible I might really suck at being a tour guide.

Sam nods. "Yup. Lemme ask you this. What would you be doing tomorrow in Salzburg if you were here all by yourself? Without any itinerary to follow."

Anywhere else I wouldn't have a clue how to answer him, but here I don't even pause. I do not pass Go, I do not collect two hundred dollars, and I do not spare a thought for how someone like Elizabeth would answer.

"*Sound of Music* sightseeing." I bounce a little in my seat.

I expect Sam to roll his eyes, but instead he nods his head so hard I'm afraid it might come off his neck. "Yes! See? I can tell just by the way your posture changed that you're excited about being where the movie filmed. Okay, so obviously we have to use this."

We? "Er, use it how?" I ask. Tomorrow we're scheduled to

tour Mozart's residence. Mountaintop spinning is not on the list.

"We need to do the *Sound of Music* movie tour."

"They have that?"

Sam looks at me like I have a second head. "Would you pay to be on that tour?"

"Any amount," I answer.

"Exactly," he says. "You and a million other fans. Which means that of course they have one. More than one. But we don't need theirs because we can make our own."

Sam's energy from before is back and he looks like a squirmy puppy as he pulls an iPad out of his bag and sets it on the table between us. "We can make this epic!" he says.

I gape at him a second, but his enthusiasm is contagious, and we *are* talking about one of my favorite movies of all time, so clearly there's nothing else to say but "Let's do it!"

Again, I know it would be way smarter to keep Sam at arm's length. But on the other hand, this is legitimate tour guide business we're working on. So it's officially all official.

SEVENTEEN

"*Deep breaths. Don't* be nervous," Sam tells me, squeezing my shoulder gently as he boards the bus behind me.

I don't even know why I'm jittery (aside from the fact that Sam finds an awful lot of little ways to touch me). It's not like I haven't been a tour guide for the last six days. Except I realized yesterday that what I thought was me handling the tour and all its obstacles uncharacteristically well was really only me acting in survival mode, ensuring everyone stayed together and made it to the next city intact. And Dolores's sling in my peripheral vision reminds me *intact* is a relative term.

So, really, today is my first official day actually engaging as a tour *leader*. Which, duh, makes it pretty obvious why I'm jittery, I guess. Sam was very convincing over breakfast this morning and it took him zero seconds to persuade everyone else to abandon our existing plans and embrace our new and exciting schedule for the day. Mary and Emma nearly swooned when Sam mentioned *The Sound of Music*, so I know I have at least two fangirls along for the ride.

Then why do I feel like Fraulein Maria being summoned to Mother Superior's office?

I glance at Sam, who's settled himself next to Dolores and is busy peeling a banana for her. When he catches me staring, he flashes a thumbs-up.

My eyes land on Mr. Fenton and he flashes me double thumbs-up. At least I know he's rooting for the real, authentic me, which is nice.

I clear my throat. "Um, so . . . everyone? If I could have your attention?"

Hank sounds a catcall from the back and directs all eyes to me.

I take a deep breath.

"Okay, well, so thanks for being flexible today. I know Sam mentioned at breakfast that we've come up with an alternative plan and I just hope you love it."

I smile the biggest smile I have in me and reach beside Bento to the bus's radio. Of course I'd noticed the TV mounted above Bento's seat, but I never even thought to use the DVD player until Sam mentioned it at our coffee date. Well, not date, but, um, work outing. Pushing play, I return to the front seat to grab the small bags Sam and I assembled in the lobby last night. I have to give the guy total credit. He was instrumental in scrounging together a bizarre arrangement of items from various shops all over Salzburg.

I dispense party favors the length of the bus.

"Here you are, Hank, Maisy." Hank takes his hand off his wife's knee long enough to reach for two bags, and I work my way to the front just as the screen is zooming in on a spinning Julie Andrews and the words "The hills are alive" flash at the bottom.

Mary asks, "Is this close-captioned? If so, I'll turn down my hearing aid."

I smile, a genuine one this time. "Nope. It isn't. It's the sing-along version, so the lyrics will show on-screen anytime there's a song. I found it in the hotel gift shop. I thought we could have the movie playing in the background today, and if anyone wanted to sing along as we watch, all the better! So, if you'll open your bags, you'll find props. The little flower is to wave when Captain von Trapp sings 'Edelweiss.' And the popper is to set off when the captain and Maria kiss for the first time. Also, according to the DVD case, we're all supposed to hiss whenever the Baroness is on-screen and boo whenever the Nazis appear."

"What about Rolfe? He's not a Nazi to start, but then he becomes one. Do we wait to boo until he rats out the captain?" Emma asks, clearly very invested in the whole thing.

Sam pipes up from behind her. "I say we boo him the whole time. He's an asswaffle."

I nearly fall over with Sam's choice of words, but no one else blinks.

"Agreed!" Mr. Fenton is nodding.

Oh. My. God. I think they actually like this idea. I was

worried Mr. Fenton might have planned his own lecture for today and been put out, but no. He seems totally into this. Now I'm smiling even harder.

On screen, Maria hears the church bells and realizes she's late for the prayer service. As she races down the mountain, our bus climbs it, following directions Sam wrote out for Bento last night while I pretended to be too busy "researching" to scribble them myself.

"We're going to start in Mehlweg, near where Maria does that hilltop twirl. It's about a half hour away," I tell my riders, but they're all glued to the movie's start. Wait until they see what other DVDs Sam ordered for them online last night. We had to have them delivered ahead to Prague, but they should help pass the time on the second part of our trip.

Sam moves into the empty row behind me, slinging an arm over the back of my seat and leaning in to talk to me. "So far, so good, huh?" he asks.

I grin in reply. "Yup," I say, twisting a little so he can see my expression.

Our faces are so close I can smell the peppermint gum he's chewing. He looks over his shoulder at Dolores and calls out, "You good, Gram?"

She must nod because he comes around and slides into the seat next to me, slouching low and propping his feet on the half wall that separates my row from the steps.

"Hey, sorry for crashing out on you like that last night," he says.

"Right. One second you were stuffing goodie bags and chatting away, and the very next you were facedown on the arm of the couch."

Sam laughs. "I know! Jet lag catches up with me like that. I feel bad you had to witness it."

It was totally sweet the way he'd drooled on the armrest of the sofa, but I'm not about to admit that to him. Sam looks torn between laughing at himself and being embarrassed.

In the end he settles for laughing at himself, which I knew he would because I've never met anyone so comfortable in his own skin. Not even Elizabeth.

"Did I say anything mortifying when you woke me up?" he asks.

"Oh, you mean like 'Mom, I swear, I brushed my teeth already!'? Would you consider that mortifying?"

Sam drops his face into his palms and pretends to be upset, and I laugh at him. He grins back, but then he gets a tiny line between his eyebrows as his grin fades and he studies me. His head tilts and I start to get self-conscious. Do I have something in my teeth?

"I have something very alarming to tell you and I don't want you to freak out," Sam says, still examining my face closely and with concern. Um, how am I supposed to not freak out when someone says that to me while looking at me the way he is? I swallow. Do I have some kind of skin thing I didn't notice this morning in the mirror? Is there something hanging out of my nose? What the hell?

Sam takes a deep breath and says, "One of your dimples has disappeared."

Oh. Oh, *phew.* "I only have the one."

"Yes, well, I see that now. I would have sworn it was two when I stalked your passport picture, but I guess there must have been a smudge on it or something."

Thank God my sister and I look enough alike. If he were holding that picture up to my face right now, he'd see way more differences, but if the dimples are all he noticed, I should be good.

"This is tragic, you know," he says.

I try to fight a smile. "Tragic? How so?"

"Well, it means I'm going to have to reorder the hand towels I was having monogrammed for our guest bathroom. Dimples and Watson just won't work anymore."

I grin. He's really cute. And really impossible not to flirt with. Harmlessly, of course. "Maybe we could just X out the *s* or stitch something over it."

"Ooh, yes, good call. We could have them embroider a flower in its place."

"Nah, we can do better. What about a skull and cross-bones?" I ask.

"*Très* romantic, Dimple. See what I did there? I dropped the *s.*"

I open my mouth to reply, but he raises his head and holds up his hand to silence me.

"Do you hear what I hear?"

I tilt my head and listen hard, but all I can make out is the movie playing to a rapt audience.

"I don't hear anything."

"Exactly. No one behind us is wondering in verse how we're going to solve a problem like Maria. Which begs the question: How's your singing voice?"

"Um, well, I tried out for chorus in seventh grade."

"Okay, that sounds promising," he says, grinning.

"I didn't make it past round one."

"And I, for one, would like to hear why." Sam's fingers stroke his chin and his eyebrows raise as he issues the challenge. Is he serious? I think he might be serious. The song has ended and Maria is now being assigned the governess job by Mother Superior. Sam gives me a pointed look and drums his fingers on the half wall.

Oh, no. No, no, no.

"Sam. I really don't think I can lead a sing-along. I'm already at the far edges of my comfort zone here."

When he smiles at me, I flush. "Lizzie, pushing your comfort zone is what traveling is all about. Now, what do you think about getting this sing-along off the ground?"

"Sam, I can't."

"The *t* is silent. Try it again."

"What? I—"

"Say it."

"I can—"

His finger shoots out and covers my lips before I can get the last letter out. "That's what I thought."

He jumps up and points at me. "Ladies and gentlemen, who would like our fearless tour guide to conduct our sing-along this morning? Because Abustus Caesar is entirely too quiet."

There's a smattering of applause from my passengers. I shoot Sam death rays with my eyes, but I ease myself out of my seat and turn to them, gulping at the eager faces looking back at me. Well, if I completely suck at this, at least I'll never have to see these people again in my life after our tour ends.

The statistical likelihood that any of the seniors knows how to post videos to YouTube is somewhere between low and not a chance. Which still doesn't keep me from cringing at the prospect of singing for them.

I steal a quick glance at Sam and he smiles up at me, looking completely serene. I'll bet if the tables were turned, he'd be on verse three of a song by now. So would Elizabeth. It's so unfair. Why does everything come so easily to certain people? And why is it that no amount of close studying of those people on my part seems to be unlocking any magical answers to that one? What if it never does?

Above me on the screen, Julie Andrews pushes out of the abbey gates, swinging her guitar. Well, if ever there was a more appropriate song about faking it till you make it, I can't think of one.

Here goes nothing.

"Okay, just remember you all asked for this," I murmur. Hank answers with another catcall. I angle my back so I can't see Sam at all and take a deep breath. Above me, the song has started already and Maria is wondering what this day will be like. You and me both, sister. I fix my eyes on the road out the back window, open my mouth, and join in.

"And here I'm facing adventure / Then why am I so scared?"

Oh Maria, I have all the feels for you right now.

I manage to get the next few lines out, willing myself to project the words. It's not like there are documented cases of people dying from extreme embarrassment, right? I force myself to make eye contact with my passengers and find them all smiling back at me. Sam, Emma, and Mary join in for the next verse, and then Mr. Fenton. By the time I get to the middle of the song everyone but Dolores is singing along. I steal a glance at Sam and almost stop midverse to gasp because of the way he's looking at me. He blinks fast when he catches my eye, and before I can interpret the look further, easygoing, confident Sam is back and he winks and belts out the next line with gusto.

I am in the Alps. I am in the Alps, on a bus with a Spaniard, a cute boy, and six senior citizens. And I am singing. Loudly and (mostly) without shame.

I collect my breath for the last line.

"I have confidence the world can be all mine / They'll have to agree, I have confidence in me!"

EIGHTEEN

As it turns out, only Emma and Mary have confidence in me. Or at least they're the only ones who agree to hike with me to the mountaintop meadow, which also involves a bit of sneaking through someone's farm. I can't decide if it's the Alpine-flower-scented air or the illicitness of tiptoeing through private property, but the three of us are cackling like the Wicked Witch of the West when we get back to the bus, having had our fill of arms-flung-wide spinning.

Even though I knew to expect it from my *Sound of Music* trivia research, I was still ever so slightly disappointed that the winding brook and the bank of birch trees really weren't there. I was having a hard time believing the movie production would have built a grove of trees and a burbling brook just for one scene, but, yep. They did.

"Have fun, ladies?" Sam is wearing his trademark grin. I'm beginning to wonder if he even owns a frown.

"Tiny bit, yup." I answer his smile with one of my own.

And we *did* have fun. With so much more to come. I'm giddy about that and I think, for not the first time, that I might be a little too invested in my *Sound of Music* fandom. But so far no one is complaining, and in fact, Mr. Fenton is rewinding the opening scene so Emma can compare her moves to Maria's.

Hank and Maisy are, of course, making out in the back of the bus.

We head back down the hill to a lively chorus of "Do-Re-Mi," which even Bento knows the words to. "*So Do La Fa Mi Do Re*," my merry troop sings as our bus careens down the hill and back into the city. By the time we reach Hellbrunn Palace, where they've built a replica movie gazebo in the middle of expansive gardens, we're all as breathless as Maria trying to work all the billy-goat puppets while yodeling.

When I've composed myself, I say, "All right. If you want, you can take a *Sound of Music* break for a bit and just explore the gardens. The gazebo from the film is here, but this place is actually more famous for the water games designed by the prince archbishop. All over the grounds are hidden spray fountains that were designed so the prince could play jokes on his guests. So, fair warning: you may get wet."

It's amazing the kind of tour one can give when one has had full access to the internet. Sam's iPad is a godsend. It's not my missing binder, but it's pretty damn close.

"And no whining if the fountains get you. There is a strict no-whining rule on Aubustus Caesar." Sam places his hands on his hips as he says this.

I wait as everyone files off, then whisper a *"gracias"* to Bento. He's been following Sam's written directions to the letter and not giving any indication that he and I do not share a common language. I get a smile and a nod in return.

When I catch up with everyone, we're at the entrance to the palace and it's beyond amazing. To think one person lived here (well, along with his staff of a billion) and it wasn't even his full-time house. I'm fairly sure mine back in Ohio would fit inside a broom closet in this place, and it's not like I live in a shoe box or anything.

We're really here to see the gardens, though. This prince archbishop dude who built the place was seriously obsessed with water. There are fountains everywhere, and that's not even counting all the ones we won't be able to see because they're camouflaged in the bushes and under trees. I read there's even one hidden in all the seats of an outdoor table. Except, of course, for the chair the prince sat in. That way, when he wanted everyone to sober up and go home, he could give them all a good dousing. There's a reason certain people should not be allowed to be obscenely rich.

Mr. Fenton wants to get up close and personal with some-place called the music room, and Mary and Emma trail off toward the gift shop. They try to include me now that we're newly bonded from our alpine adventure, but I'm not quite ready for my *Sound of Music* break. I'm on a quest to find the gazebo from the movie. Hank and Maisy have their hands in each other's back pockets as they wander off toward the grottos and I feel sorry for any school group that stumbles upon them. Dolores, Sam, and I move toward the gardens, in the direction of the gazebo.

Since I'm the one who researched this place online yesterday, I'm also the one who knows to watch where the employees leading the garden tours stand if you don't want to get wet. See, us tour guides know the lay of the land. Okay, fine, today is the first time this trip I've known the lay of the land, but I intend to revel in it. And maybe not share all my tour guide secrets with Sam.

I race after him along a narrow pathway with sprinklers forming an arch over our heads. Dolores was first through, so she's standing off to the side watching when, just as I reach the end, the sprinkler pressure changes and the water lowers to waist level. Two seconds earlier and we'd have been drenched. A tourist behind us rattles off a string of words in what I assume is Chinese as he reverses course, and Sam turns to me with a satisfied smile.

"Ha!" he says. "They missed us. I'm telling you right now, I'm making it through this entire visit without getting—"

A hidden fountain of water bursts from the sidewalk directly under Sam's feet. The surprise of it throws him back a step, so that the water sprays into his shocked face. In five seconds it switches off, but it's still long enough for Sam's hair to soak into clumps, dripping rivulets down his face.

He sputters and stares at me, mouth open. I can't help it. I dissolve into giggles. Dolores hides her smile behind her hand, but I'm positive it's there. She's been way more relaxed since her grandson joined our trip. Still quiet, but definitely more engaged.

"Quit laughing at me." But he's laughing himself, so I don't hold back. Over his shoulder, I spot the gazebo across the lawn and point it out to Sam, who groans at its distance from us.

"I'm going to rest on this bench where it's nice and dry. You kids go on ahead," Dolores offers. Sam tries to join her, but he's dripping so much that she shoos him away. He turns to me with a shrug.

"Race you," I challenge.

"Hold on, I need to empty my shoes." He pulls them off and lets a river of water tumble out of each. "Ha! Don't Liesl and Rolfe duck into the gazebo to *keep* from getting wet? Looks like that's not gonna work for me." He replaces his shoes and bunches his T-shirt to wring it out. I try not to stare at the strip of exposed skin above his waistband as he twists the fabric. Whoa. Hello swimmer's abs.

Instead I cover with, "Just as well because you can't duck into it anyway. I read last night that they had to close it to the public when too many people got hurt trying to re-create the bench jumping."

Sam hunches over to slide a shoe back on and says, "We'd have totally tried to re-create the bench-jumping scene, wouldn't we?"

"Duh! How could you not?"

Although I blush a little thinking of how that scene finishes with Liesl and Rolfe crashing into each other on their spins and ending up in a kiss. I'm pretty sure Sam's having the same thought because when he straightens, his ears are turning slightly red. Just as I get my composure back, Mary yells out a "Helloooo" from the far left side of the lawn. I steal a last sideways peek at Sam before turning toward Mary and Emma.

"Hi, ladies. Having fun?" Sam is alongside me as we jog to reach them, effortlessly casual again.

"This place is beautiful. Oh, I'm so glad we added it to the schedule today. The whole morning has been a blast so far."

"Speaking of a blast," says Emma, arching an eyebrow at Sam's soggy appearance. "Had a run-in with a hose, did you?"

"More like one of the hidden sprinklers. You be careful, Emma, they're evil and they're everywhere."

"I'm sorry, young man, but weren't you the very one who instituted a no-whining rule a short while ago?" Mary has him there. I raise my hand to high-five her and we all smile at Sam as he hangs his head in mock shame.

"May I escort you ladies to the gazebo?" he asks, holding up two dripping elbows to Mary and Emma.

Emma wrinkles her nose and says, "What you may do is venture down this pathway ahead of us. That way if any of those fountains are hiding, you can suss them out for us."

Sam gamely heads up our procession, taking steps that are exaggeratedly slow. He peers at the ground with great concentration. When we reach the gazebo, nice and dry still, I'm shocked to find how small it is. I knew they built a larger one on a soundstage in Hollywood for that scene, but I still didn't expect this one to be quite so tiny. We spend a few minutes taking pictures of Emma and Mary in front of it with their cameras. They insist I join them for a couple, which is super sweet.

As Sam hands Mary back her camera, she says, "Oh, but we need one with Sam in it. Lizzie, you hop in there too. I'll take it and Emma can, uh, help me."

I raise my eyebrows at this, but Sam just laughs, so I play along. We stand next to each other and paste on smiles.

"Step in closer, you two," calls Emma.

Oh, I am soooo onto them. I slide an inch nearer to Sam, but he surprises me by closing the gap between us, draping an arm over my shoulder and settling his hip against mine.

"Gotta give the guests what they want, Lizzie," he says out of the corner of his mouth, keeping his smile in place. Um, I think there are limits to that, but I don't protest. I'm too busy absorbing the feel of his leg on mine and I don't even care that his wet clothes are pressing against my dry ones. Mary takes an extra long time framing the shot and I have every suspicion that's on purpose too.

She finally says, "Got it," and I step quickly to the side, blushing *again*.

As we walk back toward the palace, Emma steals a last look at the gazebo. "Oh, that scene is my absolute favorite, even if Rolfe does turn out to be a—what did you call him, Sam?"

"An asswaffle," Sam answers, stepping gingerly along the path, his eyes still searching the ground for hidden fountains.

"Right. He may have been an . . . asswaffle, but there's something about Liesl getting her first kiss and that squeal she gives when she does. So sweet and innocent. I get teary every time."

"Remembering Corporal Anderson?" Mary teases.

"A lady never divulges intimate details." Emma swats at Mary before winking at me. "But she also never forgets her first kiss."

"You go, girl," says Sam, bending over to inspect something on the pathway more closely.

"That song from the movie got it all wrong, though. Not all girls need someone older and wiser, telling them what to do," Emma says.

"You don't say?" Sam's head comes up, and he suddenly seems less concerned with attacking sprinklers.

I avoid looking at him. "Was your corporal a younger man, then, Emma?" I ask.

"No, *he* wasn't. But my husband, Stanley, was three years younger, and that didn't keep us from forty-one happy years together. I'm just weighing in with my own opinion here, but if you ask me, plenty of girls do all right by a younger man."

"You know, Emma, I, for one, couldn't agree with you more," Sam says.

He's just turning to me with a smirk on his face when another water fountain explodes underneath his feet.

After the palace, we take a funicular (this train built into the side of a mountain and pulled up on a cable) to a fortress overlooking the Nonnberg Abbey, where Maria was a novice, and have lunch in a café on the battlements. Then our afternoon is spent visiting another palace (the one that provided the facade for the Von Trapp residence) and the church Maria and the captain got married in. We also manage plenty of hissing at the on-screen Baroness. From the front of the bus, I deliver movie trivia I dug up online, like the fact that Christopher Plummer had all of his songs dubbed because his singing voice didn't hack it, and how the bell cord on the abbey was put there for the movie and never actually worked, but the nuns liked it so much they asked the crew to leave it up.

As I collapse onto my bed back at the hotel, I'm exhausted but happy because the day was pretty much perfect. I had a big test with Sam looking over my shoulder all day and the pressure of actually engaging with my tour, but it turned out better than I could have hoped. Everyone seemed to really like it. To like me.

We're off to Vienna tomorrow. A whole new city.

And tonight I feel energized, because I've decided I'm taking this tour into my own hands. As we headed off to our rooms after dinner, I asked Sam if I could borrow his iPad for the night under the pretense of keeping up with the latest in Ohio political news.

Obviously I'm not reading any policy initiatives, but I do

send an email to Mom and Dad, telling them how amazing camp is, and a very brief one to Elizabeth, telling her I am in Austria and fine. I'm grateful to not have to talk to her. I may have been wrong about hanging up on her the other night, but I feel like my other feelings were valid and I'd rather have some space from her until I sort them all out.

Once I hit send on those, though, I spend the next several hours researching everything I'll need to know about Vienna and the stop after that, Prague. I spend longer on my work than I did on most of my high school papers.

As I clear the browser history so Sam won't see the websites I looked at, the only thing dampening my mood is how crazy bad I feel lying to him. But it really is for the greater good.

My last act of the night is a postcard to Madison. I found one of Julie Andrews on the hilltop, arms spread wide, and I draw a little arrow to her head and write *Me today!* beside it. On the back I scrawl *Got to live out my* Sound of Music *fantasies in the Alps! I missed your voice on the "Do-Re-Mi" rounds. Holy snowcaps, you should see these mountains—you'd die!! Miss you, love you, eat some campfire s'mores for me. XOXO, Bree*

As I switch off the light, I'm still singing snippets of "Sixteen Going on Seventeen."

"Timid and shy and scared am I, of things beyond my ken."

Never mind that I don't have a clue what a ken is, I can completely identify with how Liesl feels. But I'm making progress.

NINETEEN

Vienna is only a three-hour drive away, but we have to be there by ten a.m. to catch the morning workout session of the famous Lipizzaner stallions, and I happen to know that Mary, for one, would kill us if we missed it. Apparently she was quite the rider back in the day. So it's extra early when we all gather for breakfast in the hotel restaurant.

Emma and Mr. Fenton immediately begin debating whether it was the Turks or the Austrians who introduced coffee to Europe, and Mary gets busy wrapping pastries from the buffet into napkins and stuffing them into her purse. Sam and Dolores have claimed a quiet table in the corner where Sam is cutting up Dolores's plain pancakes for her.

No Maisy. Or Hank.

"Has anyone seen our favorite couple?" I ask.

Everyone shakes their heads. I return to the lobby and do a quick scan. Nope. Grabbing a list of room numbers from my pocket, I punch in their extension on the lobby phone. It rings six times.

Argh. It's 6:22 and we're cutting it close as is, so I guess I have no other choice. I researched half the night, dammit. No one's messing with my day.

I make my plea at the check-in desk. "Um, I don't know if you remember me from yesterday. I'm the one who was asking you if a binder and a cell phone had been delivered here for me? Anyway, I'm the tour guide for a small group staying here and two of my guests haven't shown up for breakfast. Would it be possible to have their room key?"

The employee checks my credentials and hands over a key card just as Mr. Fenton crosses the lobby to stand next to me.

"Like some company for this bed check? No telling what you'll walk in on with those two."

We both shudder and grin as I follow him into the elevator and push the button for the sixth floor. A few moments later we're standing in front of their room. Mr. Fenton gives a gentle knock.

"Just a second!" we hear from inside. Okay, phew. I won't need my key. Inside the room a shower turns off. So that's good, right? If one of them is in the shower, it's pretty unlikely the other is in a compromising position. I exhale in relief.

Hank flings open the door and we're treated to the sight of him with only a towel around his waist. His belly spills over the top and practically into the hallway. I take an involuntary step backward.

"Uh, good morning, Hank. I just wanted to be sure you both were, um, awake. The bus is leaving in ten minutes."

Maisy steps into our line of vision. She is also dripping wet and wearing only a towel. Oh dear Lord! Do these two ever quit? I guarantee most honeymooners do not get this kind of action the *first* time around.

Mr. Fenton coughs into his fist. Real subtle.

"Okay, then. So, uh, if you could just get downstairs as soon as possible, I'll grab some pastries for you and we'll be waiting on the bus."

I don't even give them a chance to answer or react. I turn and retreat before they have any thoughts of dropping those towels.

Mr. Fenton catches up with me at the elevator doors, barely containing his glee.

"Those two are worth the price of admission."

I would prefer not to have a ticket to that particular show. But I *am* glad to have Mr. Fenton alone.

"Could I talk to you a sec?" I ask as we wait for the elevator.

"Of course, Lizzie."

"Um, I know I asked you for a big favor before in having you fill in on the lectures, and then I switched things up on you yesterday, but, um, I was wondering if you'd be okay if I backed out of our deal today too."

"Backed out?" he asks, raising an eyebrow.

I study the ugly carpet under my feet. It must be a rule or something that hotel carpet has to be hideous beyond belief.

"It's just, I thought I might try to do some of them myself.

I was able to borrow Sam's iPad to do research—although technically he doesn't know it's for research, so please don't tell him. Anyway, I covered Vienna last night, and, well, I just thought . . ."

The elevator dings and the doors slide open. Mr. Fenton gestures me on ahead of him.

When I look up and into his eyes he's smiling. "I'm glad to see you taking some ownership over this tour, Aubree. It's a very mature thing to do."

Maybe it's just because he's a teacher and he has the kind of presence that makes you crave his respect, so that when you do earn it, it feels super sparkly. Maybe it's because he remembers my name is Aubree after all. Either way, I'm feeling pretty good when I board the bus ten minutes later.

We roll out of Salzburg and toward our next adventure. Sam is sitting with his gram, helping her work through the arm exercises her doctors prescribed, and when I peek back a short while later, he's sleeping on Dolores's shoulder.

I haul out my jewelry kit to work on a Baltic amber-beaded necklace, but then I remember my new directive to myself to engage the other tour members whenever I can. I turn my neck and catch Mary's eye.

"Would you be able to help me pick out beads for this?" I lift my arms to show her the necklace I'm knotting. I don't mention that I've decided to make one for each of the women on the trip and this one is for her.

"Oh gracious. That's lovely. May I?"

She holds up a hand and I pass the necklace back to her.

"What's this knot thing you're doing called? It looks a little like the macrame we used to do back in the seventies. Lord, all that macrame. Remember that, Emma?"

Emma's head pops up from her book. "Macrame? Of course! I had hanging macrame plant holders, macrame wall hangings, a macrame lampshade, you name it. Couldn't give that stuff away now, but it was fun to do. This looks a bit like it, but the knotting was somewhat different."

I gather a breath. "Do you think you could show me? If the technique is similar, maybe it would work even better than what I'm doing."

Mary and Emma grin at each other and gesture at the empty seat across the aisle from them.

"Oh, this is gonna be fun. I haven't done macrame in decades. Lean over so you can see what my hands are doing," Emma says.

The ride passes quickly and I love the way the knots hold my beads in place. I'm positive I can put a modern spin on what they've shown me and I almost wish I could burrow into my hotel room and work on new designs for the rest of the day.

Almost.

As we near the outskirts of the city, everyone is awake again. I move to the aisle and face my tour. I hold a notepad from last night's hotel in my hands to glance at when I need prompting.

"All right, then, everyone. We're now headed to the

Imperial Palace, where the Spanish Riding School has resided for close to four hundred and fifty years and cultivates classical equestrian training using the famed Lipizzan horses, who are bred specifically for the purposes of dressage performances. It might interest you to learn that these pure white horses are actually born jet-black and turn gradually white over the course of five or six years. They are also bred from only the very elite of . . ."

I continue to talk right up until we disembark at the palace (another freaking palace! What's so wrong with a three-bedroom colonial, people?) and, judging from Sam's and Mr. Fenton's grins, I do okay.

We follow the crowds into the most elaborate riding ring I've ever seen. Seriously, it looks like royalty could host a dinner party there. It's three stories tall, with the rink in the center surrounded by second- and third-floor balconies on all sides. But even more impressive, it's all white arches and columns and in the center of the ring dangle enormous crystal chandeliers that have seven hundred and eighty-nine lights each. Approximately.

It doesn't even smell like farm animals.

We're just getting settled along the balcony railings when the horses high-step it into the ring. Each rider salutes a portrait of King Karl, the founder of the academy, when he enters. Classical music fills the ring as they all prance about (literally) and line up in a whole kaleidoscope of configurations.

I try to think about what I'd be doing if I were at home.

Ten a.m. on a summer weekday? Probably just waking up, maybe texting my friends Claire and Hayley to come hang at the pool. There's a good chance they'd swing through the KFC drive-in for a bucket of chicken to eat before we claimed our lounge chairs and spent hours flipping through back issues of *Us Weekly*.

Instead I am listening to Mozart and watching horses a billion times better groomed than me.

I look around for Sam, thinking he might want to share my can-you-believe-this-is-our-life-right-now? epiphany, but he's not anywhere I can spot. Everyone else is absorbed in the horses below, so I force my eyes back there and refocus on marveling at the riders' ruler-straight posture.

Sam is in the very back seat of the bus when we wander outside. He's talking intently into his phone in quiet tones, so I don't bother him. We proceed to our hotel, where I take everyone inside as Sam still yammers away. I sure hope he has a good international calling plan.

Our afternoon is technically free time, but Emma and Mary ask me if I want to come with them on a horse-drawn carriage ride through the city and really, who in their right mind says no to that? We spend the rest of the afternoon visiting the crown jewels at the treasury (which also has a giant narwhal tooth everyone once believed was the horn of a unicorn) and even riding a giant Ferris wheel where the boxes you sit in are so big they hold seated wedding receptions in them.

Um, can you say perfection? Vienna is, no surprise, beautiful beyond belief. It's a thousand times different from anything in Ohio. It barely even looks like anything from movies I've seen. I'm in love. Again. How on earth do people pick a favorite travel spot?

We're back at the hotel by three and I'm fantasizing about a long nap. I'm just stretching out on my bed when there's a knock.

Sigh. This being-in-charge thing can really be a drag.

I swing open the door to find Sam picking at a tiny piece of peeling wallpaper in the hallway outside my room. It's so not good how excited I am to see him. We barely got to talk at all today and, well, I sort of missed him.

"Hello. What's up?" I hide a yawn behind my hand. Check me out, Miss Super-Casual.

"Sorry to bore you," Sam says with an easy laugh.

"Oh, no, that's okay. I was just getting ready to take a nap. Is everything okay? You seemed pretty intense on the phone earlier."

"Oh yeah, fine. My mom was just giving me a hard time about Gram's elbow. She made me talk to a physical therapist she found back home so he could make sure I was doing all the strengthening exercises exactly right. I guess there's a concern if it doesn't heal properly, Gram will need surgery. Which, of course, puts pressure on me, but it's all good."

Hmm. So Sam knows pressure too? He hides it well.

"How was your afternoon?" he asks.

I smile as I remember Emma leaning out the Ferris wheel window to shout "How ya like me now?" to the world below.

"Great. You?"

"Good, yeah. Gram and I checked out the Kunsthistorisches Museum of Art."

"Wow. Try saying that ten times fast."

Sam takes a deep breath like he's actually going to do it. But then he exhales and grins. "It was fun. Mr. Fenton wanted to tag along and I swear it was like having a docent with us. He knows everything about everything, that guy."

"Tell me about it."

Sam doesn't follow up my comment with one of his own, so there's an awkward silence, which is the absolute worst.

"So, um, did you need something?" I finally ask.

"Oh yeah. I was swinging by to see if you wanted to grab dinner tonight. But if you'd rather do your own thing . . ."

Sam shrugs and glances at the carpet.

Say no, Aubree. You should definitely say no. Alone time with Sam is full of opportunities to slip.

"Sure, yeah."

Sam's eyes come back up and his smile is in place. "Cool! Just a heads-up, the restaurant I had in mind is a little bit dressy. But totally worth it, I promise. The food's amazing. Are you up for a costume change?"

Dressy? Dressy means fancy, and fancy food and I do not tend to get along. But what am I supposed to say: "Hey, thanks, but can we find a pizza joint instead?"

"Uh, sure. I just need to make sure everyone else has dinner options sorted first."

"Good thing they like to eat dinner at five, then, huh? Lobby at seven thirty?"

I nod, and he gives me a last grin before turning in the direction of the elevator.

So I'm going to dinner with Sam. And there really isn't any way to spin this one as official tour business. Am I crazy? Maybe.

I just have to be sharp and on my game for Elizabeth's sake, but I can do that. I know I can. I've been doing it so perfectly these last few days. Besides, the longer I'm on this trip and the more I'm handling things, the more I'm convinced the crazier thing would be saying no to a dinner in what has to be one of the most beautiful cities ever built. Even just the memory of a night dressed up and strolling through Vienna with an adorable guy should be enough to get me through a few future nights in boring old Ohio (gah! Since when am I thinking of home sweet home as boring?! What's happening to me?).

TWENTY

When Sam sees me step into the lobby he whistles, which of course makes me turn bright pink. He just smiles and ducks his head. Speaking of whistling, he doesn't look half bad himself in suit pants, a white button-down, and a polka-dotted tie.

I've changed into a black jersey dress Madison lent me. She insisted it was perfect for travel because it would never wrinkle and she was right. With a few bracelets of my own design and a pair of sterling wishbone-shaped earrings, I feel pretty and light and summery and ready for a night in this perfect city.

We head outside and walk side by side along the narrow sidewalks of Vienna. Sam's shoulder keeps bumping mine, although neither of us acknowledges it. Eventually he turns us into a wide, pedestrian-only square paved entirely with cobblestones. Little red café umbrellas dot the street and the restaurants seem to spill out of their buildings and into the courtyard. Sam leads me toward one of the doors and we step out of the crowds and into the hushed gold-leafed entrance of a clearly upscale restaurant.

"I love when I get to introduce someone to something amazing. You ready for a fantastic meal?" he asks.

"Absolutely." (Not.)

There was a period of time (from age two until, um, last year) that my dinner order almost always consisted of "plain pasta, only butter. No sauce, no cheese, no parsley, no foreign substance of any kind." I'm way more adventurous now. By which I mean I tolerate the occasional fleck of parsley.

This is the main reason I'm a teeny-tiny bit stressed out when the waiter floats a napkin onto my lap and hands me an opened menu encased in a heavy leather portfolio. It's ultra-fancy-schmancy.

I hold out hope there's gonna be a burger listed somewhere on here, even as Sam is saying, "This place is where all the locals come for the best of the best in Austrian food."

I've never even heard of Austrian food, which I'm thinking can't be a good thing. I sneak a peek at the menu. Oh, just wine. I mean, not like I know my way around a wine list or anything, but it's way preferable at this point to reading about weirdo food.

Sam says, "Great thing about Europe. Drinking age: eighteen. Although, what am I saying, you can drink back home too. Can't wait for that day. My fake ID is the absolute worst."

"Right, well." I lower my eyes so I don't have to look into his.

I am going to hell. This totally friendly, totally cute boy

is being so nice, and all I've done since meeting him is lie to his face.

"So do you have a favorite vintage?" Sam asks.

"Um, not really, just red? I guess?" I would be much better at faking being a college grad here if I had the first clue about wine.

Sam's eyebrows scrunch down a little, but he orders us two cabernets. The waiter nods and replaces the wine list with an even heavier menu.

I'm scared to open it, but Sam is studying me now. I prop it on my lap and peer down at it to avoid Sam's gaze.

Vorspeisen / Starters
Item 1. Schafkäseterrine an Vogerlsalat mit
Kürbiskernpesto

I try not to gasp when I read the English translation just below. Sheep cheese terrine on lamb's lettuce salad with pumpkin pesto.

What exactly is *that*? And who would order it willingly?

I move on to the next item, but there is NO CHANCE I'm eating smoked goose breast with horseradish and mango-ginger compote. Compote sounds waaaay too much like compost.

The waiter returns with our wineglasses. I've never ordered wine in a restaurant before, so I'm a little bit giddy about this, even though I'm not much of a drinker.

"What looks good?" Sam asks, peeking over his menu.

Um, a dine-and-dash, minus the dining part? Think, Aubree, think. I take a sip of wine to stall until an idea hits me. Then another sip, before one does.

"Um, I should have mentioned this before," I say, "but I have some, uh, food-allergy things going on. I usually try to stick to simple items on the road, so I don't accidentally eat anything, uh, dangerous."

I avoid his eyes. What's one more lie to heap upon the pile, especially if it lets me save face in front of this guy I really shouldn't want to impress, but definitely do? What I really am allergic to, as it turns out, is the truth.

"I'm so sorry, I didn't even think to ask. How severe is your allergy? Do you need to carry an EpiPen and all that?"

"Oh, nope. I mean, no. I have . . ." I try my hardest to remember what Madison's mom has. She's always going on about stuff she can't eat. Something to do with wheat or something. Gluten, that's it! ". . . a gluten allergy."

"You have celiac disease? My roommate does too. Wow, I guess I didn't even notice what you were eating the last few days. I know meals out can be kinda tough with that one. Do you want to talk to the chef and see what would be safe for you?"

"I feel really stupid right now. I probably should have said something before we sat down."

Although what I *should* have said was that I'm the least adventurous eater on the planet and could we please just dive into my stash of PowerBars instead? Why can't I just be honest with him about this one stupid thing, especially because I can't be about anything else? But he's so in control and worldly and I'm so . . . not . . . and I can't stand having him think I'm this sheltered little girl from the suburbs.

Sam is nothing if not sweet. "You know what, we don't have to stay if you're nervous about it. We'll just finish our wine and venture out in search of something gluten-free. Sound good?"

I smile gratefully. "Sounds perfect. Thanks." He holds my eyes as he lifts his glass to flag down the waiter. So sweet.

It's true that the more time I spend with Sam, the more possibilities there will be for me to blow my cover, and that would be so very, very bad. It's also true that if Elizabeth were here, she'd find some excuse to leave and head straight back to the hotel.

But I never said I was Elizabeth.

Well, that one's *not* true. Although I never said I was *as smart as* Elizabeth. Which is why, twenty minutes later, we're sitting in a booth at McDonald's.

"This isn't exactly the 'meal' I had in mind for us tonight," Sam says.

He seems a little reluctant to term a #1 Extra Value a meal, but the knowledge that McDonald's actually exists in Austria makes me happy for some unknown reason that probably has to do with the effects of a glass of wine on a total lightweight. It also takes away a little bit of the sting of having to order my cheeseburger without a bun. I really should have thought this celiac thing through, because it's not like I can so much as nibble down a baguette in Sam's presence from here on out. Thankfully he's way more up to speed on celiac than I am because of his roommate, so he knows that McDonald's fries are gluten-free. I am *not* prepared to sacrifice fries for the whole rest of the trip.

"Are you up for a walk?" Sam asks as we crumple our wrappers and deposit them in the trash before heading back into the square.

I tell myself I owe it to Sam to end the night on a high note after the lame meal I just subjected him to, but the truth is I don't want tonight to be over yet either. The air is warm but not sticky and all around us people are outside enjoying the summer evening.

I nod and we're both companionably quiet as he weaves us alongside churches advertising Mozart concerts (seriously, just try to go five feet without being reminded Mozart was Austrian. Total overkill) and beautiful white buildings with window boxes overflowing with flowers, until we reach a set of steps leading down to a walkway along a river.

"The Danube Canal," Sam pronounces. "A little dingy by day, but perfect by night."

It *is* perfect. Where we reach it, the pedestrian walkway is wide and there are restaurants lining its edges and, in the water, waiting riverboats. Sam gestures at one. "Now there's a tour I'd like to take one day. No buses. Just a slow-moving boat cruising through Austria and down into Hungary. Have you been to Budapest? It's unbelievable."

Ha. Have I been to Budapest? I haven't been anywhere.

I shake my head and pretend to be fascinated with the low, flat ship awash in lights. I step closer and Sam grabs my hand to stop me. "Careful. There's no railing."

He's right. The drop is several feet straight to the murky water. I nod my thanks, but Sam doesn't release my hand. Instead he laces his fingers through mine and resumes walking. I force myself to ignore the internal reaction that causes and instead take in the medieval architecture and the way the moon is hanging in the sky, so low it almost touches the church spires.

"Do you ever think about what it would be like to be their age?" Sam asks pensively, and I know he's speaking about our passengers.

"You mean old?"

"Well, yeah. I mean having most of your life behind you and knowing it. Like, obviously there's still plenty you can do or see—I hope, or else Mom would be out of business—but all the major decisions would be behind you. What to do for a living, how many kids to have, where to live, the kind of person you want to be. Don't you think that would be weird?" Sam asks.

I consider his question. "In a way. But in another way there's something kind of comforting about that. You can just do whatever you want to do at that point. You don't need to try to impress your relatives, or please your parents, or anyone, for that matter. You don't need to worry about choosing the wrong career or the wrong person to marry. You just get to enjoy the time you have. It sounds kind of nice, if you ask me."

"Yeah, I hear ya. I stress all the time about the whole 'what do you want to be when you grow up' thing," Sam says.

"Yeah?"

"Well, mostly because I don't want to grow up in the first place," he says, ducking his head.

"Okay, Peter Pan." I squeeze his hand and he answers with a squeeze of his own.

"I'm just saying. For example: this whole thing with the swim team suspension. It sucks and all, but at the end of the day people sort of expect kids our age to mess up. We get this limited-time pass where it's like, 'Oh well, kids will be kids.' And I feel like I'm so close to the end of that. In a few years, when I graduate and I'm out on my own, no one will be saying that anymore. If I mess up then, I'll just be some loser."

He shrugs and I laugh. "What makes you think you aren't now?" I ask.

Sam punches me on the arm with his free hand. "Okay, smart-ass. What do *you* want to do with your life?"

"For a career, you mean?"

"Sure, career, yeah. Or not. However you want to interpret that question . . ."

I tuck my hair behind my ear and study the cobblestones. I think of Elizabeth and try to answer like she would. "Well, I want to work for the congressman and learn all that I can about running a campaign. Of course, I have experience on the college level, but I mean professionally. The idea is that one day I'll be able to run for office on my own platform of women's rights. I want to promote strong, independent women everywhere."

Screw this. I draw a deep breath and speak from my heart.

"To be honest, I don't really know what I want from the future."

Sam's eyes widen and he studies me, encouraging me to continue. I look out over the river and say, "I know I don't want to end up the old lady who eats dinner with her forty-seven cats every night. And I want kids. Marriage, white picket fence."

I grin as I think of something else. "Actually, I don't need the fence, but I do want a big old house with a walk-up attic I can convert to my bedroom. I always thought that would be like sleeping in an indoor tree house. And a fireplace in the kitchen. I mean, in every room, if I could ever find that, but definitely in the kitchen because my feet are like icicles even in August and I like hanging out in the kitchen best."

Sam smiles his encouragement, so I keep going. "I always assumed I'd stay in Hudson or nearby, close to my family. I can't imagine not having them around." I study the ground. "But I never knew all *this* was out here. I'm thinking maybe I should start to venture outside my comfort zone a little bit more."

His hand squeezes mine again and his eyes are on me when I bring my chin up.

"Well, you do lead a kick-ass sing-along. I think you outside your comfort zone is a sight to see," he says.

I cover my face with my hand. "Ugh. Can we never speak of me singing again?" Then I take a deep breath and get serious. "But what happens between now and then? That's a giant question mark. When I even try to picture me at a job, it's as if my brain can't find any picture that works."

Sam stops walking and turns to me, dropping my hand in the process. Confusion wrinkles his brow. "But what about the campaign?"

Oh. Crap.

For two measly minutes, I let myself forget. And look where it's gotten me. I slip my hand behind my ear and subtly work loose the hair I tucked there so that it dangles in front of my face, forming a curtain between Sam and me.

Think, Aubree, think.

"The thing with the congressman, well, it's a job, and not many of my classmates have managed to land one of those, so when I got it I figured I'd better not turn it down if I don't want to have to live on ramen noodles for the next five years." Oh shit. Are ramen noodles gluten-free? Double shit. Does he know the congressman? I wouldn't want him telling the guy his newest employee is anything less than thrilled. I barrel on before he questions it. "And I mean, the campaign of my own? That's just a bit of a pipe dream, if you know what I mean."

I force a laugh to cover my nervous rambling, but I'm not convinced Sam is buying it. He studies me for a second, then says quietly, "Right. Of course. Makes sense."

Does it? Do any of my lies make sense?

Sam turns to study the water below us. We've stopped in front of a café and this section of the canal has a railing lining the edge. Sam rests his elbow on it and he leans over to peer down. "You know that thing you said a few minutes ago about getting past an age where you feel like you have to impress relatives?"

"Yeah?"

"Do you think that happens?" he asks.

I think about the events of the past few weeks and I so badly want to answer honestly because I certainly have a lot to say on the subject, but I'm not at all prepared for where that conversation could lead.

Beside me, Sam raises his eyebrows, and I realize I haven't answered him. "Sorry," I say. "I sort of wandered off there. Um, to tell you the truth, I don't really know."

"Who are you trying to prove yourself to?" Sam asks.

I lie and say, "My mom. You?"

"My mom too, I guess. Mostly my dad."

"I thought you said your dad wasn't around."

Sam yanks a leaf off an overhanging tree beside us and begins shredding it, dropping tiny bits into the river below and watching the current carry them off. "Yeah, he's not. I haven't ever met him. But I want to. I'm just waiting for the right moment, ya know? I want to do something really cool first. Something that will show him what he missed out on."

"Wow. I can't believe you've *never* met him." I try to imagine life without my father—goofy as he is—and can't.

"Nope. In fact, for the first twelve years of my life, I thought he was dead. And then we had this project in history class where we were supposed to research our family tree. I snuck into my mom's room when she was at work to look for my birth certificate and instead I found their divorce papers. Turns out he hadn't died at all; he'd just deserted us."

"Your mom told you he was dead? That is . . . but . . . *why*?" I'm floored by this.

Sam laughs, but there's no humor in it. "She thought she was protecting me. She says I'm better off without him in my life. I didn't get it for a long time. I'm not sure I totally do yet, but she insists I'll understand when I have kids of my own. She claims that she would have said and done anything to keep me from hurting or thinking any of it was my fault because abandonment like that could scar a kid for life and she didn't want that for me. To be honest, I think all she did was heap onto the pile. It's not like she saved me from the abandonment issues. She just added trust issues on top of them. I mean, I was completely upset that she'd lied in the first place, but it was worse the way she kept it going all those years. If I hadn't found those papers, I'm not sure she'd have ever confessed to me, which is like a total kick to the gut, you know?"

Um, yeah. I do. I feel like shit right now. Obviously I'm not deceiving him about anything on that scale, but the guy just came right out and admitted his trust issues and I'm lying right to his face twenty times a day. "Wow. I'm—I'm so sorry," I say, not knowing what else to add to make him feel better.

Sam shrugs and pulls down another leaf, continuing to tear off pieces. "It wasn't your lie."

Maybe not, but I've told him plenty too. If he ever finds that out, he's going to hate me. The certainty slides like a brick to the bottom of my stomach and lodges itself into place. Once again, my brain screams that I need to put a lock on any feelings I might be starting to have for this guy. Once again, my feet stay planted.

"I'm sorry, I completely dumped on you there. I didn't mean to bring the mood down," Sam says.

"That's okay," I say. I'm quiet, though, still taking it in. His issues, my issues.

"It's your fault, you know. You shouldn't be so easy to talk to." Sam loops one arm over the railing, the rest of his body facing me.

I shiver when a breeze comes off the water and Sam nudges closer. I counter with a small step back before saying, "I think maybe it's just easy to talk to someone on a trip like this, you know? We're completely removed from our real lives, we're in this foreign place, and you don't have to see me after the trip. . . ."

Sam studies me for a moment, his gaze locked on me, and I forget to breathe. "You think that's all it is?" he asks. The lights from the nearby café are reflecting off the water and making Sam's eyes shine. In the corners are the featherlight lines that deepen when he smiles, but he's not smiling now. In fact, he's looking at me so intently, I might melt into a puddle.

"Probably?" I whisper, still caught up in his stare.

"Nope. Sorry, but I don't think that's all it is," he murmurs, leaning over to me in slow motion. His eyes dart to my lips, then back to my eyes. Lips, eyes.

Before I can react, he places his mouth softly on mine. His arm leaves the railing, settles on my back, and tugs me closer, while his other palm rests warmly on my arm. My eyes flutter shut.

His kiss is soft and hard at the same time. Sweet but questioning. I sigh into his lips. It's perfect.

When I pull away, his hand at my back steadies me as I blink at him a few times. A breeze blows strands of my hair across my lips, where they stick. Sam reaches up and gently frees the tendrils.

"I'm sorry for that," he murmurs, and I don't even want to guess what emotions he's seeing on my face. Because I'm feeling all of them. Surprise. Guilt. Total giddiness. His eyes haven't left mine and I open my mouth and close it again. What is it I even want to say to him right now? Sam's eyes drift to my lips again.

"No, actually. I'm not. Not even a little bit," he says. His hand tangles in my hair as he pulls me into him and uses his other hand to cup my face. Without taking his eyes off me, he lowers his head until his lips are on mine, their warmth chasing away the cool breeze off the water.

After the initial surprise wears off, I snuggle closer, kissing him back.

So much for a clean escape.

TWENTY-ONE

Prague has a McDonald's too. I know this because the next day I'm sitting at one, blissfully inhaling a cheeseburger *with* a bun AND a crispy apple pie (which, joy upon joy, they actually fry here instead of baking like at home) before anyone from my group (well, more specifically, Sam) spots me.

I may be recently converted to the wonders of the world outside the 44236 zip code, but being open to new discoveries does not yet include cuisine. Especially in a place famous for goulash.

To be honest, I'm also hiding out a little bit while the rest of the group wanders through Prague Castle. As in love as I am with Europe, I am palace'd and castle'd out at the moment, so I jumped on Sam's offer to stick with everyone on their guided tour while I grabbed a coffee.

Coffee, fried apple-y goodness. Potato, po*tah*to.

To be even more honest, I also need a little more time to process last night's kiss—check, make that kiss*es*, because we stayed by that canal for a long, long time.

I experienced major jitters this morning when I saw Sam outside the hotel loading luggage and they didn't really go away during the bus ride here, even though he was sitting with Dolores three rows behind me. The way he smiled at me like we shared a delicious secret the one time I snuck a peek back at him was positively heart-melty and I don't know if I can handle heart-melty. Oh God, but I kind of want to.

Hence the current head-clearing space.

In other not-so-shocking news, I have a new favorite city. I know, I know. But Prague is so beautiful and ancient that it feels like medieval (400–1500 AD—yes, I remember, Mr. Fenton) knights should be walking down the street. All the buildings have clay-colored red roofs and there are cobblestones and gas streetlights everywhere. We're staying in a hotel in the castle district of town, right by the river and the base of the Charles Bridge. It's like something out of a dream, complete with swans floating around in the water. For real.

It's a pretty intense climb between our hotel and the top of the hill where the castle sits but it was too short of a distance to take the bus, so we just moved slowly and gave Mary and Emma the option of going into every store selling marionettes and Czech crystal (I guess it's world famous), which was basically all of them. Since Prague is part of Bohemia, Emma also insisted on buying a long flowy skirt and a bandana for her hair. The woman sure likes her getups.

I toss the evidence of my Mickey D's binge in the trash can and sneak a peek up the street for my crew before ducking out of the restaurant. I told Sam I'd catch them back at the hotel, and I'm heading in that direction when I spot a sign for an internet café at the base of the hill. I've sent Elizabeth one email since our talk in Germany five days ago and I'm overdue for a call. Maybe a face-to-face conversation over Skype will help get rid of some of the tension our last one had.

I pay for fifteen minutes and log on to the Skype account Mom had me set up so we could video chat with Elizabeth at college. Within seconds I'm checking the corners of my mouth for ketchup remnants while I listen to the computer ring.

A small square appears and then blows up. Elizabeth's face fills the frame, her familiar room in the background.

My pesky throat lump is back at the sight. Everything looks so, just so . . . *home*. A tickle forms just north of the throat lump and my eyes get a tiny bit watery.

"Aubree!" Elizabeth's eyes are wide. "Where are you? Prague today, right?" Her expression is wary, like she's not sure what version of me she might get. Maybe I deserve that.

I smile to let her know I've moved on from our last call, when I said "screw you" and hung up on her. To my relief she smiles back.

"Yep, I'm in Prague. It's so beautiful, you should see it."

Her eyes get wistful and her voice is soft when she says, "Yeah, I wish I could."

I know Elizabeth is way more concerned about losing out on her dream job versus having to give up this trip, but it still must sting that I'm here and she's not. We never even discussed that and she definitely never complained about it even once. It suddenly hits me that I've been doing all this grumbling about Elizabeth being self-absorbed, but what if I have been too?

I never considered what missing out on this trip to sit home would feel like to my sister, who not only has the travel bug big-time but also hasn't stopped go-go-going in the entire time I've known her. I wonder what this last week has been like for her? I bite my lip and feel a thousand times more sympathetic toward her than I have since our scene at the airport.

She studies something over my shoulder. "Is that a real stone wall behind you?" she asks.

I glance behind me at the exposed stone on the inside of the internet café. "Yeah, I guess. This whole city is about a million years old."

She laughs. "More like a thousand. Haven't you been keeping up with my binder?"

But the way she says it is teasing, not accusatory, and I grin. Obviously there's no way I'm telling her that binder could be anywhere between here and whatever trash dump is nearest the Philadelphia airport.

It feels good to laugh with her.

"Okay, *now* are you ready to tell me about all of your adventures?" she asks.

"Are you sure? It won't bother you?"

I tilt my head and study her, but she seems completely sincere when she answers. "Of course not! I wanna hear."

"Okay, so, not to rub it in, but man the Alps are crazy

huge. They make a total mockery of the top of the ski lift at Mad River Mountain," I tell her. "And get this! We went off book a little to do a *Sound of Music* tour in Salzburg." I add, "With the tour operator's permission, of course!" when I see her expression turn a little hesitant. (FYI: not telling her about Sam, but he shares blood with the tour operator, so I'm figuring that counts. Plus, it was his idea[ish] to begin with.)

Elizabeth smiles. "Hey, do you remember how funny you were when I tried to get you to reenact the wedding scene from *Sound of Music* with me? You must have been, what, six? Seven?"

"Ten," I answer. I remember it perfectly. Elizabeth's high school was rumored to be staging the musical that fall and, in typical Elizabeth fashion, she was determined to rehearse ahead of time so she would be a shoo-in for a leading role, even though she was only a freshman (she got it, by the way). Her two best friends were at Girl Scout camp that summer and it was also the year our pool had gone in, so we'd been spending a ton of time in the backyard, swimming and playing badminton. But that day Elizabeth wanted to practice the wedding scene, while *I* was very insistent there was no wedding scene.

"You could never stay up past the part with the party whenever it came on TV," Elizabeth said with a giggle.

"Well, *you're* the one who told me it ended right after that!"

"I didn't want you to feel bad about not seeing, basically, the whole last hour!"

We grin at each other from opposite sides of the ocean.

Elizabeth says, "I remember the minute Mom got home that day you made her take you to Target to buy the DVD so you could see what you'd been missing out on."

I remember too. Elizabeth had popped popcorn and had the living room all set up for movie night when we got back. And then she held my hand when I cried over Rolfe blowing the whistle on the Von Trapps' hiding spot.

I wish we could go back to being little kids and liking each other just because we were sisters.

"I'll bet it was fun to see where it was all filmed," Elizabeth says, so I fill her in on the mountaintop spinning and the gazebo with the hidden water fountains (conveniently leaving out Sam, of course. No need for her to freak out that I'm under round-the-clock surveillance by both the owner's son *and* mother).

Instead I tell her about the epic make-out sessions Hank and Maisy have in the back of the bus and the costumes Emma keeps buying. A tightness in my chest releases as we talk and laugh.

When I realize I'm doing the exact same thing I accused her of doing on our last call and making it all about me, I ask, "So what's it like to be living at home this summer? Weird?"

She pauses. "It's . . . quiet. Mom and Dad are at work and you're gone, so I'm just hanging out alone all day. I don't even have any summer reading for fall classes I can get ahead on, like I usually do. It's really strange to be back in this life, which doesn't even feel like *my* life anymore. I mean, not that home won't always be home, but just, well . . . you know what I mean. It's not really where *my* life is anymore, if that makes sense. I feel like I'm in a time warp back to high school or something. Except you're not here, which is equally weird, because you're always here."

I hadn't thought of that. I'm totally used to the house without Elizabeth, but of course she was only four the last time she lived there without me. I try to process that.

She grimaces. "I've been trying to find a part-time job, but so far, no luck. And I don't even know if I'm supposed to check 'yes' on the application when it asks if I have a criminal record or what? I haven't been, but . . ."

"What's new with the court case?" I ask, cringing at the reminder.

"Nada. Still set for mid-July."

I nod and swallow. After we hang up I get to go back to marionette shows and the astronomical clock and the Kafka Museum and Elizabeth doesn't have anything to look forward to besides a date with a judge. That sucks.

"Hey, Bree?" she asks.

"Yeah?"

"Nothing. I'm just glad you called." She shakes her head a little and smiles, and I return her smile.

I'm glad I called too.

I'm still riding the high from my conversation with Elizabeth when we venture as a group onto the Left Bank to take in all of the sights of Old Town.

This could take a month, considering it's been forty minutes just crossing the Charles Bridge—oldest stone bridge in Europe, according to Sam's iPad—because Mary wants a picture of every statue along the way. There is one approximately every six steps. I wonder what exactly she plans to do with these pictures when she gets home. Talk about the world's most boring slide show. Don't get me wrong, they're really beautiful in person, but . . .

Hank and Maisy have stayed behind because they noticed the same internet café I visited earlier also caters to their American clientele by broadcasting sporting events via satellite. Tonight's showing is of a classic Texas Rangers game. We left them hunting for peanuts to smuggle in.

Sam angles himself next to me as we pause in front of a statue of St. Wenceslas. He hums a few bars of that Christmas carol about King Wenceslas and the feast of St. Stephen, then asks, "Wanna hear something totally grotesque and weird?"

I laugh. We haven't been alone together since our kiss last night and I'm not quite sure how to act around him in front of the other passengers. On the one hand, I don't want him to think I didn't like our kiss or that I don't want to do it again—and again and again and again and again—as soon as possible. But I also don't want to be unprofessional.

Mr. Fenton is all of two feet away reading a plaque and Mary is snapping another photo just to my left. So I carefully avoid touching Sam, but I do lean in closer.

"That's a rhetorical question, right? Who would say no to that?"

Sam smiles. "Okay, so Mr. Fenton just told me this. You know how we're headed to the Old Town Square to see the astronomical clock?"

I roll my eyes and gesture with a head tilt to Mary, clicking away. "*If* we ever get off this bridge."

"Seriously." His fingers brush mine and I jump. A smile twitches in the corner of Sam's mouth. I sidestep to put more distance between us. Sam doesn't comment on that, instead continuing, "Fenton says it was installed back in 1410."

"Wow." For our school field trips we used to go to Ohio Village to see a replica of a nineteenth-century village, where all the people working there dressed up in long dresses and bonnets (or straw hats and suspenders for the boys) and pretended they were from that time. They'd look at you with fake wonder if you chewed gum or pulled out a cell phone. I thought that was the coolest thing when I was in fifth grade.

And now I am going to see a clock installed in 1410.

Sam tugs gently on my backpack to pull me along to the next statue. "We're gonna try to wait it out until it strikes the hour because this row of figures parades out, including Death himself."

I pause and a group of tourists streams around us on either side. "That sounds creepy."

Sam stops too, then steps backward to reach me. "Nope. Not the creepy part. I've seen it—it's actually really cool. But

I never knew the next part. Okay, so check this out. Legend has it that the city was so proud of its unique clock that they ordered the clockmaker blinded so he couldn't re-create it anywhere else. He got so ticked off after that, he broke it, and no one could figure out how to fix it for over a century."

"Whoa. So just because he was awesome at what he did, they blinded him for life?"

"Yup. Pretty sick, huh? You might want to mess up here and there on this bus tour, Lizzie. I'm just saying."

Sam mimes slashing across my eyelids as I laugh.

Pretty sure messing up frequently will *not* be a problem for me.

Sam moves closer, his eyes on mine. That small smile is still dancing in the corners of his mouth, and I know this because I'm completely staring at his lips like they're on fire. Which, now that I think back on our kiss last night . . .

For a second I wonder if he's going for a repeat performance, right here in front of all the seniors and I stumble, eyes wide.

Sam's hand on my elbow steadies me. I sigh at how delicious it feels, then jump away. Out of the corner of my eye, I'm positive I see Emma nudge Mary and point in our direction. Great. Just great.

Sam tilts his head, and his expression is somewhere between puzzled and amused. "Not here," I whisper/hiss, jerking my head in the direction of Mary and Emma.

Sam follows my head motion and bites his lower lip as his

eyebrows go up. Now there's no hiding his amusement. "I get it. We're on the down low, Agent X?"

"The very down low," I whisper, because Mr. Fenton and Dolores are making their way toward us.

Sam steps closer again, hands raised in surrender. "If you insist, but it's gonna be tough not to touch you all day."

His voice is low and warm and teasing and I just want to grab his hand and run us to a hidden spot under the bridge. Instead I force myself to turn my back on him and very deliberately march over to Mr. Fenton. "How are you enjoying Prague, you two?"

Mr. Fenton smiles easily. "Very much, Lizzie. I was just telling Dolores that if you stand on this bridge during the summer solstice and look up at the St. Vitus Cathedral, the very last ray of sun to touch the cathedral hits at the exact spot where St. Vitus's remains are buried. Is that impressive planning or what?"

I nod and shuffle lightly away from Sam, who has come up beside me and is feigning great interest in Mr. Fenton while trying to surreptitiously brush his fingers against mine again. I swat them away with a small smile on my lips this time and from the corner of my eye, I see Sam grin. My insides go all bubbly, like someone just opened champagne in my belly.

The rest of the afternoon we spend wandering very slowly around Old Town. I'm ready to jump out of my skin, having Sam so close and not being able to touch him. Actually, I'm about to jump Sam. I can tell he's every bit as attuned to me, because whenever I "accidentally" bump my hip against his or I step so close behind him that my breath tickles his shoulder, I feel his whole body tense up.

We're trailing a few feet behind the seniors and I'm about to go certifiably crazy from all the amazing tension between us when Sam, in one fluid motion, grabs my hand and tugs me into a doorway tucked into the cobblestoned alley we're walking down. He pushes my back against the wall and tangles his hands in my hair, kissing me so passionately that I now get that whole "weak in the knees" expression. My legs feel like rubber glue. Just as quickly he pulls back and steps into the alleyway, whistling innocently as he catches up with the others. I, on the other hand, can't move. Like, physically can't move.

When I join the others a full three minutes later, Sam is the picture of innocence when he asks, "Stop to tie your shoe?"

I'm wearing sandals.

I need another doorway right this very second.

I glance at him and he subtly winks at me. God, this boy.

I do my best to throw myself into playing doting tour guide, fishing out the first aid kit from my backpack when Dolores gets a blister and finding Mary's reading glasses in the bottomless pit she calls a pocketbook. All afternoon, every move I make, I can feel Sam's eyes on me. It's . . . well, it's kind of thrilling.

After dinner (no roll, plain chicken breast, a PowerBar in the stall of the ladies' room), we all see a performance of *Don Giovanni* at the National Marionette Theatre. Apparently, this is some big thing in Prague. There are smoke machines going during the performance and everything. And forget yodeling a la the *Sound of Music* puppet show. We get Mozart (the dude sure got around Eastern Europe).

I have a seat next to Sam, and he keeps shifting so that his leg brushes against mine and I place my hand low between our seats and wait for him to do the same. When he twines my fingertips with his, I have to suck in a breath. He squeezes gently and rubs circles in my palm with the pad of his thumb. To be honest, I spend way more time focused on this than the marionettes.

But when we spill out onto the street once it ends, I find the one thing that could take my attention off of Sam. Prague at night. "It's so beautiful!" I gasp.

The cobblestones twinkle under the flickering flames of gas lamps curving down the narrow alleyways of the old section of town. It feels like I'm in another century.

Emma slides into place next to me. "This here is why I booked the trip."

I understand perfectly. The night's warm and a tiny bit sticky, but the atmosphere is otherworldly.

"I'll tell you what this city is, it's romance," says Mary, never far behind Emma.

"So true," answers Emma. "Too bad we're all withered up and old. You'll have to settle for a stroll with an old friend instead, Mar."

Mary links her arm through Emma's. "Hey, speak for

yourself on that withered-up-and-old thing. Except . . ." She pauses and winks at me. "I do think we can live vicariously through some of us here who might be single *and* full of youthful promise."

I begin backing away. "Oh, no. Um, I don't think . . ."

Just then Mr. Fenton appears with Dolores at his side and Sam a few steps behind.

"You know, Dolores and I were just talking about what a nice night it is for a leisurely stroll along the Vltava River. Don't you think us old folks should trot ourselves off to bed and let our young friends here enjoy a walk?" Mr. Fenton says.

Who needs eHarmony when you have the Granny and Gramps Matchmaking Service? I catch Sam's eye and my cheeks flush pink. But he doesn't look embarrassed at all. He looks amused.

"Well, if you're sure you can make it back to the hotel on your own," Sam says, palms to the sky in a who-am-I-to-protest gesture.

"Oh, no. I'm the tour guide. I insist on getting you back safely," I say, holding my ground.

"I see. Let's settle this once and for all. Lizzie, which way is our hotel?" Mr. Fenton looks smug.

Ummmmm. I have a map of the city in my backpack for just this kind of situation, but I'm guessing from the victorious looks on everyone's faces, they're not gonna let me grab it. I point behind me and try to sound authoritative. "That way."

"Enjoy your walk," says Mr. Fenton. He gestures in the

complete opposite direction. "Anyone over the age of sixty-five, follow me."

Emma, Mary, and even Dolores smile and waggle their fingers in my direction as they fall in behind Mr. Fenton. I turn to Sam helplessly. "Did you have anything to do with this?"

"Nope."

"Are we going to let them get away with it?" I ask.

"What do you suggest? We hold a trial and hang them from the Old Town bridge tower for incessant meddling? I kind of thought meddling was what grandparents lived for."

"What do you think gave us away?"

Sam coughs. "Probably the way you can't stop undressing me with those swoony eyes. Geez, I feel like I'm on the cover of *Tiger Beat* or something."

I swat at him for the hundredth time today and he captures my hand easily and tucks it inside his own. I am suddenly filled with warm, happy thoughts about my mutinous crew.

"Who cares what gave it away," Sam murmurs, stepping close and gently backing me against the wall outside the theater. He takes my other hand in his too. "Cat's out of the bag, so now I can do this any time I want. Which has basically been every second of this day."

Stepping in, he places his lips on mine and steals my breath. Even as my eyes close, I can still sense the flickering gas lamps on the street corner. I hear the soft strums of guitar music from a street café a little ways off and feel the uneven cobblestones under my sandals. This place is magical. All of it.

Sam brings our entwined hands up and tucks my elbows against my hips as he sighs into my mouth. I think he's feeling the spell of this place too. His kiss isn't urgent like earlier, but soft and sweet. I untangle our hands and wrap my arms around his neck as Sam deepens our kiss. It feels like I could float away as his hands circle my back.

How could I have ever imagined *this* would be my summer?

TWENTY-TWO

"Up for a walk? It's a free-choice afternoon and I choose you." Sam slides behind me and whispers in my ear.

My insides feel like they're wrapped in an electric blanket and getting warmer by the second. Getting close to Sam is really stupid and potentially threatening to everything I'm here to do for Elizabeth, but not getting close to him feels completely impossible.

I turn to face him. "Sure! Give me a few minutes to grab my stuff from my room."

I'm deciding right here and right now to just let it happen. I'll worry about the fallout later. For now, we're in Venice.

Venice!

After two hours of walking around, I'm ready to make another declaration. Venice is my new favorite. Okay, I *know*. I say that everywhere. But really, it's like Amsterdam with all the canals (or probably it's more that Amsterdam is like Venice) but it's also a little bit more mysterious and just more . . . edgy.

Every time we take a turn, I'm convinced we'll never in a million years find our way back to our hotel. I can barely do that when there's a grid pattern, and here we're talking bridges everywhere. But Sam keeps saying "Trust me," so I do.

The irony is not lost on me.

He steers us to St. Mark's Square with the pigeons and the Basilica and the Caffè Florian and all the long striped poles where the gondolas are docked and bobbing in the water. But I prefer the surprises of turning corners and finding hidden squares with laundry hanging above our heads and tiny bubbling fountains.

Sam is a far better tour guide than I am. He's no Mr. Fenton with all the dates and facts, but his anecdotes come from experience, unlike mine, which come from Sam's iPad. He tells me about coming in the fall, when half the city floods with the tides and there are narrow wooden platforms people use instead of sidewalks and all the Italian women put away their fancy Italian shoes in favor of tall rain boots (which I'm sure are still somehow fabulously stylish). And he likes to point out everything, like those posh Italian women, or the little boys in an intense soccer match in the street. Or the patisseries with their colorful windows and the souvenir masks dangling from the street carts as we cross yet another bridge over a canal. I feel like he's letting me see everything through his eyes, bringing me into his world.

"I've always wanted to come one year during Carnevale. I mean, it's a total tourist trap, but they still hold the fancy balls where everyone comes masked. Don't you think it would be fun to be someone else entirely for a night?" Sam says.

As a matter of fact, I know a thing or two about being someone else entirely.

I feel like a Ping-Pong ball the way my emotions are jumping all over the place today. Walking around hand-in-hand with Sam makes me feel like we're a real couple, and just hours ago I decided to take things as they come with him and try to enjoy our time together, but the guilt about all the lies between us is killing me. It's taken up residence in my stomach and it's like I swallowed an avocado pit. (Not that I'd ever eat an avocado.)

Although speaking of eating, maybe there *is* something I can be honest with Sam about without putting Elizabeth's future in jeopardy. We pause on one of a hundred different bridges that all look alike, arching over a canal. This one even has a gondola passing underneath. I wonder if those guys ever get tired of striped shirts and "O Sole Mio"? Sam leans over the railing to watch the boat disappear underneath the bridge. When he straightens he catches sight of my expression and his eyes go wide.

"Uh-oh. I don't really like that look."

I sigh. "We need to talk."

"Four worst words in the English language." He leans over the railing again, I think to buy time. When he looks at me again, he's clearly hurt. "Don't say it. Please. I know I'm too young for you by some people's definition, but I don't care about that. Nobody here cares about that. The past few days have been . . . and I just . . ." His eyes rest on my lips for a second before he jerks them back to the water below us. He whispers, "Just please don't, okay?"

He thinks I'm putting a stop to this? Is he crazy?! And did he just give me a whole speech about how much he doesn't want to stop either? My heart does a little salsa dance around my rib cage and I can't keep the smile off my face.

"It's not that," I say.

He takes a deep breath and exhales. Then his eyes go wide. "Did I just make a total fool out of myself? Because sometimes I get ahead of myself. I'm not talking about telling someone I love them at the end of my very first phone call with that person or anything on *that* level of ridiculous or anything, but . . ."

I punch him in the arm, still smiling. Then I grab his shirt in my fist and tug him in for a kiss. A kiss I hope conveys how very much I do *not* think he made a fool of himself. And how very much I do *not* want to stop kissing him. At all.

"Wow," he says when we break apart. "Let's have this talk more often."

I laugh, then grow quiet. Sam tilts my chin up with his finger and says, "Hey. Hey, you can talk to me. About anything. I hope you know I'm not just here for the kissing. Although I'm not *not* here for the kissing, because that's pretty great too." He chuckles and brushes his lips across mine, whisper soft. He moves his lips to my ear and whispers, "But not just the kissing. Promise. Talk to me."

God, this has to go well because if I mess things up with this guy . . . plus, his reaction is going to tell me everything I need to know about how I can expect him to react to the much, much bigger lies if I can ever bring myself to confess to those someday far, far in the future.

Sam steps back and I play with the hem of my T-shirt as I finally work up the nerve to say, "Um, so, I, well . . ." I keep my eyes fixed on the water below us. Another gondola passes under our bridge and a tourist riding in the bow of the boat snaps a photo. I look away, at Sam, whose eyes are fixed on me. "I haven't been *completely* honest with you about something."

I'm scared to even utter those words, knowing how strongly he feels about lying. The last thing I expect is for him to say, "I know. I already know."

TWENTY-THREE

Sam knows. He knows?

"You . . . you do?" I sputter. What does this mean? Is he saying he knows I'm not Elizabeth? Does he know I'm not a college graduate? Does he—

"It was totally obvious from the first day."

The first day. What the heck is he talking about? I must look confused because he puts his hand on my arm and says, "Look, I know you don't speak Spanish, Dimple."

The breath goes out of me in a whoosh. Oh. Spanish. Right.

Wait.

"You do? How?"

"Oh, please. You never reacted when I talked to Bento, never joined in. Then you confirmed it for me when you had me write out the directions to Bento for the *Sound of Music* tour."

And here I thought I'd been all subtle about that.

"I figured you were embarrassed, though why you lied on your application is beyond me. Mom was desperate for a guide and that would never have put you out of the running. To be honest, her choices were you or . . . you."

I hang my head and pretend to be ashamed of my résumé fraud. "I'm sorry. I don't know why I did that. Your mom mentioned knowing a second language as being a job requirement, so I just checked the box. I didn't think it meant the driver would *only* speak Spanish."

"Don't worry about it. Bento's totally cool with everything. He really likes you."

"He does?"

"How could he not?" Sam murmurs. He catches my eye and then ducks his head, and the words "I really like you too" hang in the air between us, even though he doesn't say them out loud.

I'm so flustered I forget where I'd been going with this line of conversation and say, "Yeah, Bento's great. Do you happen to know where he goes when he's not driving us? Like today, for instance, when we don't need the bus. What do you think he's doing? Is it rude of us not to invite him along to do stuff?"

Sam snorts. "I wouldn't worry about Bento. You know that expression 'a girl in every port'? That's what Bento has. Only in his case they're men."

"Oh. Oooooooooh."

"Yeah, oh," says Sam, waggling his eyebrows up and down.

"Okay, then. Well, his secret is safe with me," I say.

"Pretty positive he's not keeping anything secret. But I'm sure he'll be glad to have your blessing." He gives me a conspiratorial wink. "You, on the other hand, *are* keeping secrets. And yours is safe with me."

I bring my eyes up to meet his. They're staring back at me with such complete trust that I consider saying "Thanks" and calling it a confession, but it isn't the one I need to make. Because I really like him too. Oh, and plus, we're in Italy and the pasta dishes look unbelievably amazing since, hello, it's *Italy*. I'd be lying if I said that wasn't factoring in here.

I drop my eyes again.

"I wasn't talking about the Spanish. Even though it's a huge relief to not have to try to hide that from you anymore. I think Bento was at the end of his acting rope, so it was only a matter of time." I manage a laugh, but Sam is now studying me with scrunched eyebrows.

"If it wasn't the Spanish, what was it?"

I blush. "So, the thing is, you have to understand that you're super worldly and all and I didn't want you to think I was just some typical American girl from the suburbs who doesn't appreciate foreign culture."

I look at Sam, but he just waits for me to continue.

I take a deep breath. "I don't have celiac," I rush out.

"You . . . ? What?"

"I don't have celiac disease. I'm just a ridiculously picky eater and I was embarrassed, but there was no way in hell I was eating goose brains or whatever else was on that menu and I didn't want you to think I was some brat, so I lied."

"You made up a disease because you didn't want to tell me you don't like Austrian food?"

"Um, yes?"

I expect him to get angry or maybe roll his eyes, but instead he blinks at me a few times and then starts laughing. Loudly. A few passersby glance our way.

"Sam!" I tug on his sleeve. "Sam, you're making a scene."

"I'm making a scene?" he says between gulps for air. "Are you telling me we gave a waiter in arguably the best restaurant in Vienna a total line about you not being able to eat gluten? That is priceless."

I don't think it's *that* funny. But his laughter is kind of contagious and at least he's not mad, so that's something. In fact, he's handling this all surprisingly well. He says he has trust issues over the stuff with his mom lying to him about his dad, but wow. He's being very mellow about all of this. I help him straighten up and hold him by the arms as he collects himself.

He swipes at a tear of laughter in the corner of his eye. "You are completely adorable, do you know that? When I read your résumé back at the office, I thought you were some classic overachiever, a Goody-Two-shoes know-it-all who'd be bossy and snobby. And then we talked on the phone and you weren't like that at all. At all. I don't know if you felt it too, but it was like we just . . . clicked."

I nod.

Sam bites his lip. "As long as we're making confessions, I have one. I wasn't annoying my mom around the office. In fact, I had to spend three hours *begging* her to send me here instead of a home health aide. All because I was dying to meet you in person."

"You were?" A laugh tickles my insides and burbles out of me, but Sam is very serious as he tucks a strand of hair behind my ear.

"Yep. Best use of three hours ever, too. C'mere."

He tucks me under his arm and gazes down at me. "You are so cute." His finger hooks beneath my chin again and he tilts it up. His presses his lips against mine and I happy-sigh into them.

His reaction to my confession is not *at all* what I expected. But I will for sure take it.

"Is there anything else I need to know?" he asks, breaking away but not releasing me. "Are you actually a spy for MI6? Part of the Witness Protection Program? Any other dark secrets hiding in your closet?"

Um . . .

I shake my head. "Not a one," I say, keeping my eyes on his lips.

Okay, so in spite of all the happy feels I'm having, underneath it all, the avocado pit is still there. Which I sort of suspected would be the case. On the upside, Sam seems to roll with things pretty well. Maybe I can find some way to confess to him once we're back home. Maybe he won't see a need to tell his mom everything. He'd have to really like me a lot for that, but that could totally happen, right? All's well that ends well? And at that point, this whole trip will be a (hopefully) happy memory in our rearview mirrors.

It could happen.

Right?

TWENTY-FOUR

Aside from Emma looking ridiculous in the glittery mask she bought in a street market and insisted on wearing nonstop, Venice was a hit. Three days of wandering churches and museums and piazzas and strolling along canals. And pizza! And pasta! All things I can now safely eat out in the open, versus PowerBars in the confines of a ladies' room stall.

But now we've left all the mystery of the foggy city behind for sparkly sunshine on the Mediterranean and a couple of quiet days of lounging in the small hill towns of Cinque Terre.

Cinque Terre is really five towns (hence the name, which in Italian means—drumroll, please—"five towns." Well, "lands," actually, but same difference) connected by train and mountain passes. There are no cars allowed so we had to leave Bento behind in La Spezia and hop a train for this stretch of the journey. Thankfully Sam was along to help us navigate buying tickets and show us where to get off, because I may be getting better when there's a driver escorting me door to door, but there's nothing like an Italian train station to put someone in her place.

The towns are all small collections of brightly colored villas built into the terraced hillsides. The best part about Cinque Terre is that you can soak up tons of atmosphere by barely moving. You can pretty much explore the entire town of Vernazza, where we're staying, in under an hour, which means we have some much-needed lazy, hazy summer days of relaxation in our future.

I'm thinking it might be my new favorite (I *know*!) as I stretch my legs out to the side of the café table. I close my eyes and tilt my face up to catch the warmth of the morning sun.

Now *this* is the life.

A shock of cold hits my back and I jump ten feet in the air, knocking my chair over and nearly falling on top of it myself, if not for the strong arms that catch me. A slew of ice cubes tumble out the back of my shirt.

"Sam Bellamy!" I screech.

Emma, who is (or was, that is) seated beside me, tsk-tsks him. "You are a wicked boy, Sam."

He grins at her and kicks aside a few cubes. "Emma, my capacity for tomfoolery is unsurpassed."

I snort and punch his arm a little more aggressively than I intended. He yelps and rubs it. "Hey, I was just trying to help wake you up. I thought you might be sleepy after all that hiking yesterday."

Sam, Mr. Fenton, Emma, Mary, and I walked the two hours

of hillside trails carved between Vernazza and Monterosso and then caught the train back. I'm feeling those climbs today, but I can't exactly complain about my stiffness if the people three times my age aren't. So much for my stereotype about frail, helpless senior citizens just waiting at death's doorstep.

"It's Italy. I'm certain I can find some espresso somewhere around here to help with the waking-up part," I say.

"Yeah, but with all the cream and sugar you add, I'm not sure there's any room for caffeine in those tiny cups."

I narrow my eyes at him and he laughs again and pulls a chair out for his grandmother, who has been hovering quietly behind him. Luckily for Sam's other arm, Mr. Fenton approaches the table then.

"Pesto focaccia, anyone?" he asks. He's juggling a giant pizza-sized piece of flatbread.

"For breakfast?" Emma asks.

"Local delicacy. Don't think they're too particular on when you enjoy it."

"At least he didn't bring one with anchovies. That's the other local delicacy," adds Mary from her seat next to Emma.

"So's limoncello," says Hank, joining our group, plopping into a seat and pulling Maisy onto his lap. "Don't y'all ask me how I know that one."

He winces and shakes aspirin from a bottle into his palm before passing the container to Maisy. Oh great. Hank and Maisy, hangover version. That should be super fun on our boat-ride outing this morning.

"Okay, guys," I say. "You have thirty minutes for breakfast and then we need to meet the charter boat at the end of the dock. I'd say to allow about seven minutes or so to walk there. I clocked it yesterday when I confirmed the booking."

Look at me, all fancy tour guide. I'm definitely getting the hang of things. I even remembered to walk at senior-citizen speed when I timed the commute.

"Better leave now, then," Hank says, lifting Maisy back up and setting her on her feet. "Not moving too fast at the moment. I thought all those Lone Star beers I enjoy back home would have meant I could keep up with the shots they were pouring last night, but hooooo-ey!"

They wander away, oblivious to our laughter.

Thirty minutes later we catch up with our Texans on the boat dock. The water below us is the kind of blue-green you only see in the artificial waterfalls at minigolf courses and it glimmers in the bright sunshine. Even this early in the day the deck of the boat we step onto feels deliciously warm beneath my newly bare feet. We settle into seats on the small fishing boat we've chartered for the day. Our captain, who introduces himself as Marcello, looks like a crusty old seaman in a wind-breaker and a floppy hat, but his smile is wide and genuine as he welcomes us.

I don't really have high hopes for enjoying the fishing por-tion of the morning, but after so many hours spent driving on this trip, being out on the water feels like freedom. Marcello pulls away from the dock and aims us along the coastline. We follow the curve of the coast for a while and I close my eyes, soaking up the sun like a lizard on a rock. When I inhale the pure sea air, it fills my body.

This moment. Right here. This is the one I'll remember when I think back on this trip.

I open my eyes to find Sam looking at me. He smiles his yummy just-for-me smile.

Perfection.

And then Dolores throws up.

Chaos ensues as several people jump up at once, sending the little boat listing to one side. Dolores immediately bursts into tears and Sam races to her side to comfort her.

Marcello wastes no time dipping a bucket into the sea to fill with water and producing a rag to clean the mess. Lucky tour guide me, I get the honors. This was so not in the brochure.

Though I do feel awful for Dolores. I can't tell if her tears are from discomfort or embarrassment, but with the way she's clutching her stomach, it's clear she can't continue. When I finish cleaning up and swishing the rag clean, I move next to Marcello.

"Short of turning around, is there anywhere you could drop the two of us for the next few hours and then pick us up on your way back?"

I'm a little nervous about being stranded alone with Dolores since she's the one on this tour I'm most intimidated by. I love Mr. Fenton and Mary and Emma. Hank is maybe not the most PC of individuals (by a long shot!) but he and Maisy are off in their own hormone-filled world and are generally harmless. Dolores, though? She's a tough nut to crack, even if she seems much more content now that she has her grandson by her side. Too bad *content* and *engaged with our group* are two very different things. Except what kind of tour guide—much less *person*—would I be if I left her to her own devices in this state? I'm sure Sam would do it, but I know he's been looking forward to the boat trip and I don't want him to have to miss out. I can take one for the team. That's my job and I'm getting pretty okay with doing my job, if I say so myself.

"*Si, si*. We have *bellissimo* beach near Riomaggiore. Few minutes by boat." Marcello turns the boat back toward land and aims us at another terraced town with houses stacked on top of one another up into the mountains.

I fill Sam in on the plan, who in turn whispers it to Dolores. She nods, still swiping at her eyes with a handkerchief Mr. Fenton produced.

A few minutes later Marcello pulls alongside a tiny stretch of rocks that form a deserted beach. The mountainside comes right to the edge of the water, surrounding it on three sides with cliffs of jagged rock. To our left, there is a waterfall spilling over the top and into the sea below. It's breathtaking.

When Marcello has gotten as close as he can without bottoming out, he cuts the engine and he and Sam hop out and gently pull the boat in until only their knees are submerged in the ocean. Then Sam does something better than one thousand of Mr. Darcy's *Pride and Prejudice* proposals. He *carries* his grandmother to shore. Like, in his arms. Total swoon. When he sets her down on the rocky beach, it looks as though she'd like to kiss the ground. Me, I'd like to kiss Sam. I hop out behind them and splash over, which is not easy with the slippery rocks below.

"I'll stay with her," I say. "I could care less about fishing and you said yesterday you were excited for it. If you don't mind keeping an eye on everyone else, I'll make sure your grandmother is comfortable."

Sam is glancing over at his gram when Emma's voice rings out. "Can we stay too?" She and Mary are standing in the boat.

"What?" I call.

"This beach is one of a kind. I'd far rather stay here and explore than catch stinky anchovies."

"We will likely not be catching any anchovies, señora." Even as he shouts to keep those of us on the beach part of the conversation, Marcello sounds amused.

Still, what the guest wants, the guest gets, right?

"Hop out," I answer. "We'll have a ladies' day. Maisy, wanna join us?"

I'm expecting her to say yes on account of her hangover. Quite honestly, I was expecting *her* to be the one booting up her breakfast. But she's a stand-by-your-man kinda gal. She shields her eyes with her hand and shakes her head.

"Okay, well, Plan B, I guess," says Sam. "And thanks, Lizzie." He squeezes my arm before wading back through the water to grab Emma's hand, then Mary's, to help them pick their way toward the beach. When they've reached shore, he pushes the boat into deeper water and hoists himself over the side. All the men—plus Maisy—wave as the boat turns and races for open water.

"Well, this is perfectly delightful," says Emma. "I feel like we're shipwrecked. Which is much nicer knowing you're guaranteed a rescue in a few hours."

She's right. The beach is totally remote. I can see some of the rooftops of homes far off in the distance but this cove is protected from both the open water and the village. I find a grouping of rocks that look more smooth than jagged and nestle myself into them as a sort of makeshift chair.

"Dolores, is being on solid ground helping?" I ask. She still seems a bit shaken up.

"Oh, I feel fine now. More ashamed than anything else. My behavior was so unladylike. I apologize."

Mary snorts and Emma laughs.

"Ladylike? Oh, pish," Emma says. "Who cares about that anymore? I could certainly do without the tattoos on every which body part, but this younger generation is far smarter than ours, with their 'I'll be who I want to be and you'll just have to like it' attitude. When I think of all the stockings I rolled on and the girdles I wore, just to vacuum the house and make casseroles for my husband, I could scream."

"Well, I believe there's something to be said for the way we conducted ourselves, don't you?" Dolores asks, looking to Mary for backup. "We knew how to be modest, which is more than most young ladies these days can say."

I try to slink deeper into the rocks as I mentally walk through the hemlines on the outfits I've worn so far this trip. I *think* they've been okay?

"Modesty is for the birds," Emma says. "I am quite through being a proper lady. Would you like to know how through with it I am?"

She doesn't wait for an answer before struggling to her feet and stripping off her sweater (what is it with old people and their sweaters in the middle of summer, anyway?). Her blouse is next and her pants quickly follow. She stands before us in her bra and underwear.

And then those are gone.

She gives us a defiant look and begins wading—buck naked—into the water toward the waterfall.

The rest of us are too shocked to say anything.

TWENTY-FIVE

Mary recovers first.

With a whoop, she stands and begins stripping as well. My jaw drops. Dolores is practically purple with embarrassment and *she's* fully clothed. In less than thirty seconds, Mary is naked too and wading out toward Emma.

Their laughter floats across the water.

I look around, verifying that we are indeed completely isolated. Even so . . . I thought I was the one who was supposed to be young and wild, yet these two are completely putting me to shame.

I scoot closer to Dolores.

"Mary and Emma sure know how to make the most of the moment, huh?" I ask. Here I am alone with Dolores, just like I was dreading. Hanging between us is the beyond-awkward fact that *I* know that *she* knows I've been making out with her grandson all over the continent of Europe. If she doesn't approve of short shorts, who knows what she thinks of that.

"They sure do," she says, and something in her voice startles me. She sounds almost . . . wistful.

"Dolores, did you—do you want to skinny-dip?"

She covers her mouth with her hand. "What? Me? Don't be ridiculous. I could never do that. I'm nothing like those two women."

But she hasn't taken her eyes off "those two women" and her voice goes up a little at the end of her sentence. I think she might actually wish she *was* like them.

I say, "I mean, if you wanted to swim, it would totally be our little secret. There's no one around and the guys won't be back for hours."

She begins tracing the edges of the rock she's sitting on with her finger. "I don't think I have it in me. I've never been one to throw caution to the wind. That's just not the type of person I am."

Something about that makes me very sad. I think about how much Dolores has hung back on this trip because she has a particular idea about the kind of person she is and the kind of person she isn't.

"Dolores. Can I tell you a secret? Before I came on this trip, I'd never been anywhere. I mean, seriously. Nowhere. But you know what, I was perfectly fine with that. I was completely comfortable being at home and I thought my life was perfect."

Dolores nods. "Home sweet home."

"Right, exactly. And you can't miss what you don't know.

Except . . ." I lean forward so that I'm facing her. "What if we were wrong?"

"I don't know what you mean." She looks pained.

"I mean, what if we're those kinds of people back there but maybe there are other kinds of people inside us and we just need the right circumstances to draw them out? Does that sound weird?"

She nods. "A bit."

"But what if there's someone in you who *is* brave and *would* want to go skinny-dipping in the Italian Riviera?"

Dolores laughs. "That sounds so Grace Kelly."

I smile. "Then maybe you can channel Grace Kelly for the day. C'mon, Dolores. I feel like you might regret it if you don't do it. You could wear your, um, undergarments."

I can't say the word *bra* to Sam's grandmother. I can't.

Mary and Emma have reached the waterfall and their squeals carry over to us. I take Dolores's hand. "I'll go for it if you will," I tell her.

Wait, what did I just say?

Dolores studies my hand in hers.

I take a deep breath. "C'mon. We'll do it together. What do you say?"

This has to earn me a place in the tour guides hall of fame, right? But aside from any job responsibility, it's somehow really important to me that Dolores does this for herself.

Still, I'm surprised when she says, in a tiny voice, "Okay."

Okay? Okay. So here comes the striptease with my kinda

sorta boyfriend's grandma. Special.

Except it is. We undress with our backs to each other. I leave my bra and underwear on (*just like a bathing suit, just like a bathing suit*) and when I turn I see Dolores has too. Even so, I make it a point to keep my eyes averted until we're deep enough in the water to submerge the parts I can't wait to have submerged, but before we're even ankle deep, I'm relaxing. Especially because Dolores is laughing.

Laughing.

Her shoulders, which have been permanently hunched in, like she's trying to hide herself inside them, are thrown back as she calls to Emma and Mary and lifts her arm to wave. They spot us and shout, beckoning with their hands, so we move in their direction.

By the time we reach the waterfall, all four of us are giggling up a storm, and if I thought back on the boat that I was going to remember today, I am now positive it is etched in my memory for life.

I'm sure the guys (and Maisy) are wondering why we all look like cats who swallowed canaries when they pull the boat up to the beach a few hours later, but we aren't talking.

Except for Dolores. She isn't dishing about the skinny-dipping, but she certainly is newly bubbly on any and every other topic. It's like she finally woke up from a deep sleep and wants to catch up on all the gossip. She doesn't look the least bit seasick either. Sam catches my eye as we motor back to

Vernazza and mouths, "What's with her?" I shrug and give him my best Mona Lisa smile. What happens on Cinque Terre beaches stays on Cinque Terre beaches.

I can tell Sam is impressed, though, and that warms me more than the sun-soaked rocks on the beach did. It's not like I need his validation, but it's more like, when Sam first got here, he was so at ease and in control, and I was soooo out of my element. Now I finally know what that confidence feels like for myself. A laugh bubbles out of me before I can help it and Sam squeezes my knee.

The next day is our last in Vernazza and we mark the occasion by doing a whole lot of nothing. I play model for some drawings Mary does in her sketchbook, and Emma, Mary, and I have a three-hour lunch in a sunny courtyard. I dash off a postcard to Madison: *Remember last summer when you went skinny-dipping with the counselors from the boys' camp . . . well, I have stories!* (Let her chew on *that* for the rest of the summer.) Sam and Dolores head off to spend quality time together and Mr. Fenton tackles another of the hiking trails, this time up to a vineyard. Hank and Maisy also spend "quality time" together, but we all know what that's code for. When we meet up for a group dinner of family-style pasta platters later that night, they are still conspicuously absent.

I haven't had any alone time with Sam on this leg of the trip, other than a few morning hours in the laundromat watching our loads of whites tumble over each other in the dryer and chatting (there's something to be said about flirting over the folding table), but I'm hoping we can have a little extra time together tonight after dinner. I try to linger after paying the check while Sam attempts to convince Dolores she'll never get the chance to eat the leftovers she wants to bring back to the hotel, since we have three meals a day booked once we get to Monte Carlo tomorrow.

As I hang back, Mr. Fenton wanders over and plants himself next to me.

"Lizzie," he says, more a statement than a question.

"Mr. Fenton." I will say, it's a little amazing how naturally I answer to Lizzie now, like it's my real name or something.

I wait for him to say something more, but he doesn't. I sneak a peek and find him staring at me. "Um, is there something you need help with?"

He smiles at this. "Indeed there is. In fact, I suspect there's something we can each help each other with and the timing seems right."

Well, now I'm intrigued. I send one last glance in Sam's direction, then turn my full attention to Mr. Fenton. "Would you like to take a walk?"

In answer he takes my arm and tucks it into his elbow. Sam looks up and I give him a small wave. His wave back seems a little limp, which I take as a good sign that he's as disappointed as I am we won't be hanging out tonight.

Mr. Fenton must notice our exchange because as we exit the restaurant, he says, "Things seem to be going well in the world of young love."

I'm glad the streets are dimly lit so my blush won't be totally visible. "I don't know about calling anything love. I've only known him for eleven days. Or so."

"Not that you're counting," Mr. Fenton says. It's too dark to see his expression, but I can hear his chuckle just fine.

"Anyhoo . . ." I'm desperate to change the topic. "You said I could help you with something?"

Mr. Fenton laughs and it's a deep belly laugh I don't often hear from him. "Oh, Aubree. Someday you'll learn to talk about romance every chance you get. But I'll let you get away with your evil manipulations. Again. Yes, there is something I'd like to request from you."

He steers us up a small street that's really more of an alley, with the houses leaning in just a bit and rows of fairy lights strung across the expanse and looped around second-story balcony railings. A short way up the hill, Mr. Fenton gestures for me to sit on a stoop, then struggles a bit to settle in next to me.

He clutches his knees. "Not the spring chicken I used to be. All that hiking today did a number on these old bones."

I give him a concerned look. "Are you okay?"

He waves me off. "I'm fine. Just fine. And even if I weren't it wouldn't keep me down because tomorrow is the day I've been waiting for. For most of my life, I've followed all of society's conventions and been quite content to do so. But I do have a bit of a wild streak I don't often get to indulge."

He looks at me and smiles. I'm really wondering where this conversation is going. I think I've had enough "throw propriety to the wind" seniors over the last two days to last me for a while.

I exhale when he says, "The thing is, I like to gamble. And, well, the main reason I booked this trip was because the itinerary took us through Monaco."

"Oh, okay. Are there casinos there or something?" I ask.

"Yes indeed. Monaco has one of the most famous, most glamorous casinos in the world." Mr. Fenton sighs, like I should have known this already.

"Sorry. I haven't asked to borrow Sam's iPad in a few days to research ahead."

"Why don't you let me handle the talking on the Cinque Terre–to-Monaco leg?" Mr. Fenton says.

I turn to him with a smile. "That would be perfect. Thanks."

Mr. Fenton smiles back and then, ever so smoothly, says, "Well, it's not a freebie. I expect something in return. We'll pretend you're one of my students and I've got a little home-work assignment for you."

"Um, no offense, Mr. Fenton, but I'm on my summer break."

"There's no summer break from the school of hard knocks, Aubree. And if you don't want to think of it as an assignment, I'm fine with us calling it what it is."

"Which is?"

Mr. Fenton shrugs and grins. "Blackmail."

Great. Skinny-dipping grandmas, blackmailing elderly

gentlemen, nonstop-sex-having honeymooners. What next?

I sigh. Something tells me I am not going to like this assignment. "What is it?"

"You have to tell Sam who you really are."

I let my feet thud to the ground. "Mr. Fenton! I can't tell Sam. Of everyone on this trip, he's the absolute last person I can tell."

"I disagree. I've seen the way that boy looks at you. He'll forgive you. He's an old soul and old souls know their way around forgiveness. I've been on this planet a whole lot longer than you and you'll have to trust me on this one."

"But, but . . ." I'm having trouble forming words beyond that. After a few deep breaths I manage, "For one thing, there are things you don't know about Sam that make him way less likely to forgive and forget. Plus, what if he decided to tell his mom and then Elizabeth gets in trouble. Why would I chance that?"

"Two reasons." Mr. Fenton places a hand over mine to settle me. "One, every day you lie to him is a day your relationship will suffer. And yes, I know it's only been eleven days, so don't think you need to remind me."

He must spot my open mouth, all ready with an argument.

"But when you see it, you know. And you two have something going on that I think could continue past this trip."

I don't even know what to say about that since I know I haven't felt the way I do around Sam with other boys, but there is the small matter of the fact that he'll probably hate me the second I tell him the truth. I let my thoughts swirl for a while as Mr. Fenton sits calmly next to me.

Finally I say, "I'm not sure I can."

"And that is the second reason. You say Elizabeth is your older sister. Is it just the two of you?"

I nod.

"And she's the more accomplished."

"She's pretty perfect. Four-point-oh student, president of every club, never disheveled, and always totally on top of things. She's never messed up a day in her life."

"Except for whatever she did to keep her from this trip?"

"Right. Except for that."

"Hmm. So responsible Elizabeth did something irresponsible?" Mr. Fenton asks.

"Well, yeah, but she didn't mean to. I mean, it wasn't even her fault. There were extenuating circumstances."

"But to get herself in that position, she must have been at least a little irresponsible, maybe made a bad choice. Of which you were understanding. And you forgave her. More than forgave her, I'd say, to be willing to take over this trip from her." He fixes me with a stare. What is it he wants from me?

"Of course I forgave her."

"So you can be understanding toward Elizabeth's mistakes, but not willing to consider that others would be equally understanding about a bad choice you made? A choice that had pure motivations behind it?"

Oh. Yeah, I get where he's going. But Elizabeth didn't lie

to anyone. I mean, okay, she has me lying *for* her, I guess, but she didn't lie every day for weeks straight into the faces of people who trust her. Except maybe Mom and Dad. Sure, but she didn't lie to a boy who likes her.

"I don't think it's the same thing, Mr. Fenton. Anyway, I *have* to forgive her. She's my big sister."

"And you're the baby sister." Mr. Fenton looks amused, but it's not funny to me.

I sigh. "I'm the baby sister." I try not to think about how much it means to me that Elizabeth start seeing me as something more than that. Which will never happen if I mess this charade up. The avocado pit grows to the size of a watermelon in my stomach. Mr. Fenton won't really make me tell Sam, will he?

As if he can read my mind, he says, "I think you're selling yourself short, Aubree. You've been doing quite the job of it ever since you decided to take ownership over our tour. So you have that success already. And taking ownership over your *mistakes* is about as grown up as it gets. I'll let you think that one over. And I'm here if you need to talk. But you do need to tell Sam. Soon."

I study the ground. "I'll think about it."

"Do more than think."

Geez, for someone so nice, he sure can be pushy. He stands and brushes his pants off before offering me a hand.

"Anyway," he says. "Let's move on to what else I'd like you to do for me in the meantime. We can file this next request under the favor category. . . ."

After Mr. Fenton fills me in on his plan, he leaves me alone on the stoop to think. When I get back to the hotel, the front desk clerk hands me Sam's iPad with a note from Mr. Fenton taped to it.

Perhaps a call back home will remind you of all that's waiting there . . . versus all that could be.

He means all that could be with Sam. *If* I tell him *and* he forgives me (which is no guarantee), Sam could be waiting for me at home.

I think about going back to Ohio and picking up where I left off. Obviously I'll be starting college in the fall, and that will be exciting in its own way, but otherwise I'll be going home to exactly the same life I left behind last month. And while a few weeks ago, that was all that I wanted, it isn't enough anymore. I want more.

Mr. Fenton's right. I have to tell Sam. But first I have to tell Elizabeth. I owe her that much.

TWENTY-SIX

I connect to Skype and plug in my sister's username. Before I have time to change my mind, the iPad is making a ringing noise. This time I hear Elizabeth before I see her.

"Bree? Hang on, I'm turning on the video. Don't go anywhere!"

She sounds cheerful and I smile, thinking about how well our last Skype talk from Prague went.

"Hey! Hi!" she says when her face appears on the screen. She's on the couch in our family room and the TV flickers beside her.

"Are Mom and Dad home?" I ask first.

"Nope. Both out. We're safe. Although maybe you could find some pine trees to stand in front of and make one of these calls to them. I think they're getting really antsy to talk to you. The postcards Madison's been sending 'from you' aren't quite cutting it anymore."

I peer out my hotel window at the glittering lights of boats bobbing in the Riviera. Pine trees? She must be kidding.

"I'll see what I can do," I say.

"Yes, please. You should just watch Mom's sad anime eyes every time she boxes up another care package for you. It's driving me crazy having to put on the whole act of wondering what you're up to at camp with her all the time." She makes a face, then tugs a pillow into her lap.

I swallow. "Yeah, lying is the worst. That's, um, that's kind of why I'm calling."

"Okay, but first can I say something?"

I nod, waiting.

I'm not at all prepared for her to say, "I want to apologize," which she does.

"Huh?" I reply.

"Look, Bree." She twists a strand of her hair around her finger and I wonder if she might actually be *nervous* to say that to me. I didn't think Elizabeth "did" nervous. She continues, "I'm really, really sorry you overheard the things I said on the phone at the airport, but I mean, just look how wrong you've proven me."

My eyes have to be as big as saucers as she asks, "You're in Italy now, right? That means you're past the halfway mark and disaster-free!"

Disaster-free(ish), but she doesn't need to know that.

Elizabeth leans in to the computer so her face fills my screen. "I know you're gonna accuse me of being condescending again, but I'm really proud of you and I don't know any way to say that without sounding all big-sister-y."

I'm flustered, but her words mean a lot. So much. I'm actually proud of me too. I set out to show my sister I could handle things on my own, and I did. I am.

I twirl the bracelet on my wrist as I give her a shy smile and a soft, "Thanks."

She smiles back. "You're welcome."

Are we really having an adult conversation?

Knowing that she might actually see me as someone worthy of her respect gives me all the courage I need. Well, mostly. I take a deep breath and say, "Everything's really good as far as the tour is concerned. It's going perfectly. But, um, the thing is, there is this tiny twist I haven't told you about."

I puff out a breath and, before I can lose my nerve, fill her in on Dolores's fall. Her eyes grow wider and wider as I mention the words *ambulance* and *hospital*, but I'm quick to reassure her. "Dolores is fine. In fact, her sling is off and Sam's been working with her on exercises every day, so I really think she'll be good as new."

Oh shit. That wasn't how I planned to introduce Sam. Maybe she didn't notice.

My sister cocks her head. "Sam? Which one is he? Is he the non-PC guy from Texas?"

I swallow and dart my eyes away as I choke out, "Um, no. He's, um, well, he's sort of Dolores's grandson."

"I don't—"

"The tour company sent him after the fall to help out. So her injury wouldn't be an added responsibility for me."

Elizabeth's nose scrunches up. "And they were cool with

just adding an unexpected guest midway through? Why wouldn't they have arranged for her to come home instead? Adding someone else seems kind of extreme. He'd need a hotel room in every city and—"

I cut her off. "Okay, I might have left out the fact that Dolores is actually the owner's mother, and Teresa didn't want her mom abandoning the tour."

I gulp and wait for my sister's reaction. The pillow on her lap drops to the ground as she stands suddenly. I can only see her torso now as she paces the room. I try to remind myself that ten seconds ago she was all relaxed and gooey apologies, because her voice is decidedly *un*relaxed as she says, "Are you telling me the owner's mother is on your trip? The trip where we're deceiving the passengers and the tour company and relying on glowing reviews to keep my career out of jeopardy? The owner's mother! Is on your tour!"

In the background she plops onto Dad's recliner and covers her face with her hands. I wait for the rest to hit her. It doesn't take Miss 4.0 GPA long.

"Is Sam . . ."

"The owner's son," I murmur.

"Her son!" Elizabeth wails. "How could you have kept all this from me? I don't know what we were thinking! We're doomed."

Dramatic much? I mean, I get it. If I remember back to the way I felt when I first found out Dolores was related to Teresa Bellamy and then how I flipped again when I found out where Sam fit into the equation, I guess I wasn't reacting any differently than Elizabeth. But now that I know both of them, I feel like my evaluation is safe. It might even be safe after I tell Sam the truth. I don't know yet, but my gut is saying Mr. Fenton could be right. It might not be the worst thing.

I just have to convince Elizabeth of that.

"Look, I know it *sounds* bad, but I promise you, everything is really awesome over here. I get along great with Dolores and, um, with Sam." I cough a little and Elizabeth moves back to the laptop and brings her face right up to the camera. Her eyes squint.

"Why did your voice just do that when you said 'Sam'?" she asks.

"Do what?"

She pulls back a little and studies her screen, which means she's actually studying me. After a second, her eyes widen.

"How old is Sam?" she asks.

"Um, nineteen, I think. He's a sophomore in college."

"Nineteen . . . ," she says, sinking back into her chair and looking at the floor. "And you like him." She sounds resigned when she says this.

"Yeah," I whisper. "A lot."

Her head snaps up at that. "A lot?"

I can see different emotions play across her face: annoyance, fear, but mostly curiosity.

"Huh," she adds.

"We've been spending most of our downtime together," I tell her. This is weird. I never talk about guys with Elizabeth.

"Wow. Leave it to you to find a boyfriend on a senior

citizen trip." She almost smiles then, but just as fast her face falls. "Wait. Wait, hold up. He only knows you as Elizabeth . . . as *me*. Please tell me he only knows you as Elizabeth!"

Lizzie, actually, but probably not the time to break that nickname to her either. She'd hate it and I need her pliable. "He does. Which is what I need to talk to you about. Things are kind of progressing with us and, um, I really feel like I need to be honest with him."

Elizabeth's eyes widen. "You can't, Bree. You cannot."

I hold up my hands. "Hear me out. Please! I think I might have real feelings for him. And the lying thing totally sucks. What's even worse is he has this whole thing in his past with lying and I know about it, so every day I do it too, it's like I'm giving him the finger. It's completely not fair to him."

Elizabeth slumps back against the couch cushion. "Not fair to *him*? Bree, do you hear yourself? You're willing to throw your own sister under the bus over a *guy*? A guy who you just met and who you admitted might not even stick around once he learns the truth? You know what's at stake here. My future. Please don't make me regret that I trusted you with it."

It feels like she just reached through the computer screen and slapped me. My fingers curl around the edges of the iPad and my knuckles turn white.

She sighs and gazes at something offscreen for a second, then turns her eyes back to the camera. Back to me. "The thing is, if you could try to see this from my perspective. It's not like I'm asking you to perpetuate this lie forever. I just need you to hold strong for a couple more weeks and then you're home and I have my court date and this could all be behind us. I might be wrong, but from my side of the ocean, it just doesn't seem like that much more to ask when you've already come this far. We're talking about less than two weeks versus my entire career. Everything I've worked toward for twenty-one *years*. Years versus weeks? I don't know, does that make any sense?"

I nod slowly. It does. It does make a little sense. Maybe I'm being selfish putting my own feelings above hers when I did go into this eyes wide open and I did make a promise to her. Mr. Fenton is older and wiser, but that doesn't mean he's right about this. Elizabeth and I were just starting to make some positive progress and I don't want to jeopardize that. She's my sister, which means I *have* to put her ahead of a guy. It's like an unwritten law.

"I guess maybe I see your point," I say softly.

"So you'll stick to the plan?" she asks, and I can see the hope glimmering in her eyes.

I nod again, as if my head is being controlled like the marionettes in Prague. "Sure."

"Thank you. Best sister ever," she says, relief coming off her in waves. Her head turns toward a sound I recognize as the garage door opening. "That's Mom. Bree, listen, I can't even begin to tell you how much I owe you. Seriously. For life."

I force a smile and wrap my arms around myself to mimic the hug she's giving me, but really I feel like crying.

TWENTY-SEVEN

As it turns out, Mr. Fenton gives only an abbreviated talk the next day because Sam has found a DVD of *To Catch a Thief* and we pop it into the bus's media system. It has two things going for it: it's Mary-approved, and it takes place right in the area we're driving through.

In the film Cary Grant and Grace Kelly go zooming along the cliffside roads in their convertible, but our bus takes things a little more cautiously. This makes me exceedingly grateful, especially after Emma tells me that in real life Grace Kelly died when her car crashed on these very same treacherous roads.

For most of the trip we're inside the mountains. No sooner do we emerge from one tunnel than we are entering the next. There are approximately a hundred and ten of them between La Spezia and Monaco, which I know because Bento told Sam, who is now more than happy to translate for me. It turns out Bento has as much information about this area as Mr. Fenton *and* a wicked sense of humor. Who knew?

While I love Bento, I do not love Monaco. Even though every place we've been so far has become my new favorite, Monaco isn't. It's not because it isn't beautiful, because it is. It also climbs into the mountainside, like the towns of Cinque Terre, but that's where the similarities end, because everything in Monaco is flashy and new and shiny. And after how sleepy and laid-back Vernazza was, it seems a little much.

Mr. Fenton does *not* share my opinion. He's practically hanging out the window, taking it all in.

"Have you ever seen *GoldenEye*? James Bond movie?" he asks me.

I shake my head, while next to me Sam says, "Of *course*."

"James Bond striding into the Monte Carlo looking all dashing, ordering his signature martini, beautiful girls all around? That's me tonight, Sam. You mark my words."

Sam laughs. "Whatever you say, Mr. F."

What Sam doesn't know is that Mr. Fenton speaks the truth.

"Hello, we called earlier about the car rental? My name is Elizabeth Sadler." I step to the counter and smile at the woman behind it.

She lets her eyes sweep over me and tiny frown lines show in her forehead. "Hmm. Yes. You were asking about our sports car selection, were you not?"

"That's right," Mr. Fenton says.

"For how many days?"

"Just the afternoon," I say.

"Of course. We have several available. You will have your choice of a Lamborghini Aventador, a Rolls-Royce Phantom Drophead, a Bentley GTC, a Ferrari FF . . ."

She trails off as if there are all kinds of other luxury vehicles she could mention, but Mr. Fenton doesn't even hesitate. "The Lamborghini."

"Very well. I will begin the paperwork. You may drive anywhere in Monaco and France, but not into Italy. The daily fee is three thousand euros."

My jaw hangs open. Three thousand euros! That's a small fortune. That could pay for my textbooks for the next two years. We're talking about *one* day. Is Mr. Fenton crazy?

"Are you crazy?" I ask when the woman steps away to retrieve the car keys.

"Absolutely." Mr. Fenton's grin is wider than the Ohio River. "Aubree, I've dreamed about this for years. Besides, I'm a confirmed bachelor whose closest relative is a niece I haven't seen in ten years. I've lived frugally my whole life, saving for a rainy day." He peers at the sunlit Riviera sparkling below us and shrugs. "I see a cloud or two. Close enough. It's time to have some fun with it."

Mr. Fenton seems totally calm at the wheel of his temporary ride. If it were me driving a four-hundred-thousand-dollar car, I'd be a wreck. Then again, I got my license half a year ago and have barely even used it.

"Um, do you think you could drop me at the hotel first?"

I'm afraid for what he has in mind. I know from all the signs everywhere that Monaco is the site of the Grand Prix races every year, but I'm not quite up for a qualifying run today. Mr. Fenton looks disappointed, but not for long.

"Will do. You're too nervous to be good company. Besides, you have tasks to accomplish yet. And if there's any time after *those*, you'll need it for all that deep thinking about honesty you're supposed to be doing. But run inside and see if any of the ladies are around."

Oh sure, I can just picture Dolores's hair whipping in the wind as Mr. Fenton screeches around curves. She'd totally be up for that.

But she *is*. She actually is.

Mr. Fenton helps her down inside, then burns rubber away from the admiring valets. Now that is a sight I never thought I'd see.

Sam is rounding the corner when they peel off and he uses the next few hours to give me a hard time for not letting *him* be a passenger in the pretty, pretty car. At least he also spends the time helping me arrange for an assortment of dresses to be sent to our hotel for Mary, Emma, and Dolores to choose from. Even though Mr. Fenton instructed me to get something for myself as well, I can't bring myself to spend his money.

I'm sure Sam can tell my attention isn't completely in Monaco with him, but I can't very well tell him about my call to Elizabeth or how in knots it has me, going back and forth between my own self-interest and being a good sister. Luckily he doesn't push me for answers on my mood.

We return to the hotel after a stop in a café to find Mr. Fenton and Dolores pulling in. Thankfully the car and both occupants seem to be in one piece, though the two of them are hoarse from laughter.

"Was it amazing?" I ask.

"Worth every penny and then some," he assures me.

"Time for your spa appointment, Mr. Fenton," I instruct as he hands the car keys to a valet to park the car.

Mr. Fenton steps back to allow another valet to help Dolores from her seat. "You girls make sure you're ready by six," he tells her.

She giggles. "We'll be primped and waiting."

Mr. Fenton winks at me and I know it's because of the sparkling dresses waiting to surprise the three women in their rooms.

Two hours later, Sam and I stake out a spot in the lobby, cameras in hand, waiting for our group to emerge. Hank and Maisy are the first ones down, which is some kind of unnatural phenomenon.

"We're going to take a walk over to the marina, suss out some of those yachts. I saw one out the window that looked bigger than Texas."

High praise coming from Hank.

"You might want to stick around a minute and see something," I tell him.

Seconds later three giggling ladies step off the elevator in long dazzling gowns and high-swept hairdos. A moment after that Mr. Fenton steps off another elevator, looking handsome in a tuxedo. I feel like I'm sending my kids off to the prom.

"Ladies, you look bewitching," Mr. Fenton says.

Emma giggles some more. "You'll have to take turns having us on each arm."

"However will I manage?" Mr. Fenton replies. Then he looks over at me.

"Three lovely women and a night at the baccarat tables. See what a clever man I am, Lizzie? Almost makes you think I know what I'm talking about, doesn't it? Almost makes you think you should take my advice about everything."

He doesn't win points for subtlety, that's for sure. If only he knew how much I *do* want to tell Sam. How much I want him to kiss *me*. The real me.

I watch Sam fuss over his gram. Yup. I definitely want this guy to know the real me. Whether or not he'll want to do that after learning about all the lies I've been telling him, *and* his mother, *and* his grandmother, is something I don't even want to think about. Whether or not he'll feel the need to confess to his mother is something I *can't* think about.

I push the thought away. For now, I made a promise to Elizabeth. Blood thicker than water and all that.

I take pictures as Mr. Fenton and his harem head out the door, then turn to Sam. "Guess we're on our own. What do you want to do?"

Sam smiles wickedly as he takes my hand. "Pretty sure we'll come up with *something.*"

Despite Sam's suggestive comment, he steers me away from the elevators and toward the hotel exit, where we find dinner and wander around the marina, ogling all the luxury yachts that are part of a lifestyle I can't begin to imagine.

However, we do end the night in the hallway outside Sam's hotel room, kissing against his door. Sam's lips trail up my neck and he whispers, "Do you wanna come in?" I nod against his shoulder.

Sam's next kiss is tender and sweet and makes my heart sigh. He fumbles with his key card, then drops it. He curses under his breath and it hits me that he's *nervous.* I melt.

His trademark confidence slips back into place as he tugs me gently inside and takes my face in his hands, kissing me deeply. With his lips on mine, he walks me into the room. This is new territory for us; up until now I've been too paranoid about the seniors who might need attention at any moment. The backs of my legs hit the edge of the bed and Sam continues our kiss as he eases me down onto it.

"This okay?" he murmurs.

"Definitely okay," I whisper against his lips. He nods and his kiss grows more urgent. I lose my breath in it.

Sam is perched above me, one arm propping him up and the other by my waist, but now he rolls to the right and brings me with him so we're lying pressed up against each other, on our sides. I lose track of time as we kiss. And kiss. And kiss.

His hands run along my torso and mine grasp the belt loops on his jeans, pulling him closer.

Except I accidentally knee him in the leg and he yelps.

"Oh God, are you all right?" I ask.

Sam buries his face in my neck, his shoulders shaking with laughter.

I laugh too. Steamy, with a side of laughter. It's so us. It's perfect.

Sam kisses me again but pulls back a moment later, and the humor fades from his eyes as he looks at me. "Dimple?" he says. All traces of laughter are gone from his voice. Instead it's husky and quiet and it makes my pulse thrum in my ear.

"Yeah?" My stomach does cartwheels.

He traces a finger down my cheek and runs his thumb along my lower lip. "I'm really glad you're here," he says softly. "Really, really glad."

I don't know if he means here in Europe or here in his room, but either way my answer would be the same. "I'm pretty glad I'm here too."

"It's . . . Okay, this is gonna sound corny, so bear with me, huh?"

Oh, I'm bearing. I'm totally bearing.

Sam smiles, but then his expression grows serious again. "I didn't really have a lot of expectations for this summer, ya know? I thought I'd spend most of it swimming laps. I didn't expect to be here. I didn't expect to feel—" He sighs softly. "I didn't expect *you*."

I didn't expect him either. God, did I not expect him. And

as much as this trip has opened my eyes, getting to know Sam has opened my heart. I want to tell him all of this, but I don't trust my voice. Not with the way he's looking at me like I'm one of the crown jewels.

"Sam . . . ," I whisper, and my voice catches.

He smooths my hair and smiles gently. It twists my heart like a wrung-out towel and I bite my lip. Sam leans over to kiss me and I try to put everything I want to tell him into my answering kiss.

He hooks his leg through mine and I pull him in. His kiss deepens and we're right back to steamy and all of a sudden I can't get close enough to him. I don't want even an inch of space between us. Our breaths are coming out in gasps and I shimmy up against him, aligning myself along his body.

"God, Lizzie," Sam whispers against my mouth when I fit my hips to his.

Hearing him say a name that is not *my* name feels exactly in this moment the same as the ice cubes sliding down my shirt in Cinque Terre and snaps me back to reality fast. I'm completely falling for this guy and he doesn't even know something as incredibly basic about me as *my freaking name*! How messed up is that?

I jerk upright, trying to catch my breath and process the thoughts in my head at the same time. I leap off the bed. Sam sits up too, obviously confused, and trying to control his own breathing.

"Dimple. Hey. I didn't mean to . . . I mean . . . what just happened?"

I look at him, his palms up and an expression of such sweetness on his face it about breaks me in two. How did I let things go this far with our relationship? Why am I letting myself have so many feelings for Sam when there are all these lies between us?

But I can't tell him any of those thoughts, so I sink down next to him and say, "I'm really sorry. That was kind of intense and I . . . would it be okay to . . . could we just hit the pause button for a bit?"

Sam puts his arm around my shoulder and pulls me close, my face nestling against his shoulder. When I peer up at him, his expression is gentle and protective. "Anytime at all. You call the shots."

I smile weakly. I really could cry right now over how much I like this guy. He smiles back. "Wanna stay awhile?" he whispers. "I promise to keep my hands to myself."

He puts his arms up like he's being held at gunpoint and I giggle. He lowers one and pats the empty space on the bed next to him. I lie down and tuck my legs under me. Sam lifts my head and slides a pillow underneath it before setting his own head right next to mine, so close our foreheads nearly touch and our breaths mingle. In the small space between our bodies, we hold hands.

He smiles but doesn't say anything, just squeezes my hand and stares into my eyes for what could be five minutes or could be an hour. I get lost in it. All I know is that it feels like I'm under a spell, my recently expanded world narrowing down to just this boy and this bed and everything our eyes are telling each other. It's easily the most intimate thing I've ever done, letting my face show him everything I'm feeling for him. We stay like that for the longest time and I can't even believe how much passes between us without either of us uttering a single word. And yet I don't feel self-conscious at all.

I feel safe.

I feel seen.

I wake up a few hours later with my back cuddled against Sam's torso and his arm draped over me. I smile. We're fully clothed, on top of the covers, but completely entangled. I savor the sensation of Sam's chest moving up and down and smile even bigger when I realize he's on the right side of the bed. I make a note to give Mr. I Can Only Sleep on the Left a hard time about it when he wakes up. For now I savor his warm breath against the nape of my neck, and the memories and the feelings from last night come rushing back. The frustration over Sam only knowing me as Lizzie is there in the background, but overriding all of that is the intensity of staring into each other's eyes the way we did. It sounds totally cheesy to say it like that, but when it was happening it wasn't cheesy at all.

At all.

Outside the sky is just beginning to brighten and I stare out the window at the yacht lights in the harbor below, lost in my thoughts.

I replay my conversation with Elizabeth and wish I'd said

everything differently. I made her think my wanting to be honest with Sam was all about my feelings for him, but as it turns out, it isn't. Not totally, anyway. It's about me.

The thing is, this trip is forcing me to get to know myself more than I've ever had to at home, where everything is comfortable and easy. And what I'm learning is that the kind of person I want to be isn't the kind of person I am right now. I hate being a liar and a fraud and a fake. Even beyond telling Sam, I want to be honest with *all* the people on my tour. They've trusted me to take care of them these past couple weeks and I really, really want to be the kind of person who's earned that trust.

Elizabeth's logic was that waiting a little bit longer when we've already come this far couldn't hurt anyone. But it *is* hurting. It's hurting me. I'm worried about Sam not forgiving me, but what if I can't forgive *myself*?

And I know Elizabeth is my sister and Sam is just this guy I barely know, and that should make my loyalties clear, but Sam doesn't feel like just some guy. It doesn't feel like I've only just met him either. Something happened last night.

The way I feel about Sam . . . the way I think he feels about me . . . can I trust him? And if not, what does that say about us? If I believe my gut, which says Sam will keep my and Elizabeth's secret from his mom, and I end up wrong, I've lost Sam *and* my sister.

Why can't I figure any of this out for myself?

Mr. Fenton thinks it's so black and white and that of course

I should tell Sam, but he doesn't know Elizabeth's perspective.

A seagull streaks by the window and I blink.

Mr. Fenton.

Of *course*. He'll help me make heads or tails of this. He's a mostly neutral party (despite the fact that he and Sam *have* bonded pretty hard ever since their Aubustus Caesar moment) and he's already proven trustworthy. He's got years of wisdom. I'll tell him all the details he doesn't know yet and then he'll tell me exactly what I should do.

It takes thirty full seconds to slide out from under Sam's arm. That's how careful I am not to wake him. Instantly I miss his warmth next to me. Slipping out of his room, I ease the door closed with the tiniest of clicks.

I take the elevator to Mr. Fenton's suite. Yes, suite. All part of the high-roller package we put together. I reach it just as a uniformed waiter with a room service cart stops in front. Oh, phew. I was worried about knocking at such an indecent hour, even if I know by now that Mr. Fenton is an early riser.

"Good morning, mademoiselle," the waiter says.

"Good morning," I answer. We both wait for the door to open.

He turns to me. "Would you like me to bring up another place setting? The monsieur placed his breakfast order upon check-in yesterday and it only included service for one."

"No, thank you. I'm fine." He nods and we both shuffle our feet a bit as we listen for signs of movement on the other side of the door.

"He did request five-thirty a.m.," the waiter says when a minute stretches to two.

"Do you have a key?" I ask. "He had a big night last night, so he may be sleeping it off."

Please, please, please do not let me walk in on Mr. Fenton and Emma.

Or Mary.

Or Dolores! I imagine if I told Sam *that* tidbit, he wouldn't care if my name was really Chewbacca.

Shrugging, the waiter pulls a key card from his pocket. He swipes it through the reader and when it beeps twice, he steps aside to allow me to enter before rolling his cart in behind me.

"Mr. Fenton?" I call. Good Lord, this suite is HUGE! The living room is brightening from the rising sun through the open curtains and the bedroom door is ajar enough that I can see an unmade bed. Maybe Mr. Fenton is in the bathroom. I call out extra loudly from the doorway, not daring to venture farther. Hank in a towel was quite risqué enough for me.

Behind me, the waiter makes himself busy, removing silver domes from plates and pouring coffee into a rattling cup. Inside the bedroom, it's eerily quiet.

Something isn't right.

I can't put my finger on it, but the air is too still.

I step into the bedroom and turn toward the bathroom, but my eyes rest on something by the foot of the bed. It's a slipper. With a foot attached. I race over and cover my mouth with my hand.

Mr. Fenton is on the floor, one arm splayed out. The other lies across his chest. His legs are crumpled, and the right one is at an awkward angle. He's unnaturally still. I take a step backward and collide with the waiter.

"Is everything all right, mademoiselle? You gasped."

I did?

"I think . . . I think he might be . . ." But I can't say the words. Instead, I brush past the waiter to race out the door and down the hallway, down the stairs next to the elevator, not stopping until I reach Sam's door, which I bang on with all my might. Then I slump to the ground. When he answers, his smile falls from his face as he sees me on the floor. He drops to his knees beside me so he can look into my face.

"Lizzie? Lizzie, what is it?"

I stare at him and then burst into tears.

"I think Mr. Fenton is dead."

TWENTY-EIGHT

Mr. Fenton is dead.

Mr. Fenton is *dead*.

I still can't comprehend the words, even after returning to his bedside with Sam and waiting until the paramedics summoned by the waiter burst in and started checking for vital signs. I already knew what they'd find.

He's gone.

Sweet, kind, wise Mr. Fenton. I'm sure I can't have any tears left in me, but every time I picture his face or think of him standing at the front of the bus all aglow with his facts and stories about things that happened a million gajillion years ago, I lose it all over again.

The paramedics tell us they suspect a heart attack. He'd complained of aches several times yesterday, but always in jest at his old age and always attributing them to his hike in Cinque Terre. But maybe something had been happening even then. Dolores mentioned he'd had several drinks after dinner, and that plus his age plus the excitement of the trip and the day yesterday . . .

It's not fair. I don't care how "long and full" his life was. It's still not fair. I just . . . he was so . . . he was alive. Hours ago. And now he's not.

Thank God for Sam. He's a rock. When he's not holding me and wiping my tears away with his fingertips, he's on the phone with his mom, and giving statements to the hotel manager and the police they called, and making sure everyone else is checked in for another night and settled into their rooms. I don't know how the rest of the group is passing the morning, but I hope they're all together somewhere.

Mr. Fenton's suite overlooks the harbor with its dozens of luxury yachts bobbing in their moorings, and I can't even comprehend that there are people out there enjoying a beautiful sun-filled day on the French Riviera. It should be dark and gray and stormy out. It shouldn't be cloudless blue.

He was *just* here. He was smiling and helping Dolores out of a ridiculously expensive sports car. He should be standing in front of me, telling us all about, well, I don't really know about what because we're headed to Barcelona next and I haven't researched much about the history of Spain yet.

"Lizzie?" Sam's touch is gentle and so is his voice as he brings me back from my thoughts.

"Yeah?"

"The hotel is sending up some breakfast. You should probably try to eat something. And then we need to go to the

embassy and work out the details for getting his . . . his . . ."
He stumbles a bit and I hear a tickle in his voice. "His body
home," he finishes.

I can't speak, so I just nod.

We have to go to Marseille now. Well I do, at least. Marseille
is the closest office of a US consulate and I need to fill out the
paperwork necessary when an American dies abroad. Or so we
learn from Mrs. Bellamy. She's been nothing but caring and
concerned, much like her son, despite being woken with the
news in the middle of her night.

The only issue we've had has been an argument between
Sam and his mother over whether or not he could accompany
me to the consulate. His mom wanted someone to remain with
the other group members and Sam refuses to leave my side.
Given that he's on this continent and she's not, he won that
one; we compromised by leaving Bento and the bus behind
and allowing the hotel to arrange a car for us.

I was prepared to go on my own—it *is* my duty, after all—
but I'm glad Sam insisted on coming too. I'm not so worried
about everyone else. Emma and Mary have organized a shiva
of sorts in their room, despite the fact that neither one of them
is Jewish. Even Hank and Maisy seem to have acquired some
decorum; when we stopped in to say good-bye, they were sitting a perfectly respectable distance from each other on the
couch. Mr. Fenton probably would have made some joke
about dying earlier if he'd known that was all it would take to

separate the horndogs. I stuff my hand in my mouth to keep from giggling at such an inappropriate time, but it's either that or cry more.

Emma squeezes my hand. "You be brave," she says. I choke back more tears. I don't deserve a group like this.

We arrive at the embassy just after lunchtime and we're taken to a quiet office by an American dressed in a fancy suit that fits in well with all the French fashion. He gestures to seats and faces us across a desk.

"First, let me say that I'm so sorry for your loss." His accent is a southern drawl and seems out of place.

Sam and I answer with tight smiles.

"I understand there's some paperwork I need to fill out?" I ask.

The man passes a form to me. We've already spoken on the phone, so he knows which hospital has Mr. Fenton and what the circumstances of his death were. This part is just a formality.

"This is a consular report of death of an American citizen abroad form. It'll be for our records, but will also serve as official documentation to settle any legal and estate issues back in the United States. I understand his next of kin is his niece?"

"Yes," I murmur.

Sam elaborates. "She's who he listed on his emergency contact form. Our tour company owner is just waiting for a decent hour to call her in California."

"Of course," the man answers.

I pull out all the information Mrs. Bellamy sent to Sam's email, including Mr. Fenton's date of birth and his home address, and turn his passport over to the man behind the desk.

"Another formality, but we like to have a statement on file from those he was traveling with or those who were witness to the, er, event. Would you mind giving me the details of how you came to discover the deceased?"

Sam takes my hand and holds it firmly in his as I tell this stranger about finding Mr. Fenton's body. The man types as I talk and when I finish, a small printer beside him spits out a page.

"Thank you for going through that. I'll have you on your way shortly. Just need to grab your signature on this. I also need a copy of your passport to include with the file, please."

I thought he might ask for this. When I fastened my money belt around my waist back at the hotel, I took a moment to replace Elizabeth's passport with my own. I'd put mine away after the flight, using hers instead for all the hotel check-ins in case anyone from the tour was beside me, but I thought a US consulate was probably *not* the best place to practice out-and-out fraud.

And even if it was, I can't do that to Mr. Fenton. I'm glad he got to know me as Aubree, even for a short time, and I'd be letting him down if I signed these documents as Elizabeth. I fork over my passport, keeping it tightly closed as I do so.

The man takes it without glancing down. "Be right back."

He steps out of the room with the documents, leaving the door open so we can watch him place my passport facedown on a copy machine in the hallway.

I study my hands in my lap until the man returns and passes my passport across the desk, saying, "I'm so sorry. I've been calling you Elizabeth all this time. I don't know why I got that name stuck in my head. Anyway, my apologies, Aubree."

Sam opens his mouth to correct the man, but I grab his arm and say, "Oh, uh, it's fine, no worries. Thank you for your help." Sam looks baffled and stiffens in his chair, but says nothing.

The man reaches across the desk and shakes both of our hands. "My pleasure. I'm so sorry again for your loss and I wish we could have met under better circumstances. Please have good travels and a safe return home."

Sam waits until we're on the curb before turning to me. "Why didn't you correct him when he called you Aubree?" His eyes are nothing but confusion, but I know his expression is about to get a lot worse as I swallow away the lump in my throat. It had to happen sometime.

The thing is, this trip has turned me into an excellent liar. I've had a few minutes to think and I'm confident I can talk my way out of this. But I've had a few minutes to think. And the one thing I can't get out of my mind is Mr. Fenton's words to me about how owning up to my mistakes is the sign of a true grown-up.

I need to confess.

Not to hurt Elizabeth or even to try to preserve things with Sam, but to be true to the me I'm becoming. I need to be honest for myself.

I wordlessly hand Sam my passport.

He opens it and studies the picture. He takes in the name. And the date of birth. Then he looks at me.

"I don't—" He sounds like a little boy.

It turns out I'm not all cried out after all. Fresh tears form in my eyes. But I force them aside so I can give Sam a proper explanation. He at least deserves that.

I put my hands on his arms and silently will him to hear me out. "My older sister is Elizabeth and she was the one your mom hired. She knew how much your mom was counting on her, and my sister is not one to shirk her responsibilities, trust me. She got into an, um, situation and couldn't come and she thought this would be the best way of solving the problem."

Sam just stares at me. Oh boy. This is not good.

"I don't understand," he finally says.

I sigh deeply. Telling him is so much harder than I thought it would be and I fight to keep my voice from cracking. "The thing is, my sister got arrested. It was a huge misunderstanding and she's completely innocent. But the conditions of her bail meant she couldn't leave the state and at that point it was so close to the time the tour was going to start and she couldn't think of what else to do, so . . ."

I trail off and wait for Sam to say something, anything

at all, but he's still silent. I know I'm bungling this. There definitely won't be any Sam clutching his sides and laughing at how adorable I am, the way he did when I confessed I didn't have celiac disease.

"Sam, could you please say something?" I beg. "I know it wasn't the smartest thing to do and if I had known any of this was going to happen or that I'd meet you, I never would have agreed to it. I swear, I wouldn't have. But at the time we thought it was the perfect solution to make everyone happy."

Sam gives me a sad smile. "Do I look happy, Lizzie? No, wait. What do I even call you now?"

"Aubree." I drop my head. And no, he doesn't look remotely happy.

I'm quiet, waiting for Sam to speak again so I can gauge his feelings. He studies his nail beds and then gives a tiny shake of his head before bringing his eyes to mine. "Last night?" he asks in a small voice.

Last night things changed with us. We didn't say anything with words, but we still said a whole lot. I felt it and I know he did too. "Last night was—it meant everything to me, Sam."

"Just not enough to be honest with me. I really thought . . ." He's silent as he studies the ground. At one point in the trip I questioned if he even owned a frown, but the one he's wearing now makes my heart twist. The ache is so physical, it makes me wonder what Mr. Fenton felt from his in those last minutes. I let the tears fall down my cheeks. I thought the time was right to tell Sam, but this coupled with Mr. Fenton—it's too much at once. I step toward Sam, seeking the comfort of his arms the way I have all day, but he counters with a step backward. His eyes are still on the ground as he mumbles, "I'll meet you back at the hotel."

"What? But—!"

Sam glances up at me and I see every bit of the betrayal he's feeling on his face. "I need some time to process all this," he says softly. "I'll hop a train and see you back there."

"Sam. Sam, wait, I—" But I'm speaking to his back, because he turns and walks away.

I return to the hotel to find no Sam, no seniors, and a series of messages for me. The first tells me the group has gone with Bento to Nice for the afternoon to "clear their heads." The next few tell me Elizabeth has called. Three times.

My mouth goes dry. Did Sam call his mom from the train? Did his mom already confront Elizabeth? Could this day get any worse?

I make my way to the manager's office and ask him if there is a computer I could use. We've become close friends since this morning. He directs me into an empty office and signs online for me, before slipping out and leaving me alone.

Moment of reckoning. I Skype Elizabeth.

She answers with a tentative smile. "Hey. I can't stop thinking about our call the other day and I just wanted to check in with you and see if everything's, you know, okay."

So she doesn't know. She just wants to make sure I'm still

toeing the party line. I force a smile, but can only sustain it for half a second before I burst into tears. Again.

Elizabeth's eyes go wide. "Aubree! What's going on?"

Through sniffles, I fill her in on Mr. Fenton while she continues to mutter a lot of "oh my God"s. When I finish she has tears in her own eyes.

"I don't even know what to say. I feel so responsible," she says. "You'd never even be there if it wasn't for me and my stupid idea. I honestly didn't mean for things to turn out like this. I swear, I wish I'd never gotten us into this mess."

My brain flashes through scenes from the last few weeks. The mad rush through the Amsterdam airport trying to get back to the binder, seeing all the castles on our drive along the Rhine, singing "Do-Re-Mi" in the Alps, Sam getting blasted by the fountains in Salzburg, horses and Ferris wheels in Vienna, riverside kisses in Prague, canalside kisses in Venice, skinny-dipping in Cinque Terre.

Mr. Fenton in his tux in the lobby last night.

"I don't wish that," I murmur.

She's quiet as she studies me. "You really mean that, don't you?"

I shrug.

She looks . . . I don't know. Impressed, maybe? I want to savor it for as long as I can before it turns into something closer to the expression Sam just had on his face. For now she says, "It feels like you're this whole different person over there, Bree."

"It does kind of, doesn't it?" I look directly at her and her eyebrows scrunch up.

"You just seem really mature all of a sudden."

"I guess." I shrug again.

She tilts her head to the side. "Can I ask you something? And you have to be honest."

I hide my snort. If only she knew how far my honesty streak extended today. Which I'll tell her, of course. But for now, I really need to know what she has to ask.

She gathers a breath and asks in a small voice, "Do you think I'll be an okay politician? I don't have much to go on in terms of how I'd conduct myself in a crisis except this experience with you, and I feel like I totally screwed things up. And I just keep thinking, how can I do right by my constituents if I can't even do right by my sister?"

My emotions tumble over one another. Somehow it's still all about her. How do I get her to see things from my perspective?

I say quietly, "You're not a bad sister." This day has kicked my ass already, so what do I have to lose? I might as well lay it all on the line. "You don't . . . you don't exactly make it easy for a girl to stand out. But that's not really your fault. Let's just say you shine pretty brightly, so of course I wanted to be just like you, and it used to really bother me that I never measured up."

Her eyes are wide, but, duh. Of course she's always known I idolized her. I force myself to stare into the screen. "The thing is, I don't really feel like that anymore. It's more like, I don't know. I guess . . . I guess I just want you to say that who I am is good enough for you. Even if that's not your clone."

She's quiet for a long time as her eyes study the keyboard.

When she looks back up, they're glistening. Of course, that makes tears stream down my face. Seriously, at what point do I need to worry about dehydration from excessive crying?

"Oh, Bree. How could you think you're not?" she finally says. She swipes at her nose with a tissue. "But to be fair, I probably don't spend enough time recognizing it. I have to be honest, it feels pretty good to be put up on a pedestal by your little sister, you know? I don't know, maybe unconsciously or something, I thought if I paid too much attention to all the reasons you were cool in your own way, you wouldn't look up to me as much. I swear, I didn't realize that until just this second. You probably don't have me all that high up there at the moment, huh?"

This is hard. Never having been disappointed by my sister has meant never having to tell her she let me down, but the truth is, I feel like she did. I didn't do a good job explaining why it was important for me to come clean to Sam, but she didn't do a great job listening either. And if I want to be a grown-up, that means saying the hard stuff, right?

"I don't know, I guess I just feel like . . ."

I have a hard time finishing my thought. Elizabeth waits for a second, then prompts me. "Well, don't hold back *now*. Geez."

I glance over at the framed certificates on the manager's wall, then back at her. Gathering a deep breath, I talk fast. "Fine. I wish you'd trust me to make my own decisions and make the right ones for me, even if it might not be the way you would handle things."

"Even if those decisions might mean I don't have a job this fall?" She practically whispers the words.

"Yeah." I can't look her in the face, knowing I've probably already ruined that for her. Though it's not like she isn't going to find out for herself soon when the fallout from my talk with Sam happens, so I might as well rip the Band-Aid off with Elizabeth too. Argh. This being-mature stuff is craptastic.

"About that . . ."

I fill her in on the events at the embassy.

"Oh" is all she has to say. Her eyes drop to her lap.

"Oh? That's all?"

"I mean, it's done now, isn't it?" she answers. "I think it's just going to take me a little bit to process what this means. I know I got myself into this mess, so I have to be willing to accept the consequences, but I guess . . ." She's quiet for a second. "I don't know, after all this time and everything going so well, I really thought this plan could work."

Now it's my turn to say "Oh." I follow up with, "But, um, I mean . . . well, I was just hoping maybe you'd understand why I felt like I had to do it. Do you at all?"

"I don't know yet. I guess, maybe." She tries out a tiny smile, but it doesn't reach her eyes.

I wasn't expecting jumping jacks and cartwheels, for sure, but I thought she'd be at least a little reassuring. Especially with the way the call started and how honest we were being with each other.

Are we gonna be okay after this?

I'm about to speak again when there's some kind of

disturbance behind her. I see Elizabeth's eyes widen and her hand reach up to close her laptop, but a split second after it goes dark, it gets bright again, and Mom's face fills the screen at a sideways angle as she leans across a horrified Elizabeth.

"Aubree? Is that you? I didn't know you had access to a computer, honey. How are you? How are the mosquitos? Did you get the bug spray I sent?" She squints and moves her face closer, like that will also bring the objects on the other side of the screen—namely, me—closer.

"Aubree?"

"Yeah, Mom?"

"Out the window behind you? Is that—? Aubree, why is there a yacht with an enormous French flag passing behind your head?"

TWENTY-NINE

"This is unbelievable. I mean that. I really *cannot* believe this," my mom says for about the twentieth time in as many minutes. Dad is over her shoulder pacing back and forth while Elizabeth is on the couch, hugging her knees to her chest. I don't know which of us my parents are more furious with.

"I can't *believe* your sister got you into all of this, Bree. I can't *believe* you went along with it. *I can't believe* I thought you were in Maine this whole! Entire! Time!" Mom takes a deep breath and puts her hands on either side of the laptop as she leans over and hangs her head. "Who the hell got all my cookies?"

Behind her Elizabeth covers her mouth with her hand but is smart enough not to laugh out loud. Mom straightens. "I'll tell you right now, Aubree, you are on the next flight home. The very next one."

I sit up straight in the hotel manager's chair. "That's not fair, Mom. I can't just walk out on my job. I have six senior citizens depending on me."

Mom exchanges a look with my dad. "Are you hearing this, Mark? She can't even remember to water the fern in her bedroom once a week and now she's in charge of six senior citizens."

I remember Mr. Fenton and it hits me like a punch to the gut. "Five, I mean," I murmur, and a tear slips down my face.

Elizabeth looks up and bites her lip. "Mom, she's almost eighteen. You can't ground her like she's a ten-year-old."

"Like hell I can't. She's living under my roof, isn't she?" Mom has a hand on her hip and has turned to face Elizabeth, who stands too and put both hands on *her* hips. She's always been way less afraid to stand up to our mom than I have. Then again, of the two of us, she's had *way* more practice asserting her independence.

"Give her a break," she says now. "Bree's been doing an amazing job. You should hear all the stuff she's done with them—you'd be so impressed. I know for a fact I couldn't have handled things any better."

Whatever Elizabeth is feeling toward me after our talk, it means a lot—a whole lot—that she's standing up for me with Mom and Dad. If there's one thing that unites a divided sisterhood, it's forming a solid front against the parental units. I give her a grateful smile and she returns it.

"Mom, I don't know how things are going to play out from here," I say, "but I want to do whatever the tour wants. If they think I should stay and finish the rest of the itinerary, I'm going to. It's only fair to them and it's the responsible thing to do."

My father stops pacing and studies me with a thoughtful expression. He comes and stands next to Mom, putting his arm around her and squeezing before saying, "I think she's right, Nancy."

My mom deflates. Dad looks at me and says, "I guess our baby's growing up."

I half smile, half whimper. I miss him so much right now. He's wearing his Indians T-shirt, which means there's a game tonight. If I were there in my living room I could curl up in his arms and he'd stroke my hair while I cried and then we'd watch baseball. But I'm not and I can't. Instead I whisper, "Guess so, Dad," and put my fingertip to the screen so he can touch it with his.

My mom sniffles too and nudges my dad out of the way. "I can see I'm outvoted, but I'm really not sure about this, Aubree. It makes me crazy to think of you all the way over there by yourself. Do you need anything? Do you have enough sunscreen?"

In spite of how miserable I am, I have to laugh. My mom will never, ever stop taking care of me, no matter how old I get or how far away I am. At the moment, that's a really reassuring thought.

The conversation loosens up from there. Elizabeth says, "Now that we have that straightened out, tell Mom and Dad that thing about the girl in the tower in the German castle.

Oh, and tell them about how small the gazebo from *The Sound of Music* is in real life!"

I know that's probably not the end of the discussion about all this—or even close to the end—but for now I dry my tears and tell my family a little about my adventures. At one point, Elizabeth winks at me when I catch her eye while Mom is asking a question, and it makes me feel as though, even if things aren't perfect between us at the moment, we'll figure it out.

I feel a small weight lift off my shoulders. Even if Sam never forgives me, at least my family will. I'll always be the baby, but maybe I don't have to take my role quite so literally.

There's only one more set of people I need to confess to.

I make myself comfortable on a bench outside and wait for someone to return, whether the seniors or Sam. As it turns out, no one does for two hours. Just as I'm getting ready to give up, the bus pulls up in front and my group piles off.

I greet them as they come down the stairs. When everyone is clustered outside the bus, I say, "Do you think we could find a place in the lobby to talk?"

Emma looks at the expression on my face. "Is this about Mr. Fenton?" she asks.

"No. This is about me."

I wait until everyone is gathered in a grouping of chairs to one side of the lobby. I look at the trusting faces peering at me and I almost lose my nerve. I started this trip asking WWED, but today it isn't about what Elizabeth would do. Besides, I think I might be better off from now on asking WWMFD: What Would Mr. Fenton Do? Or better yet, What Would Aubree Do?

Aubree would do this:

"I need to tell you all something and I want you to know that it's really hard for me to say to you when you've all been nothing but kind to me."

I look at each face. Emma with her tiny frame that completely out-hiked me in Cinque Terre, and Mary with her not-so-tiny frame that she didn't let hold her back from skinny-dipping with style. Hank and Maisy, back to sitting on top of each other again. I guess the death-of-a-tourmate grace period has ended. I save Dolores for last because she's the hardest to face. I feel like we formed a bond back on that beach, but that doesn't trump the fact that she has her grandson to defend.

This sucks. If the skinny-dipping day in Cinque Terre is going down in history as a top-ten day, then surely today must be a bottom-ten day. But I have to do this. I have to.

"The truth is that I've been lying to you about who I am. My older sister, Elizabeth, is the one who was supposed to lead this tour, and I'm Aubree. I'm here in her place, but I couldn't be honest about who I was because we didn't want anyone to know Elizabeth couldn't fulfill her job duties. I was trying to help her, but helping someone shouldn't mean hurting others, and I realize that now."

I spit it out in one breath and then hold my next one. No one so much as blinks. Are their hearing aids turned off?

"Um, did you all hear what I said?"

"We did, honey. It's just that we already knew."

My mouth drops open. "How did you—"

I can't even finish I'm so shocked.

"Well, it turns out our Mr. Fenton, may he rest in peace, is a total lightweight when he drinks, as he did a wee bit of last night, and the people he confided in are old biddy gossips," Hank says with a grin.

"Who are you calling old biddies, you . . . you . . . Texan, you?" Mary swings her pocketbook in his direction.

Um, what is going on here? Why are they joking around with one another and not screaming at me?

Emma watches me carefully. "It's true, Sweetpea. After his third bourbon, Mr. Fenton was confessing to crimes he committed when he was seven."

"Crimes?" I gape at her.

"Oh, just breaking the neighbor's window with a baseball. Nothing major. But then he got to you and we couldn't shut him up," Mary adds.

"So he told you—"

"Everything," Emma says.

"And you told—"

"All of us," answers Hank. He's smiling too.

"I don't understand. Why aren't any of you angry?"

"What's the point in that? Are you sorry?" This from Emma.

I nod, confused.

"Were you trying to hurt us?" Mary.

I shake my head. This is so strange.

"Was your heart in the right place?" I can't believe this is Dolores talking!

I nod again, slowly this time. But it was *her* mom and *her* grandson and their company I messed with. Why isn't she angry?

"Don't see what the problem is, then," says Mary. "C'mon, ladies. I don't know about you, but I'm beat. It's been one hell of a day." She grabs Dolores and Emma by the hand and pulls them in the direction of the elevator. Hank and Maisy remain cuddling, so I turn to them.

"I—I don't know how to apologize enough, I—"

Hank looks up from gazing into Maisy's eyes. "Did you say something, darlin'?"

But as I turn from them, he tips his hat and winks at me.

Never have I been more aware that I am *not* wise to the ways of the world. But I'm also not complaining about that just now.

After more time on the bench outside, I finally give up on waiting for Sam and head upstairs. Mary was right. It has been a hell of a long day, in every sense of the word, and all I want is to crawl between my sheets.

I'm just drifting off to sleep when the phone by my bedside rings.

"Sam?" I hope against hope I'll hear his voice calling me

Dimple on the other end of the line.

There's a pause and then a sigh. "No, Aubree, this is Teresa Bellamy." Oh. I can't get a read on her tone. Is she furious with me? How much does she know? She called me Aubree. I sit up in bed and clutch the phone, my heart pounding.

"Um, hi. Hi. Before you say anything, I just want to say how completely sorry I am. I never meant for any of this to happen. I . . ." I trail off, unsure what to say next.

Teresa's voice is kind, but resigned. "I'm sure you are. I've spoken with Sam and he's brought me up-to-date on the situation. I appreciate how hard you've worked these past few weeks, but I'm afraid I can't let you continue as guide for the remainder of the tour. You understand this, I suspect?"

I murmur a "Yes" while my heart sinks into my stomach. I expected as much, but I wasn't really prepared for it.

"Good," she answers. "I heard you and Mr. Fenton had gotten quite close and I'm very sorry for your loss. I know you've had a difficult day, so we'll save any further discussion about this other issue for when you're back in the States, alright? I've arranged for a ticket on the eleven o'clock train to Amsterdam tomorrow and the front desk will have it printed and waiting first thing in the morning. By the time you get to the Netherlands, I'll have sorted out the date change on your flight as well, so please call in when you arrive there."

I'm numb, nodding, until I realize she can't see that. "Okay," I murmur.

"Get some sleep now, Aubree. We'll talk more tomorrow."

The line goes dead and I stare at the phone in my hand for a second before replacing it in the cradle.

That could have gone so much worse. She could have screamed at me, demanded I be brought up on charges of fraud (okay, I'm not entirely sure about that, but still. It could have gone much, much worse).

She sounded as deflated as I felt. I wonder what Sam's version of events was, how much he told her about us. Anything? Everything?

My day ends the same way it began (minus the boy next to me, which is a definite key difference): curled up in bed, staring out the window, going over and over things in my mind.

THIRTY

The doors to the elevator slide open to the opulent hotel lobby, where a cluster of senior citizens sits in a grouping of chairs arranged in a circle. The smallest woman wears an Austrian woodsman's hat, a knight's breastplate, a gypsy skirt, and a pair of tulip-painted wooden clogs.

I get a lump in my throat because they're holding hands and I'm guessing they're praying for Mr. Fenton. I've only thought of him a hundred times since waking up forty-five minutes ago and it still doesn't feel real. None of yesterday feels real. I wish like I've never wished for anything before that we were all back in Cinque Terre, lounging at one of the outdoor cafés, sharing Mr. Fenton's pesto focaccia and people-watching. Sam could dump all the ice cubes he wanted down my back and I would just laugh.

But no.

Sam is very definitely not interested in laughing with me or kissing me or even talking to me, as evidenced by the total radio silence on his end. I stood in the hallway outside his door this morning for something like ten minutes, trying to work up the courage to knock, but in the end I chickened out.

If he's too hurt (or angry?) to reach out to me even though he has to know I'm on a train in three hours, I need to respect that, right? It doesn't feel great. In fact, it feels like crap.

If Sam is determined to avoid seeing me, I'm going to have to live with that. But no way am I leaving without saying good-bye to everyone else. No way.

I was crossing fingers I'd find them here, ready and waiting despite the fact their bus doesn't depart for Barcelona for another hour. I glance around to see if Sam is somehow here too, but I don't see any sign of him so I step into the lobby.

Emma smiles when she sees me and extracts one hand from Mary's to wave me over. "Wanna join our sit-in?" she calls.

I cross the room quickly. "Um . . . sit-in? Like they did back in the sixties?"

"Oh, darlin'," Hank says, "you should have been there. The sixties was quite the experience."

Emma says, "Bah. I had three kids under the age of five when that decade got revved up. I'm making up for some lost time here. That Sam better listen good or else I'm liable to take things to the next step."

"Next step?" I'm afraid to know. What does she mean by *sit-in*? And what does Sam have to do with any of this?

"Bra burning, of course," Emma answers.

"Uh, sorry I have to ask, but what would a bra burning have to do with Sam listening good? And what is Sam listening to anyway?"

"To you, of course."

To me? This is for my benefit? I love that after everything I did, these guys are fighting my battles for me, and I'm sure I don't deserve it. I can't believe I don't get to finish this trip with them. I was just getting good at things.

"You all are the best," I say, smiling sadly at each of them. "But I don't think Sam is very interested in what I have to say and I found out last night that I'm heading home. So you'll have him as your tour guide from here on out. I couldn't let you leave without saying good-bye."

Mary rolls her eyes. "Well, Sam's made up his mind, but his mother is another story. You see, *we're* the paying guests. And as such, we have a say in this. We called her this morning, woke her up and everything. We told her we wanted you to lead our tour or else."

"But I—"

"Don't get your panties in a bunch, she said no," she continues. "She's not carrying insurance on you, so she can't have you stay on even if she wanted to. But she did give us the option of cutting our trip short. She's gonna refund our unused days and give us a generous credit on a future tour. We took a vote, and without Mr. Fenton and without you, well, the trip just wouldn't be the same. And we don't want to be on it anymore."

"So we're all headed to Amsterdam with you, on our bus,

to catch flights home," says Dolores. I'm as surprised to hear her speak as I was yesterday, considering it's her daughter and Sam on the other side of this mess.

She sees my surprise and nods. "I'd rather get my follow-up X-ray at home anyway. I talked to my daughter about you. Said how wonderful you've been to me. I believe she actually fell out of bed when I told her how much I was enjoying myself. I know she'll come around and I intend to see to it personally. Now, I'm not going to get involved where you and Sam are concerned, but you're a good girl and you deserve to have him hear your side of things in person."

"I'd love to have the chance, but I don't think he's too interested in talking to me," I say, sighing.

Dolores scrunches her face up. "Well, if I have to pull the 'do it for your dear old gram' card, you better believe I will."

"Not necessary, Gram."

At his quiet voice, I spin. Sam is standing directly behind Hank with his hands stuffed in his pockets. My breath hitches in my throat, but he's avoiding my eyes. He also looks terrible. His clothes are rumpled like he slept in them and there are dark circles under his eyes. Worst of all, the trademark grin that *is* Sam is entirely missing.

When he says "You want to talk?" his eyes are still on the ground, so I'm not even completely sure he's addressing me until Emma gives me a shove. I trail him out the door and when I glance behind me at the group, everyone gives me a thumbs-up. I can't help but manage a grateful grin back.

It fades as I follow Sam to a bench outside the hotel, the same one I sat on for hours yesterday waiting for him to show up. I know Sam won't let me off the hook as quickly as the other members of this tour, and I wouldn't expect him to. They're friends and sweet people, but at the end of the day I'm their tour guide. I really hope I'm more than that to Sam.

We sit for a moment in silence before I can't take it anymore. I have to know where his head is. "I'm really sorry, Sam."

He nods, still not looking at me.

"Sam?" I ask, pleading with my voice. Finally he risks a glance in my direction. When his eyes find mine, I say it again.

"I'm so, so sorry."

He doesn't respond, but he doesn't look away either, so I gather my courage.

"It's not like I set out to lie to you. I didn't even know there *was* a you when we were concocting this. My sister and I thought we were planning things out so well, but it turns out we didn't think any of it through. Not how it would feel, anyway. To have to lie so often and for so long, to so many people."

"Are you asking me to feel sorry for you?" Sam asks. His voice is soft and low.

"No! No." I sigh and we're both quiet for a moment. A fancy sports car pulls up in front of the hotel and its purring engine sounds like the Lamborghini's, which makes me think of Mr. Fenton. The reminder feels like a fresh sucker punch. I wait for the worst of it to pass, then try again with Sam.

"You have to believe me, I wasn't trying to hurt you. Or anyone on the trip. But especially not you. Especially not after everything we—after everything you told me about your dad—and, well, after everything." My hands flutter helplessly to my lap and I know I'm not explaining this well at all. When we were lying in his bed, I felt like we opened up to each other, like we made promises, even if we weren't saying them out loud. I know we got close on a totally different level and I also know how much worse that made it for Sam to find out I was lying to him. If the situation were reversed, I would be incredibly hurt too, except I could never imagine the situation being reversed because Sam would never do that to me. Of course, I'm sure he thought he could say the same about me.

"I hated lying to you," I say plainly.

"But you still did it. Hundreds of times. Actions speak louder than words, Aubree," he answers.

My name on his tongue sounds foreign.

"And sometimes the reasons behind the actions speak louder than the actions," I reply, raising my voice just a little. I need him to hear me. He has to hear me. "It wasn't about deceiving you, it was about *protecting* my sister."

He's quiet again, and his gaze returns to his hands in his lap. "I really don't understand why people feel like they have to protect others with lies." I know he's referring to his mom and her deception about his dad and I feel like the dirt caked in the bottom of my sandals.

"It's not the same thing, Sam, and you know it," I whisper.

"Well, *you* knew that lying is a pretty big sensitive spot for me. When you lied about speaking Spanish, it made total sense to me that you would just check that box to land a job you thought you wouldn't qualify for. It wasn't *that* big a deal. And then the celiac thing. To be honest, I thought it was sweet you would go to such measures to impress me. I was flattered you liked me enough to come up with that crazy story. But this, Lizz—sorry, *Aubree*. This is different. How could you let things go so far with us without telling me the truth?"

He's not wrong. He steals a glance at me and I bite my lip.

"I know," I whisper. Then I face him. "But Sam, it *was* me this whole time. Me, Aubree. No matter what name I was using at the time, it was all me inside."

His voice is rueful when he says, "Yesterday I went through this loop of all our conversations, trying to figure out what parts of them were a lie. Everything? Just some? Like, when you told me you were taking graduate classes at Kent State."

I murmur, "I really am going there this fall. But as a freshman."

"Right. What about 'confessing' to me your big dream about running for office."

"I don't have a clue about my future," I whisper.

Sam nods. "I have an easier time believing that. The campaign stuff didn't feel like you. The *Sound of Music* geekdom?"

My heartbeat quickens and I'm desperate for him to know the real Aubree. "Me. All me! I promise."

He nods and I finally get a tiny smile from him. "I kind

of thought so. Hard to fake that much enthusiasm. The picky-eating thing, the way you take your coffee?"

I take his hand in mine and place them on my heart. "One hundred percent Aubree. I couldn't eat a bratwurst right now even if you told me that would be all it would take to forgive me."

This time his smile is a little wider before he drops his eyes back to his lap. "I was sort of hoping those were the real you."

It hurts to breathe. That's how much I'm holding in how badly I want to kiss him, to show him that part was all me too. Every time.

"I wish Mr. Fenton was here," Sam says. "I feel like he'd know what to say right now."

Me too. Then my stomach gives a flutter when I realize he already *did* say it. I squeeze Sam's hand. "Mr. Fenton, he, well, he figured things out pretty quickly . . . about who I am, I mean. He didn't completely approve, but he did help me a lot. And he pushed me to be honest with you. I know you have no reason to believe me, but I swear it's the truth. . . ."

Sam squeezes my hand this time when I break off speaking. It's not much, but I'll take it.

"The reason I was going up to Mr. Fenton's room in the first place yesterday morning was to talk to him more about how to tell you. He'd been helping me sort things out about that."

Sam looks at me, his eyebrows raised. "You were planning to tell me on your own? Before you got caught at the embassy?"

I nod as hard as I can. "Mr. Fenton thought I owed it to us—you and me, us—to be honest with you. I did too, but I told him I was afraid you wouldn't forgive me." I wait for him to react, but he doesn't. He's back to studying his lap, but at least he hasn't removed his hand from mine.

"Mr. Fenton said he knew you would, because you're an old soul and old souls know their way around forgiveness."

Sam still doesn't say anything. Finally he turns his eyes to mine. "He said that about me?"

"Yeah."

Another long silence.

"The whole train ride back, talking to my mom, walking around every square inch of Monaco, I kept telling myself that you're just some girl I've only known a few weeks. I should be able to just brush this aside and get back to my regular life."

Tears prick behind my eyelids as I whisper, "Yeah?"

"But if it were true that you were just some girl, it wouldn't hurt this bad." He says the words so softly I almost can't make them out. "You're not some girl. Not even close." Then he's quiet for another long moment and I ache from head to toe. I wipe a tear from my cheek with the back of my hand as Sam watches, then looks away.

The silence stretches on until finally he says, "I really can't take lying, Aubree. I just . . . can't. How do I know you wouldn't do it again?"

I whip my head up to look at him as my heart squeezes with hope. He glances at me but then back at his lap, where he picks at the hem of his shorts. I don't care. He opened the door a crack and I intend to push my way in. I peer into his face until he looks at me.

"Because I wouldn't. I won't hurt you, I promise. And I won't lie to you. Ever. I'm just figuring some of this stuff out for myself, Sam, but I swear, this is one lesson I've learned for life."

He holds my gaze, searching my eyes for something. I will myself to show him everything I did the other night. What's in my heart. Finally, after what feels like a hundred years, he exhales and drops his eyes and my stomach falls into my shoes. Until he looks sideways at me with a small smile that makes the corners of his eyes crinkle in the adorable way they do when he teases. He says, "This is going to take some getting used to. Me being the older, wiser one of us."

I exhale too, trying to process his words and the smile in his eyes. Is he saying what I think he's saying? My insides start doing a Snoopy dance, but I try to keep my face composed.

"I mean, you're definitely older, I'll give you that, but as for wiser . . . ," I say. It's risky, inserting a joke here, but it pays off when his face relaxes into his famous (well, with me, any- way) smile.

"There's something else I need to know," he asks, and he gets all serious again.

"Anything. I'm an open book." I hold his stare and refuse to blink. I will do whatever it takes to convince this guy I'm trustworthy.

His lips twitch. "The stuffed hedgehog you sleep with? That you or Elizabeth?"

I groan. "Mr. Pricklepants? All me."

Sam leans in close to my face and his eyes fall to my mouth. Just before his lips meet mine, he whispers, "Hoped so, Dimple."

THIRTY-ONE

We're facing a nice, long drive to Amsterdam. But I don't care. I'm exactly where I'm supposed to be.

At first, no one talks much, and the morning's camaraderie fades into the background as everyone is alone with their thoughts. Mary and Emma play a quiet game of gin rummy behind us and Hank and Maisy are, well . . .

Dolores hums under her breath as she knits.

"Toblerone?" Sam asks, slipping the triangle-shaped container into my palm. As gestures of forgiveness go, chocolate trumps all. The hand he tucks into mine isn't too shabby either. I snuggle against his arm and say a giant thank-you to the powers that be for letting Sam be here next to me. When I lift my face to his, he's waiting for me with a kiss, and my heart contracts. I honestly did not think it was possible to experience so many intense emotions in one thirty-hour period.

Lyon becomes Dijon and eventually I add another new country, Luxembourg, as we skirt its border before turning into Belgium. We watch movies. We zip in and out of rest stops without any lingering in the gift shop sections. Even though we're still on the road, the trip is over, and everyone seems to acknowledge it.

Sam takes over for Bento, so our friendly Spaniard can take a nap in an empty seat. Night falls and the bus grows even quieter.

In the silence, Maisy's voice is soft. "Does anyone else think we should say a few words for Mr. Fenton? We sat together yesterday but we didn't really talk much."

Speaking of a few words, this is practically the most Maisy has said this whole trip.

"I think that's a great idea," calls Sam from the driver's seat. "Who wants to start?"

We all speak at once. Eventually we sort it out and each take a turn telling our favorite memory of Mr. Fenton from the trip. Dolores talks about the time he chased the pigeons around St. Mark's Square in Venice, and Emma has us laughing with a story of him correcting the tour guide at Marksburg Castle. Apparently, the poor man insisted the dates he was giving were right until Mr. Fenton marched off and returned with a book from the gift shop that conclusively proved otherwise.

When it's my turn, I tell everyone about the way he looked about five years old when he slid behind the wheel of the Lamborghini. I'm glad his last day was such a memorable one.

After we finish, we're all quiet for a minute, lost in trip memories and Mr. Fenton memories, when Dolores suddenly says, "I'm sorry, but I just have to ask. WHAT is that smell?"

Out of habit, we all turn toward Hank. "Wasn't me!"

Then he grows quiet for a second and something passes over his face. Wordlessly he bends down and reaches under his seat. When he straightens he's holding something that, at some point, used to be a giant wheel of cheese.

"Y'all think it could be this?" he asks.

Amsterdam welcomes me back like an old friend. The bathtub at the Kras is just as Dutch-sized and the burgers just as good. I know exactly which way to turn at the penis statue to reach an actual coffee shop, and not one that's a euphemism for anything else.

"Told you there was a Starbucks." I smirk, pointing it out for Sam.

"When did you tell me that?"

"On the phone. The first night we talked."

Sam grins. "I know. I was just testing you. I wanted to know if you remembered our first conversation as well as I did." He steers us away from the Starbucks and over to the canal edge instead.

"Know which first I'd rather remember?" he whispers, and I squirm in pleasure. I love being in his arms. He dips his head down and touches his lips to mine, briefly, before saying, "Our first kiss in Vienna. Also by a canal, I might add." He nods his head at the waterway beside us.

I stroke my chin with two fingers. "Hmm . . . I don't recall that. I might need more reminding."

"Oh yeah?" Sam asks with a grin. Then he reminds me. He reminds me very well. When we come up for air, I say, "We seems to do a lot of kissing by waterways. Vienna, Venice . . ."

"Prague," he adds.

"Not so many waterways in our part of Ohio, huh? What will we do?" I pretend to pout.

Sam playfully pokes my side until I smile instead. "Something tells me we'll figure it out," he says very earnestly. "In fact, I can promise we most definitely will figure it out. I'm planning on a lot of this in our future, Dimple, and I don't care if we have nothing but a McDonald's for a backdrop."

"Mmm . . . McDonald's. Hey, did you know their fries are gluten-free?" I tilt my head and blink wide eyes, the picture of innocence.

Sam rolls his. "You are one of a kind, you know that?"

"I'm going to pretend you meant that as a compliment."

"Good," whispers Sam before stealing a kiss.

A riverboat cruises beside us and the passengers chatter as they take in the sights. But all I have eyes for is the guy in front of me. He opens his stance and I step between his legs. He places one hand at the small of my back and I reach up to twirl one of his curls around my finger.

I can't keep a happy sigh from escaping. "Remind me to thank my sister for getting arrested."

Sam's laugh is shocked, then amused. I stand on tiptoes to kiss him again and his laugh becomes a small groan as he pulls me tight against him.

I may have to revise all previous statements. I'm pretty sure my old favorite, Amsterdam, is claiming new favorite status too.

At seven the next morning we wave good-bye from the sidewalk of our last hotel of the trip, as Hank and Maisy interrupt their groping session to toss a quick "safe travels" our way before claiming the back of the bus one last time on their ride to the airport.

Emma and Mary are on the noon flight and they're harder to say good-bye to. We spend what must be twenty minutes hugging in the lobby before Bento points at his watch.

"You take care of you, Aubree," Emma finally says.

I pull her into another hug. "I'm not going to forget you *ever*. At the very least you'll be on my mind each and every Halloween." She laughs and swats at me with her Austrian woodsman's hat, which she's decided to wear on her return journey.

Mary tugs her away and wraps me in her arms.

"You're a lovely girl. And thank you again for my necklace. That's quite a talent you have."

I laugh and snuggle against her shoulder. Being hugged by her is exactly as I imagined, like getting wrapping up in a load of towels fresh from the dryer. Sam and I follow them outside and they step onto the bus as Bento loads their bags.

We all jump when Emma honks the bus's horn.

She giggles when we spin to face her. "Oh, I've wanted to do that this whole trip. Anyway, move it, Bento. We have a flight to catch."

A few hours later, Bento is back for Dolores, Sam, and me. When we reach the terminal, he helps us with our bags, then stands awkwardly beside his bus. I throw my arms around him too. No one who made it through this trip with me is leaving without a hug.

"*Adiós*, Bento."

"Good-bye, Aubree," he says, in halting and heavily accented English. "You are," he continues, pausing to search for the word, "adorable."

He looks to Sam for confirmation. Sam grins and loops an arm over my shoulder. "I taught him that one."

I duck out from under Sam's arm and throw my own around Bento again. "Bento, you are even better than adorable, you are priceless."

He shrugs to make it clear he has no idea what I'm saying, but he hugs me back just as hard.

We get Dolores settled in a comfy chair inside the terminal with her knitting and a lemonade and I follow Sam to the ticket counter for AirEuro Airlines.

"Hey, do you mind if we take a quick detour?" I ask as we head for the end of the line. "There's someone who helped me a ton when I first landed and I kind of want to tell her how much that meant to me."

He looks at me, curious, but lets me tug him down the escalator to the counter where I met Marieke a few short weeks and a lifetime ago.

I figure, what are the odds she'll be on duty today, but when I round the corner, there she is, helping an older, freakishly tall (must be Dutch) man who is waving his arms over his head as he tries to explain something. We hang back until he finally steps away from the counter; then I move forward into her line of vision.

"Elizabeth!" Marieke lights up when she sees me. And here I thought she'd never remember me in the mix of all the passengers she deals with all day, every day.

"Hi, Marieke." I smile at her. Her eyes widen a bit as she spots Sam just behind me. But she doesn't comment, just says, "The hotel left word for you, then. Hang on, let me grab your things."

Left word? What?

She disappears into a door behind her counter and returns seconds later with a brown paper bag, passing it across the counter. I open it to find the binder and my cell phone, safe and sound, exactly as I'd left them. I look up at Marieke in shock.

"The hotel didn't send you?" she asks. "We found them a few days after you left and the Krasnapolsky was able to track your next few locations, but your trail went cold in Austria. I didn't want to risk these things bouncing around a slew of hotels, so I thought they might be safer with me until you called for them. You really didn't know they were here?"

"No idea. I was just coming by to thank you."

"Thank me? For what?"

"For being so kind on my first day away from home ever. For taking the time to help me so much."

"Oh, please, I barely did anything. Just gave you a little encouragement and sent you on your way," she says. She glances at Sam. "You claimed that day that your whole life was in the seat back of that plane, but it looks like you did an okay job finding a new one to replace it."

I reach back and squeeze his hand. "It hasn't been *too* terrible."

"I'm glad, *meid*. I could tell when I met you, you'd be just fine."

She could?

I walk around the side of the counter and give her a quick hug. "Thanks, Marieke. I'm so happy I got to meet you."

"Safe travels, Elizabeth."

I smile. "It's Aubree now, actually. But thank you."

Sam tugs the brown bag off the counter and pretends to fall over at the waist from the weight of it.

"Geez, what's in this thing?"

I steer us to a bench and drop my luggage. When Sam sits next to me, I take the bag from him and slide the binder out.

"Sam, meet the real Elizabeth." I smile as I say it, picturing my sister bent earnestly over this binder, affixing reinforcements to every hole on every page she punched. I drop the full weight of it onto his lap, and he begins flipping through the pages. He lets out a low whistle.

"Wow. She put all this together?"

"Oh yeah. And this was a rush job."

"Wow," he says again. Then his eyes get all bright. "Do you think it would be okay for me to take this home to show my mom? It would be completely amazing to have something like this to give all of our tour guides. And maybe even a mini version for our guests that they could page through during the drives or something. Do you think your sister might be up for putting something like that together?"

"I suspect Elizabeth would be grateful for any chance to get back in your mom's good graces. And she has a sister who would really like the chance to do right by her," I say.

"I don't think you have to worry about Elizabeth. My mom was crazy impressed that your sister took the time to drive down and explain everything to her in person. I'm guessing Mom'll find all good things to say when she talks to the congressman."

Oh thank God. I wrap my arms around his waist and squeeze. "Thanks, Sam. Can you tell Elizabeth that I miss her when you meet her at the airport for the suitcase trade-off?"

"You got it. Although, have I told you how much I wish I was staying with you instead?" he says for the millionth time since plans came together yesterday.

Oh yeah. Here's the twist. I didn't change my flight. I'm staying through the end of the trip. I wasn't going to, but at some point when everyone was making return plans and talking about the things they couldn't wait to get back to at home, I realized something. I'm not done with Europe yet. Or maybe Europe isn't done with me. Either way, I'm gonna find out.

I came on this trip not even believing I could get myself across the ocean in one piece, but all that changed. And I can't really imagine being right here, with all these other countries I haven't explored yet just a short train ride away, and not taking advantage of that. Somewhere along the line, the crazy youth hostelers I kept seeing everywhere stopped looking so crazy. I sure hope they're not, anyway, since they're gonna be my new friends.

I squeeze Sam's hand. "I know you want to stay, but if you did, you wouldn't be Perfect Sam. Perfect Sam would never leave his still-recovering grandmother to navigate international flights and airport connections all by herself." I'm quiet when I add, "Besides, I think this is something I might need to do on my own."

Sam nods, then kisses me, and I almost take back everything I just said and beg him to stay and see what canals there are to find in Paris and Barcelona.

Then Mom could stop all her Scarlett O'Hara, hand-on-the-forehead swooning, insisting that I'm now taking things to a whole new level she never agreed to, and Elizabeth wouldn't have to spend all her free time bringing her back from the edge. I'm actually one thousand percent, completely amazed my parents are going for this plan at all, but never underestimate my sister's persuasive skills.

She promised to school me in her manipulative ways when I get back. And I'm gonna make it my goal for the second half of the summer to find something I can teach her too. Just to remind her I don't *always* need her telling me what to do, even if I sort of suspect she might be starting to realize that already.

Sam nuzzles my neck before whispering in my ear, "Just don't forget about me when you meet all those hostelers with accents. Those Australian guys have quite the reputation, just so you know."

I laugh and wrap my arms around him. "You're impossible to forget, Sam Bellamy."

"Good," he says, planting a kiss on the top of my head before pointing to my suitcase. "Now that you have your phone back, you better find your phone charger in here before I check this sucker onto the flight." While I retrieve the cord and slip the binder inside, he turns to his own suitcase and extracts something from it.

"Got you a present, Dimple." He places two boxes of PowerBars in my hand. "Figure these might come in handy where you're headed."

I laugh. I may be making progress on Operation Aubree, but that doesn't mean I need to be sampling tapas, whatever that is. The outside pouch of my newly acquired backpack (the real kind hostelers wear, not my safety-pinned regular one) fits the bars perfectly.

Sam stands and helps me up, always the gentleman.

He spins me around and places my pack on my back. "Ouch. Hold on." I grimace as a piece of my hair tangles around one of the strap buckles.

"Need help?" Sam asks.

"Nope." I hike the pack up my hips and pull the strand free. Sam flashes me a thumbs-up. We head back to the ticket counter and check all of the bags, then make our way to a waiting Dolores.

"Time to say bye to Aubree, Gram."

"So long, farewell, auf Wiedersehen, good-bye," she sings.

I truly love her for quoting *Sound of Music* lyrics. "Bye, Dolores. And thank you for everything. When I get back maybe you, me, and Sam could catch a movie sometime."

"Forget the movies," she says. "There's a karaoke bar in the strip mall down the road I've always wanted to peek inside. You two can take me there."

Way to go, Dolores!

She hugs me and sits back in her chair before nodding at Sam. "Walk the girl to her train like a gentleman. And take your time." I think she winks, but I can't be sure.

This go-round I know exactly where to head to reach the train platform below the airport. Sam's hand is warm in mine and I think back to the day, less than a month ago, that I trailed down here behind Marieke. Back then I had a hard fist of dread in my stomach, but all I feel now is a warm tickle of feelings for Sam mixed with excitement for my next adventure.

"I'll see you back in Ohio," Sam says.

"Are you sure you're gonna want to hang out with me in boring old Ohio after we've wandered Venice and climbed in the Alps?"

He tucks a lock of hair behind my ear. "Remember what I said before. Sometimes staying in one place is the biggest adventure of all. Of course, I didn't add that it helps to have the right company."

I snuggle into his arms for another hug. When he lets me go, he says, "Besides, next up I'll get to introduce you to college. My turn to play tour guide to you."

I wiggle my eyebrows at him. "*We-ellllllll*. It could be nice to have someone older and wiser telling me what to do. Even if we haven't agreed on the wiser part yet."

"*You are seventeen, going on eighteen, I-IIII'll take caaa-are of you,*" Sam sings. Or attempts to sing.

Then he grows serious. "I don't really think you need that, you know," he says, and I nod where once I would have argued.

The train to Paris pulls in and screeches to a stop, as a display above our heads lights up with the destination details. I glance behind me, shift to line up with the opening doors, and turn to Sam with a smile.

He steps in and tugs on my backpack's straps. "Hey, so . . . likeyoubye." He leans in for another soft kiss before I can respond. My insides are total mush as the doors to the train slide apart.

Sam nudges me gently, forcing me to take a step backward to keep my balance. "Don't miss your train, Dimple."

Overhead a bell chimes twice and an announcement says the doors will be closing. I step on, my eyes still locked with Sam's. The doors swoop shut, leaving a partition of glass between us.

Sam puts a hand to the glass and I do the same. He smiles that smile of his that makes the corners of his eyes crinkle, and I return it. I feel all lit up from within. I think he can probably tell by the way my grin is plastered on my face, because he laughs and shakes his head, then mouths, "Go. Have fun. You've got this."

He blows a kiss as the train pulls away from the station and I watch until he's gone.

Then I hitch my backpack higher on my hips as I turn to survey the compartment. I get that tickle in my chest again when I see the conductor walking the aisle, asking for tickets. I find a seat and sling my bag onto the shelf above it before fishing in my pocket for my ticket. I hand it to the conductor with confidence.

Sam is right.

I do have this. I so totally do.

ACKNOWLEDGMENTS

My editor, Annie Berger, may be an only child, but wow does she get sisters—and me. Her thoughtful comments and suggestions turned the focus dial and made everything so much sharper. I hope she never gets wanderlust, because I need her driving my bus.

For helping steer, thank you to the entire team at HarperTeen and Epic Reads, especially Rosemary Brosnan, Kate Engbring, Bethany Reis, Kim VandeWater, Olivia Russo, and everyone working behind the scenes with so much care and passion.

My agent, Holly Root, is one of the smartest people working in this industry. I'm so thankful to have her for a tour guide through the Land of Publishing.

My critique partners, Alison Cherry, Dee Romito, and Gail Nall, are along for every pit stop, and sharing all things writing with them keeps it so much fun. The fact that they never run from my scary first drafts makes me love them all the more. Big hugs and thanks also go to Lori Goldstein, Dana Alison Levy, and Elodie Nowodazkij for early reads.

All the black licorice ever (no seriously, I really don't want any!) to Marieke Nijkamp and Corinne Duyvis for walking me around Holland, fact checking, and letting me cast them as characters. Big hugs also to Kip Wilson Rechea and Bernard Rachea for their Spanish translations—in all cases, any errors are mine!

To my husband, John, and my kids, Ben, Jack, Caroline—I love exploring this world with you. You're my happy place, and wherever we're together, that's my home.

This book stemmed from a senior bus tour my grandmother, Mary O'Brien Shenkus, took to Europe, and I need to thank her not only for offering inspiration but also for instilling my own love of travel. I hope she enjoyed being sent on one last trip abroad! I also had my great-grandmother Emma Jordan Keach's day planner from 1914 by my bedside as I worked on the first draft of this book in 2014 and each day I'd see what she was up to on the same date a hundred years prior. I had fun trading her buggy for a bus in this story. No doubt both these women would have been the first under that waterfall, and I'm lucky to have had them in my life.

And last, thanks go to my parents. When I was twenty-one I had the zany idea to spend a year traveling around the world solo. They let me move back home after graduation and put off a job hunt so I could waitress double shifts and save every dime from that day on. They helped me pack and repack my backpack and search for youth hostels in Nepal. I was all bluster and bravado until the moment we were standing in the drop-off area of the airport, me in tears and reconsidering the entire adventure. Unlike Aubree's parents, my dad took me by the shoulders and said, "You have to do this because if you don't go RIGHT NOW there will be a million things keeping you home—a job, a husband, kids. I order you to get on that flight." Years later I learned from my mom that he was so scared for my safety out in the wide-open world that he cried the whole way home. But he still made me go. That's love for you, guys.

So for everyone out there with wanderlust—whether a touch or a fever—I order you to go! (Also, thanks for reading and I love you.)

READ ON FOR A SNEAK PEEK AT
JEN MALONE'S *MAP TO THE STARS*,
AVAILABLE NOW.

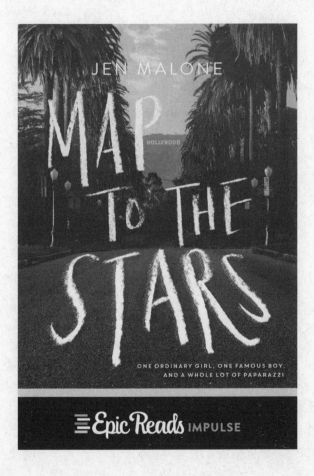

Chapter One

I never dreamed my first encounter with an A-list movie star would involve hairy feet and a bowl full of tiny fish.

Mom and I stood a safe distance from the upholstered chair of *People* magazine's Most Beautiful Man of 1990-something in the living room of an opulent Hollywood Hills mansion. His in-need-of-some-manscaping feet were stuck in a mini-aquarium of hundreds of swarming fish and he jumped every time one took a nibble at a callus.

"How is this a thing?" I whispered to my mother. I hoped the chatter from the gossiping Ladies Who Lunch (plus a few men who looked even more groomed than their female counterparts) filling the room would be enough to drown out my question.

Mom shrugged, attempting to compose her face into something resembling a California-cool "been there, seen that" look. She didn't come close. Where we were from, people hosted home Tupperware parties, not home Botox-and-spa-treatments parties.

"Mr. Glick, would you like a pomegranate spritzer?" the beautician working on the big-shot movie star asked, motioning to me as she lifted one foot out of the mini-aquarium and placed it on her knee so she could use a block of wood wrapped in sandpaper to scrub away the last of the dead skin the fish hadn't snacked on.

So. Gross.

I sucked in a breath and crossed the room, balancing my tray of mocktails in one hand. Apparently, alcohol and needles to the forehead don't play nice together. After spending half my waking hours at my grandmother's hair salon, I wasn't afraid of hard work, but I'd never waitressed a day in my life. Me plus a tray filled with deep red juice plus a room decorated entirely in white, PLUS intimidating Hollywood types, equaled certain impending disaster.

I exhaled carefully and used my free hand to grasp the stem of the martini glass. Mr. Movie Star grabbed it from me and took a sip. He made a face and handed it back. "What say we see about making this pack a little more punch?"

I didn't follow much celeb gossip, but my best friend, Wynn, was addicted to it and thus I knew a thing or two about Billy Glick's fondness for beverages with "a punch." I swallowed a snarky comment and instead managed, "Um, sorry, sir. I'm, uh, I'm only seventeen so I'm not allowed to handle alcohol. The catering company said—"

Another waitress, who looked like she'd been plucked from the audition line for *America's Next Top Model*, stepped in and whisked the glass from me. "I'll see what we can find you, Mr. Glick."

I turned back toward my mom, who was now applying fake eyelashes to a woman cradling a tiny dog wearing a satin suit. Mom could apply fake eyelashes in her sleep after decades at the salon back home, but I don't think she ever had a designer puppy audience while she did it. Never had I felt so far away from sleepy Shelbyville, Georgia, home of the World Famous (well, relatively speaking) Pecan Festival. Before I could escape back into the kitchen, a group clustered in the corner called me over.

"Do you know how many calories are in these lettuce wraps?" one asked, motioning at the tiny plate she held.

"Um, hello. It's *lettuce*," I wanted to reply, but I bit my tongue. I always have a whole host of perfect retorts that never make it past my throat. I'm basically the least confrontational person you'll ever meet, turning into a garden gnome anytime things get prickly. Stupid grin on my face, concrete legs.

When I hesitated, the woman closest to me waved her hand in a dismissive motion. "Not to worry. We actually called you over for something else." The man and woman next to her giggled and leaned in. "Okay, sweetheart, you've got us completely stumped and that doesn't happen often. We've got a thousand bucks riding on your answer. I say down your pants and my friend Ella here says bra. Which is it?"

I nearly dropped my tray. "Ex-excuse me?" I stuttered.

"Your spec script. Where've you hidden it? Your cater-waiter uniform doesn't leave many places, and we're baffled."

I stared slack-jawed at them. "I'm sorry. I don't . . . spec what?" I'd been told in training to avoid eye contact with the guests and *definitely* not to speak to them unless to answer them about which vintage pinot noir had been used in the cranberry meatballs, so I kept my voice low and glanced around the room.

The trio in front of me burst out laughing and the first woman said, "Oh, honey, you are just too cute for words. When did you get here? Yesterday?"

I couldn't tell if this was a rhetorical question or not, so I answered her honestly. "Um, five days ago."

More laughter. The one named Ella elbowed the guy next to her. "We should go easy on this one. She's just a baby." She turned to me. "Allow us to enlighten you. Spec script: a script written on speculation, i.e., not under contract with any production company or major studio. As in, one of two things every single one of your cohorts here has tucked on—or in— their person. The other option being a headshot, if they're of the struggling actor variety, versus the struggling screenwriter variety. Exhibit A. See the manicurist over there?"

I followed her head jerk to the corner of the room, where a small table was set up in front of the floor-to-ceiling windows that showcased the valley below.

"Stack of papers rolled up between the OPI bottles and the gel dryer? Script. Now . . . waitress to the left of her. See the corner of her headshot peeking out from the top of those

4

knee-high boots she's rocking? One quick unzip and that sucker's in the hands of the casting director she's passing a canapé to. That's how this town rolls, sweetie. Are you saying you really don't have either?"

I shook my head slowly. What planet had I landed on?

"Damn," said the guy as Ella adjusted her short skirt so it rode even higher on her thighs.

"Who wins this bet?" she asked.

The man shrugged and pulled out a wallet from the pocket of his fluffy robe. "You'll find a way to swindle me out of this somehow anyway. Might as well act preemptively."

With a good-natured grin he counted out ten hundred-dollar bills into her palm while I tried not to ogle them. Nothing in my small-town-Georgia life had prepared me for any of this. The house, the people, and definitely not the hundred-dollar bills changing hands like they were sticks of gum.

"Um, could you excuse me, please? I need to refill my tray."

I wove through the various spa stations set up around the room, beelining it to my mom so I could let her Southern drawl take me home for a minute or two. I found her in the kitchen, microwaving towels to warm the massage table.

"How's it going? Worth it to see the house?" she asked.

Mom knows how much I love anything and everything to do with architecture and, even if we hadn't been so desperate to make money—any money—she figured the chance to get inside a Robert Addison–designed house would be all the encouragement I'd need to don a waitress uniform.

"It's, um, different," I managed. I didn't mean the house. *That* was awesome, with its futuristic look and floor-to-ceiling sheets of glass where any normal house would have walls. No chance any place in Shelbyville would ever have the high-tech NanaWall systems built into the folding doors leading from the kitchen to a back deck. Probably no one there had even heard of NanaWalls, besides me with my lifelong subscription to *Architectural Digest*.

Mom looked up from the stack of towels. "Well, it *is* Hollywood, Annie. What'd you expect?"

I *guess* I expected I'd spend my senior year at Shelbyville High and then head off for college, while still coming home every summer to hang with her and Dad and help out with the women who'd come from three counties over to have my mama "do them up good" at the Curl Up and Dye, voted Best Beauty Salon in Shelbyville for six years running.

Not this. Not moving cross-country and changing schools and jobs, all to get some space from what my dad did to us.

And I definitely did *not* expect Hollywood, which would never even have been on my mom's radar had it not been for the movie shooting in the next town over back home last spring and the promises her new producer friend Joe made about all the opportunities for a makeup artist in La-La Land.

The door to the kitchen swung open and party sounds assaulted us until it eased closed behind the spa company's owner. She surveyed the room and her eyes landed on my mom.

"I'm gonna pull you off that, honey. Billy Glick is

complaining his face is feeling tight after his nightingale-droppings facial and I need someone to apply face cream." She ducked her head into a bag and rooted around.

"Um, I'm sorry. What is a nightingale-droppings facial? Droppings . . . as in . . . poop?" my mom asked, while I dropped the spoon I was holding.

"Oh, sweetheart, you have a lot to learn. We should do another training session before I turn you loose. Nightingale droppings are a secret of the Japanese geishas. They bleach the skin and exfoliate."

I could never imagine my mother slapping bird crap on someone's cheeks. There were some women in Shelbyville who would do just about anything to keep up the image of a Proper Southern Lady, but that was one line even they wouldn't cross. As for me, the only thing I ever put on my face was Pond's cream and strawberry lip gloss.

The owner dropped the bag onto the countertop. "Damn. I swore the face cream was in here. He's gonna freak if we keep him waiting."

My mom took charge. "Annie, grab my purse from the back closet. I've got some from my salon back home on me," she told the owner. "Made with real Georgia peaches—he'll love it."

She gave my mother a grateful look and nodded. A moment later, Mom pushed back into the party and I followed behind with a replenished tray. I was just working up the nerve to interrupt a massage in progress in the front hallway of the house when I heard the shout from the corner of the living room.

"Are you insane, lady? Did you really just put cream on my face that's been tested ON ANIMALS?"

Mom looked more surprised than she had when I'd told her I actually didn't ever envision a time I'd want to get my ears pierced. "I . . . I . . . I didn't know," she managed. She seemed pretty rattled. As the daughter of the owner, no one ever crossed her at the salon. I guess Mrs. Tipton thinking her hair wasn't sufficiently hair-sprayed to heaven was a world away from pissing off Hollywood royalty. The look Billy gave her was nothing short of venomous.

"Get out," he spit.

"But, but . . . ," she protested, while Billy stood and planted his feet, pointing his newly manicured finger in the direction of the door. My mother turned to the owner, who had reappeared from the kitchen. She looked from Mr. Glick to Mom, pursed her lips nervously, and turned her hands out in a help-less gesture.

Mom grabbed me by the arm and stormed past the owner and into the kitchen. She snatched her purse off the counter and dropped the face cream back inside. "Screw this! Annie, get your stuff."

I glanced from the owner, who had followed us, to the *America's Next Top Model* waitress dispensing drinks from a cocktail shaker into martini glasses. This could not be happening. We could *not* afford to lose this job.

I opened my mouth to plead with the owner, to tell her how Mom had left the only job she'd had since high school and the only town either of us had known since birth. How we'd moved all the way across the country. How I'd had to change schools going into my senior year. Mom could NOT get fired for something so stupid. The dude had had bird crap on his face minutes earlier. Where did he think *that* came from? Poop fairies?

But once again, I couldn't say anything. I just stood there with my mouth opening and closing while Mom fished the keys to our Kia out of her purse and rattled them at me. "Annie. Come on!"

I sighed and untied my half apron, dropping it on the counter. We were halfway across the marble floor when someone called after us.

A woman clicked toward us on towering heels. "Hold up, ladies. Look. I'm Billy's assistant. He's under a lot of stress awaiting news on the sale of his yacht. You understand. We wouldn't want this, er, *incident* to reach the tabloids. Here, I hope this makes up for things."

She smiled at me as Mom reached for the paper in her hand. Mom took a brief look and then passed it to me. It was an eight-by-ten glossy Billy Glick headshot, signed, "Keep on keepin' on. Luv, Billy."

Sigh.

Welcome to LA.

Chapter Two

"No way. You're making this up. Please tell me you're making this up." Wynn's familiar freckled face—already sunburned and peeling in June—stretched across my computer screen as she leaned in closer to her webcam. After five days of hassling the building manager, our wifi connection was finally working and I wasted no time in Skyping my best friend back home.

I laughed. "I couldn't make this stuff up if I tried."

"No. No way. It's too crazy. You wouldn't tease me with this, would you?"

I sniffed as if I was deeply offended she would question my sincerity, but Wynn only giggled.

"I swear on all that I hold sacred that this is the truth, the whole truth, and nothing but the truth," I told her.

Wynn rocked back in her chair. "Okay, that's just bizarre. It's like you moved to the moon."

"Seriously. That's pretty much what it feels like."

"Still . . . Los Angeles . . . ," said Wynn with a wistful sigh.

She and I both knew that if anyone belonged out here, it was Wynn. She was the one with encyclopedic knowledge of every single celebrity right down to their babies' oddball names and astrological signs. Even the parts of her room I could see behind her on the screen were a shrine to glitz and glamour. Gray-bordering-on-silver walls and a (faux) crystal chandelier dangling over her bed. The bedspread had ruffled edges and was shimmering silver too, except for the few remaining garnet beads from an afternoon of BeDazzling eight years ago that went terribly wrong (in our defense, we think the BeDazzler had a defect that probably had nothing to do with us not reading the instructions before beginning).

The only relief from the silver was the chunk of wall behind her bed covered in framed posters of old-time movies: *Some Like It Hot, Casablanca, Citizen Kane.* Vintage glam all the way. Only a select few people knew that on the inside of her closet door, she had one other, far more current poster. That one was a life-size cutout of one Graham Cabot, child sitcom star turned movie actor, current teen heartthrob, and the object of Wynn's unfaltering adoration (along with the majority of the world's female population between the ages of six and twenty-six). Sure, Wynn's crush was about as teenybopper as they come, but it was all part of her charm, as my mom liked to say.

Without even needing the video feed, I could perfectly picture the shelves circling the top perimeter of the room that Wynn's dad built to house her out-of-control snow globe collection. I also didn't need the camera to show me the empty spot that, until last week, held her very first one: Clara and her Nutcracker Prince ice-skating around on a small circle of mirrored paper. On my side of the country, I gave the scene a shake and watched a thin layer of flaky snow settle over Clara's ivory nightgown.

Wynn noticed. "Hey, my snow globe made it in one piece."

"Yup."

"Did you find a good spot for it yet? Turn your laptop around so I can see what your room looks like."

"Pretty standard," I said, complying. I held the laptop over my head and turned in a slow circle. The angle didn't matter much, as the view was mostly the same, 360 degrees. White walls, white drafting table in the corner with a black swivel stool tucked under it, and a black bedspread with a cityscape of buildings marching across it in chalky-white outlines.

"Jeez, Ans, it looks like a carbon copy of your old room. Need me to send you some links to decorating blogs?"

"Yeah, well, I'm still going for the clean, modern look."

"But you're in the land of movie stars and magic. Have fun with it! Set up a lava lamp and buy a puppy that will fit in your purse. Actually, you should probably buy a new purse first."

"Oh yeah, I can just see that now. How very 'me.' Besides, this move isn't exactly all about fun."

"Well, you're there now. You might as well embrace it."

I snorted. "I'm trying. Hey, but I did sign up for an event

next week at SCI-Arc."

"SCI-Arc? Is that a new nightclub?"

"Southern California Institute of Architecture," I told her. "They have this really cool lecture series and there's one next week where all the graduate students present their theses. Plus, there's an exhibit on—"

I stopped speaking when Wynn put her head in her hands and pretended to snore. When she heard my silence, she looked up and smiled. "Are you done yet? Forget columns and arches and . . . okay, I don't actually know any other architecture terms, but forget them all and get your scrawny ass down to Laguna Beach so you can send me videos of hot surfers doing their thing."

"I know, but—"

Wynn plowed on. "Better yet, take some surfing lessons of your own. Once you get a tan, you could totally pass for a surfer babe with that beachy-wavy thing your hair does. You know I've known you forever and ever and I have no choice but to love you exactly as you are, but really, Ans, you're gonna have to stop acting like my grandmother if you want to make new friends out there. And you *better* appreciate how bitter it makes me to coach you on finding my replacement."

As if I could replace Wynn. It didn't even warrant a comment. Instead I answered, "Sorry if I can't make myself get all worked up over the latest kiwi-seed diet or a seven-hundred-dollar cell phone case."

"Wasted. That place is totally wasted on you," Wynn

said with a grin. Then her expression turned more somber. "Seriously, though, what do you think this means? Your mom getting fired so fast? Think you'll pack up and move back?" Her voice went up a little at the end, like she couldn't quite hide the glimmer of hope.

"I really don't know. I doubt it, though. With things the way they are with Dad, I think she'd rather have more than just a country between them, and so would I."

Wynn gave me a look of sympathy that made me bite down hard on my lip to keep tears from spilling over. Then she said, "I saw him the other day, ya know. He looked terrible. He was at Mac's buying mulch and when he saw me it seemed like he wanted to cry. I'm not sure if you want to hear this but, um, he told me to tell you how much he loves you."

"You're right, I don't want to hear it."

Wynn dropped her eyes to her desk and quickly changed the subject. "Well, I give your mom credit. Imagine living somewhere your whole life where you were the total bomb and giving it all up for a chance at a brand-new life."

The living somewhere my whole life part I could definitely relate to. Being "the bomb"? Not so much.

I answered Wynn. "Yeah, well, her bravado's gone missing. You should see her now. She's been on a tear ever since she recovered from her mini-meltdown. Three guesses what she's doing now?"

"Uh-oh. Does it involve an apron with our kindergarten handprints on it?"

"Yup."

"Oatmeal raisin or chocolate chip?"

"Oatmeal raisin. Joe's on his way over and they're his favorite. She called him freaking out on our drive back down from the Hollywood Hills."

"Hollywood Hills . . . ," Wynn breathed in awe. "Whatever you do, you have to figure out a way to stay there through Thanksgiving. My plane ticket's nonrefundable."

"Ha! That's like a *lifetime* from now."

Wynn looked over her shoulder. I couldn't see who was standing in her doorway but I assumed it was her little brother from the face Wynn made. Confirmation came when Wynn said, "Tell her I'll set the table in five minutes. What? Just tell her, Toe Cheese!" She tossed something balled up in the direction of the door, then returned her attention to me. "Sorry, gotta go. Hang in there, okay? Text me tomorrow and let me know what's happening."

I nodded, waved good-bye, and clicked end on the session. Despite all we'd talked about after, the part of the conversation that lingered was Wynn's comment about my dad, and I sat for a moment, trying to push my feelings to a far corner of my head. I was usually pretty good at that. I needed to get my emotions under control before I saw Mom or we'd just loop right back into the way things had been at home before the move. Before the move, but *after* we found out what my dad had been up to. Even though things weren't exactly going according to plan out here, I knew how much Mom needed this fresh start, and I didn't want to be the one dragging her back into all the drama.

The timer buzzed in the kitchen and brought me out of my fog. I took a few steadying breaths before venturing out to see how many racks of cookies were cooling, which was sure to give me some indication of Mom's mood.

It was worse than I'd thought. There must have been four dozen cookies, maybe more, spread out on every surface of the tiny kitchen and spilling over onto the table in the living room. I was just yelling for Mom about the buzzer when there was a knock and a head poked around the front door and into our apartment.

"Ya know, this isn't Shelbyville, ladies. You might want to get in the habit of locking your front door."

The disembodied head waited patiently until I offered, "Come on in, Joe."

Then the rest of film producer extraordinaire (to hear him tell it, anyway) Joe Ribinowitz strode into the room. His eyes lit up when he spied the bounty of Mom's afternoon bakefest. He paused to inhale the smell of warm oatmeal and vanilla. I slid the next batch out of the oven and switched off the buzzer.

"Your assistant said this was a safe neighborhood," I accused.

"Well, of course it is. By Hollywood standards. But this complex is mostly people in the industry and you have no idea what desperate people starved for a role—and probably even regular starved from dieting for that role—are capable of. There are some kooks out here looking to land their shot at fame. And never, ever underestimate those stage moms. The things they'll do to get Junior a speaking line . . ." Joe gave a whole-body shudder that culminated with him subtly snatching a cookie off the cooling rack on the counter. "Where's your mom?"

"Not sure," I was answering, just as Mom appeared in the doorway to her bedroom at the far end of the hall.

"Hey, did you get the cookies out? Oh, Joe! Thank God. Finally a friendly face. How on earth did I let y'all talk me into this move?"

I had to admit, when Joe first started hanging around Grandma Madge's salon last winter as he recruited extra stylists for his production and, a few weeks later, landed at our kitchen table, I was pretty sure he was putting the moves on my mother right under Dad's nose. If anyone in pinprick, dusty Shelbyville was going to catch the eye of a visiting film crew, it would be Mom, with her glossy honey-butter hair and her chirpy "Hey, y'all"s. People told her all the time that she was the very definition of a Southern belle, and she had the Miss Georgia Peach sash to prove it.

My mom's sweet as a peach too—she'd probably never even see the seduction coming. But it hadn't been like that at all. Joe was every bit as friendly with Dad and he'd been a really good friend to Mom when everything went down. He was the one who made the move out here happen.

Oh, and plus Joe was gay. Kinda missed that important detail.

So now I'd finally begun to take him at his word; he was in it for the oatmeal raisin.

He answered Mom. "I'll tell you how the hell you let yourself get talked into it. Because I didn't get where I am in this godforsaken industry without learning how to get any*one* to do any*thing*." Joe polished off a second cookie and reached for a third. "Plus, you're far too talented for a town so small it doesn't even have a Starbucks. Who knew places like that still even existed? Criminal. You belong in the big time. The city of angels will open her gates for you two celestial beings." Joe ended with a typically dramatic flourish that would usually have Mom in giggles.

Instead she snorted ruefully. "I don't know about that. I can't even stay employed for an entire hour."

"Well, what did I tell you about those A-listers?"

"You said stars are just shinier versions of regular people."

"I did?" asked Joe. "Huh. I think I must have meant douchier versions, not shinier."

My mom shook her head, a small smile fighting to break free. Joe saw it too and went in for the kill. "Anyway, you, my sweet, are on to bigger and better. I had my assistant's assistant make some calls and, as they say in the biz, everything's coming up roses."

"Really?" Mom asked as she drizzled cream into Joe's coffee. I scooted my chair in and propped my elbows on the table.

"Well. It's not ideal. For me, at least. I'm gonna have to dive back into my freezer supply of oatmeal raisin. Though these batches will hold me over for a bit. I can have them, right?" he asked.

Mom waved her hand over them, eager to move past talk of cookies. "They're yours. Now, back to the job, please."

"By any chance do you ladies have passports?"

My mom and I exchanged a puzzled look. "No. Neither of us had ever left Georgia before last week, much less the country."

"Okay, no worries. We can get a rush job on a couple in two, three days tops. First stop is New York anyway, and you should be there through . . . wait, today's Tuesday, so Wednesday, Thursday . . ." He ticked days off on his hand until my mother and I both screamed "Joe!" at the same time.

Joe looked startled. "What?"

"Are you fixin' to tell us what the job is?" my mom asked with exaggerated patience.

"Oh, right. Sorry. Guess I should have led with that."

He leaned in and smiled.

"Do you two happen to know who Graham Cabot is?"

Embark on more romantic adventures with
JEN MALONE!

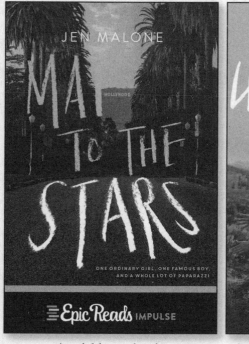

Available in ebook!

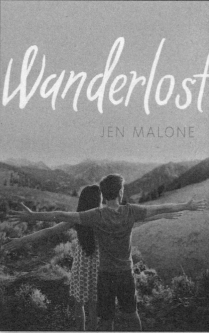

Available in paperback and ebook!

An Imprint of HarperCollins*Publishers*

www.epicreads.com